INTRODUCING

The People in the Story

When **KATHERYN FARR** became the new secretary to **DEAN ULYSSES CALDER** she replaced lovely, gay

GARNET DILLON, who left abruptly, leaving behind her a very unsatisfactory note to explain her departure.

Due to her popularity, everybody was hurt that she had not taken anyone into her confidence. Especially a group of her closest friends at the Medical School. They were

JOHN WHITTAKER, BOB HITCHLOCK, GLADYS HORST-MANN, SYDNEY VINES, JOHN GREENWOOD, THEODOR SCHWANN and his brother and Garnet Dillon's favorite, **KURT SCHWANN.**

Yes they were all fast friends of Garnet's and most of them were a little in love with her . . . yet one of them murdered her. Murdered her so cleverly that if fate had not played her part the cause of her death would have passed off as heart attack.

It was on a tour of the school by Katheryn Farr and John Greenwood that the body of Garnet Dillon was discovered in the morgue of which

MR. GRISWOLD, usually called "Grizz" was in charge.

DETECTIVE RICHARD TUCK, of the Police Department was called in to investigate and uncovered some startling facts. For instance that Kurt was —— but that would be telling and also ruining some very fascinating reading. For this is one of the most mature and absorbing mysteries printed.

MURDER AMONG FRIENDS

by

LANGE LEWIS

PUBLISHED BY BARTHOLOMEW HOUSE, Inc.
205 EAST 42nd STREET, NEW YORK 17, N. Y.

ONE

WALKING AGAIN DOWN University Avenue was like being a ghost.

A small, neat ghost, thought Kate—a ghost in business black, with sensible shoes, and a not annoyingly smart hat because some prospective employers don't like smart hats.

And it seemed impossible that only two years before she had been one of the sunlit faces walking toward her and passing by with their private laughters, their snatches of sentences that seemed heartbreakingly dear and familiar.

". . . flunked it flat, absolutely flat, and simply because it was my last final and by that time I hadn't slept for so long I didn't care . . ."

". . . never grades exam papers, so help me. He throws the whole bunch at the ceiling and the ones that land on his desk get A . . ."

". . . goes to the movies the night before finals, and gets all A's . . ."

". . . Pavlov was right, but he didn't carry it far enough . . ."

Nothing had changed. The same words were being spoken, and there were still the young women in bright sweaters, the young men in casual slacks. The same brick buildings were staunch and ugly in the sunlight. She had changed. Only she.

The Science Building was just ahead, and as usual there was a cluster of white-jacketed medical students smoking and talking before the entrance. Her heart lurched within her because one of them might be Johnny. She forced herself not to squint to learn at once whether or not he was there.

[7]

Approaching the little cluster of white jackets with her head held very high, she wished that she had repaired her lipstick in the street car. The medical students went on talking, but there was an intensification of casualness as she reached them. Johnny was not there.

She clicked briskly up three cement steps and peered into the building. Six more steps, and then a long corridor, gloomy after the sunlight. The only notice on a tan bulletin board just inside the doorway was a white card headed "String Quartet," giving the date and place of the concert. She turned and looked down at the young men outside. From her undergraduate days she remembered someone saying that you could tell medical students from dental students, who also wore white coats, because the medical students usually had circles under their eyes. These young men ran true to form. They looked up at her out of weary young eyes, each pair wearing a different type of circle. Purple, blue, and brown circles. Finals were over. The February-June semester had begun.

"Could you tell me the way to the Dean's office?" she asked.

They all said something at once; one of them pointed vaguely upward, and then a thick young man, with a thick white face and thick glasses, stepped capably forward.

"I'll take you up," he said breezily. "The last female I sent there walked into the Anatomy lab and had to lie down for a while."

"That's the deal, Vines," said an uncommonly blond young man, with light eyebrows that gleamed richly in the sun, and almost no circles under his eyes at all.

"Trust Vines," said someone else, and they all laughed.

Vines is a wolf, thought Kate, as she said,

[8]

"Thank you so much."

"Up those stairs to your left," directed Vines, and tried to take her elbow which she neatly maneuvered away just in time. Appearing not to notice, he stumped up the cement stairs beside her, chatting amiably. "This is the darndest place to find your way about in. All the doors are plainly labeled, if you can find the door you want. It was a week before I was really sure of my way to Anatomy. I kept winding up—forgive me—smack in front of the gents' retiring room. You aren't a student, are you? No, of course you're not; I can tell a scientific gal at a glance, chiefly because they're all so ghastly plain. Here we are!" He stopped in front of a tall, dark-brown door, with a ground-glass upper panel which said "Office of the Dean" in square black letters.

"Thank you very much," Kate said.

Vines airily waved a hand which made Kate think of a butcher's hand. "Pleasure. Pleasure, I assure you. I'm Sydney Vines, and if I can help you in any way I'll be one happy lad. So long." With another wave he turned to go, and Kate squared her shoulders and faced the tall brown door.

"Say!" called Vines.

She turned. He was standing at the head of the stairs, his hand on the rail. His smile displayed yellow teeth.

"You wouldn't be the new secretary, would you?"

"I hope so."

He thudded down the stairs, whistling.

Kate turned and opened the door to the Dean's office.

It was a narrow room, too full of two desks and three tall green filing cabinets. As she stepped forward, the door chunked shut behind her. The desk near the door was bare, except for a covered typewriter. The large desk in front of the window was littered. As the door shut, the small gray man sitting there looked up. Had he not been wearing the inevitable white jacket, he would have been a silhouette against the sunny day beyond the window at his back.

"Yes?" he asked, in a quiet voice.

"The University employment bureau said you might have a job for me." Kate opened her purse and found the white card Miss Gibbs had given her, and going to the desk, handed it to him. He rose mechanically, his eyes on the card. Then he looked at her. His eyes were very blue, and for a brief moment, they looked searchingly into her darker blue ones. She had the disconcerting feeling that a brief moment was all he needed.

"Sit down, Miss Farr," he said, looking again at the card, which gave her name, a record of her past experience, and a recommendation from Miss Gibbs who for some reason had always liked Kate.

As she sat down on the edge of a hard lecture chair facing the Dean's desk, he sank into the swivel chair behind it. She was pleased to see that he did not lean back in insolent comfort, but sat very straight, arranging the card punctiliously in the exact center of the green blotter.

"You will find that your work here differs from work in a business office, Miss Farr, in that you will have little or no dictation, a great number of phone calls, and all sorts of odd jobs. Odd, odd jobs, perhaps I should say. It will often be up to you to keep things running smoothly; I'm told I'm somewhat forgetful. Some of the professors are just as bad. Dr. Uman, for example. Although he's the head of the Biology Department, one of his lectures is a requirement for first-year men. You'll have to remind him about that lecture. He may swear at you in Russian."

As she watched his small flat hands move the

card to the extreme edge of the blotter, she could hear the commas and semi-colons falling into place. She couldn't help it. She smiled.

"Yes?" asked Dean Calder, very pleasantly.

"I'm sorry. But you're so unorthodox. You're talking just as if I were already hired."

"You are," said Dr. Calder, mildly.

Before Kate could savor the pleasant shock, he pointed to the wall to his right. Turning, Kate saw it consisted of a double row of small brown doors with cracked varnish.

"Use the cabinet above your desk for your coat and hat." He added, almost apologetically, "It's not nearly long enough for any respectable purpose, but it will have to serve. Supplies of various sorts are in the other cabinets. You'll have to find what you want yourself; I haven't the slightest notion where anything is. Garnet attended to that."

"Garnet?" asked Kate, as she opened the narrow cupboard and removed her hat before the little square mirror attached to the inner side of the door.

"She was my other secretary," said Dean Calder, and Kate was conscious of a change in his voice. It was cooler.

"Oh." She straightened her hair quickly, closed the door, and turned around. She found that Dr. Calder's eyes were fixed on her black suit.

"You needn't wear black unless you like it," he said. "This isn't exactly like a business office, you see."

"That's what I like most about it," said Kate, frankly.

His lids lowered and he looked briefly at the card she had given him. "I see you were an English major. Who's your favorite author?"

"Shakespeare." It was wonderful to be able to say that so simply, to know that she would not be

[11]

suspected of being strange or bombastic.

Dr. Calder nodded. "Good. Miss Gibbs told you about the salary? It's satisfactory?"

"Perfectly."

He nodded again, and put her card away in the top drawer. A bell rang, shrill and nerve-shattering, announcing the end of Chapel hour, the start of the ten-thirty class. Dr. Calder rose. "I have a lecture. Miss Farr, there is one thing I must say, and then you're on your own. Don't let the young men turn your head. There are a great many young men here, and you're the only attractive woman in the entire Science Building."

Kate asked, "Did Miss Garnet elope with one of the medical students?"

"Garnet Dillon," corrected Dean Calder. He walked past her desk and put his hand on the knob of the door without speaking, and she had the uneasy notion that she had somehow said the wrong thing. Then he turned and faced her. "That's what I thought at first," he said, slowly. "But that wasn't it. All the boys present and accounted for. No. What she did was this. Last Friday she left five typewritten lines on my desk which neither explained why she was going nor where, walked out this door, and never came back."

TWO

THE DOOR CLOSED AFTER Dean Calder, and Kate was left alone in the narrow, sunless room.

The telephone rang, and she answered in her business voice. "Dean Calder's office. . . . No, the Dean is not in. Is there any message?"

There was. She opened the narrow middle drawer of her desk to get a pencil, and stared. Bunched in the front trough of the drawer was a gold bangle bracelet, looking out of place next to three long yellow pencils and some loose paper clips.

She jotted down the brief message with her eyes on the bright gold in the open drawer, and as soon as she had replaced the receiver she picked up the bracelet.

It was a charm bracelet, foolish little miniatures dangling from a golden chain. A cocktail shaker, a skull, a sombrero—none over a quarter of an inch high. And there were at least two dozen of them. Kate tried to imagine the owner. Not serious, surely, and not very old. A gay sort of person who liked jingling things.

She heard the door open, and looked up at Sydney Vines.

"I see you got the job," he said, and then he stared at the bracelet in her hand. "Where did you get that?"

"I found it in this drawer," she said coolly. "I'm going to turn it over to the Dean when he comes back. It's rather valuable to be lying around among the paper clips."

Planting one fat palm on the desk, he extended the other imperiously. "Let me see it a minute."

She handed it to him and watched while he briefly examined it, straightening and fumbling through the charms with fingers that were like pallid sausages. Then he flung it to the desk with a clatter. "It's hers, all right."

"Whose?" asked Kate, wanting to be absolutely sure.

"Garnet's. Garnet Dillon's, the little bag." He pointed. "I gave her that skull."

Kate returned the bracelet to the drawer, and then looked up at Vines. Behind the glasses his eyes were narrowed in thought, and his hands were stuffed into his trousers pockets, making him very wide of beam but somehow not funny.

He swung toward Kate. "I can't figure why

she'd leave it behind," he said. "It was practically part of her. Sometimes she took it off when she typed, because it jangled so, but she always put it right back on her wrist. The gesture was mechanical." He shrugged, and when he next spoke his voice had lost the clear-cut thoughtfulness which had revealed his deliberate mind.

"Oh, well. I gave up trying to figure out women a long time ago. And speaking of figures, you do rather well along that line, lady."

"Don't be crude," commanded Kate. "Tell me more about this Garnet Dillon."

His small eyes mocked her. "Let's see how good a guesser you are. What kind of a gal do you think would own that bracelet?"

"Well, she was frivolous, and pretty, and gay, and I'll bet she had long red fingernails."

"Now I'll tell *you*," said Vines. He leaned over the desk again, his face unpleasantly close to Kate's. "She wasn't pretty. She was beautiful. Blond. She had a figure . . ." He made a vague, sculping gesture in the air. "She dressed in colors that knocked your eye out from a block away. You're right about the fingernails—I never saw 'em redder or longer. Everyone in pants around here was a little in love with her, and she knew it. Boy, how she knew it! She played the field, for a while, and spit in your eye when she felt like it, and then laughed as though it didn't matter at all."

Kate thought, She spit in your eye, all right.

"How about having lunch with me?"

Kate shook her head. "At lunch time I'm going to get a little more information about this job."

Sydney Vines straightened slowly, and there was something cold in his eyes when he said, "I see the way you work things, honey. If I'd had any brains at all I'd have waited to tell you about Garnet until I had you at a table in the Student Union."

[14]

Despite his stockiness he managed to saunter to the door, his hands in his pockets again. He was chuckling. He said, over his shoulder, "See you later, unless you see me first."

The door shut behind him, and it was like coming into sunlight. But the door opened at once, and he stuck his fat white face through to ask, "What's your name?"

"Kathryn Farr." It was displeasing to something in Kate to give him even this much of herself.

The door closed. She heard his voice fading down the corridor. He was singing, "K-K-Katy, beautiful Katy. You're the only g-g-g-girl that I adore . . ."

She spent the first part of the lunch hour finding where supplies were kept. The neatness of these, and of the filing cabinets, rather surprised her; Sydney Vines' description of Garnet had not led her to expect such method. Then the Dean came in, and she went to lunch. She had gone down the stairs and along the lower corridor to the entrance when she saw Johnny.

He was with another man, almost as tall as himself, and they were going down the steps just inside the wide doorway, talking earnestly.

She knew exactly what Johnny's face was like. The lips were moving very slightly when he spoke, and his light brown eyes were leaving the other man's every so often to reach out into the bright street and observe some detail—the way the sunlight warmed the grass of the parkway to emerald, the way it gleamed on the glasses of a student coming out of the Law Building opposite, the way a passing girl was wearing her hair. She knew that his eyes were blank even though he might be deeply interested in what the man at his side was saying, and she knew that the broad forehead above them was blank—Johnny never frowned. When something annoyed him, his eyebrows arched a trifle higher, but he never frowned.

Then the two men stepped out of the building, and the sunlight made Johnny's light brown hair clean and bright above the dark-brown tweed of his sport coat. She hurried on tiptoe, and fell into step beside him.

". . . decided to forget about her," the man beside him was saying, in a voice that had a foreign clip to it.

"That's all you can do," agreed Johnny, his eyes on a boy across University Avenue who had dropped a book and was stooping to pick it up. Then he became aware of someone beside him and looked down in mild surprise.

The surprise changed swiftly to amazement, and then to frank pleasure.

"Katy!" he said, and stopped walking.

"Hello," said Kate, and found herself dropping her lashes. They were rather long lashes and she at once despised herself for using them.

"Well!" said Johnny. He turned to the man beside him, and then back to Kate. "Kate, this is Kurt Schwann. Kurt—Kathryn Farr. Katy and I used to study together for exams when we were undergraduates. We picked each other's brains clean." He laughed down at Kate, and she laughed with him.

"How do you do," said Kurt Schwann, formally. Kate had the feeling that he almost bowed from the waist.

"How do you do," she echoed, and looked at his face for the first time.

She looked into the most startling pair of eyes she had ever seen. They were blue-green eyes, as lucid as water, and they slanted upward at the corners below black brows that also had an upward slant to them. Brown-black hair fitted the narrow skull almost too closely and came to a peak in the middle of the forehead. Kurt Schwann wore no polite smile common to introductions. His face was perfectly grave. The thin lips made it more than grave; they made it severe.

Kate placed his accent. "You're from Germany?" she asked, politely.

"Now that," said Kurt, "is what I consider a foolish question."

As Kate felt herself flush, Kurt glanced at Johnny. Something he saw in Johnny's face made him look down at Kate and say, "Forgive me. I was rude just then. I am not myself today."

Kate knew that she and Kurt would tolerate each other because Johnny liked them both.

"Have you had lunch?" asked Johnny.

"I'm about to."

"Fine. Have it with us." They started walking down University Avenue to the Student Union. "What are you doing around here, Katy?"

Very calmly Kate said, "I'm working here. I just got a job as secretary to the Dean of Medical School."

Over Johnny's "What!" she heard Kurt's "Gott!" quite clearly.

"Isn't that nice?" she asked Johnny.

"Very nice," he said, briefly, looking at something far down the street.

There was a silence while they walked five steps. Then Kurt said, "You see . . . we knew the former secretary rather well. She left suddenly, without saying good-by. We do not quite understand it."

"Yes, I know," said Kate. "Do you know any reason why she did it?"

"Women!" said Kurt.

"Let's talk about something else," suggested Johnny.

The Student Union Cafe was a long, high-ceilinged room; one side was windows that faced north, the other a long lunch counter. Next to the counter was a free space, and then a forest of shiny brown tables and chairs.

Kate was glad to see it again. She pushed through the turnstile at the entrance, and remembered to snatch a ticket from the boxlike machine just inside; there was the familiar click and whirr, and without turning she knew that another pink ticket had popped up for Johnny. Since it was lunch hour the cafe was jammed with color and movement, and the din was terrific.

"We'll sit at the Medical table," shouted Johnny just behind her ear. "It's our only chance for seats."

She nodded and continued walking.

The Medical table was toward the rear of the great room, a big, round table at which sat, she remembered, young men who wore their new wisdom with gravity, young men who were plainly and a trifle self-consciously apart from the prattle and laughter around them; who laughed, when they laughed, at jokes peculiarly their own.

As they reached the table, Kate glanced quickly around and was relieved to see that Sydney Vines was not there. Johnny drew out a chair for her and she sat down; he sat next to her, and Kurt next to him, turning at once to a small, sad-faced man at his other side to whom he murmured something in German. In addition to Kurt's compatriot, there was the blond young boy who had been among the group at the entrance of the Medical Building that morning, and who smiled shyly at her; a small, slender and somewhat older man with tan hair and eyes; and a heavy, short-haired, broad-shouldered young woman, exactly like dozens of girls Kate had seen down all her school years, captaining basket-ball and hockey teams with thundering proficiency.

"This is Kate Farr," said Johnny to the group at

[18]

large. "Kate, this is Theodor Schwann. . . ." **The** sad young man next to Kurt murmured something. ". . . He's Kurt's big brother. Then comes Hitch—Bob Hitchlock, I mean."

The blond young man turned rather pink and said, "Hello. Did you find the Dean's office all right?"

"Yes, thanks," said Kate.

"And this is Jim Whittaker. He's a cynic."

"Not at all," said Whittaker. "Glad to know you, Kate."

"And this," said Johnny, "is Gladys Horstmann. She's a Fellow in Biology, and she's assistant to the mad Uman. Sorry, Horstmann, I should have started with you."

"That's O.K., Greenwood," said Horstmann in a deep, pleasant voice. "You know I don't grab at my feminine prerogatives. Hi there, Kate."

"Hi," said Kate, warmed by the other's friendliness. "I've heard about Uman."

Gladys Horstmann looked around the table. "Have you heard his latest? In a spirit of frolic and fun, I proposed this teaser. If you removed the pituitary of a pelican and then placed him a reasonable distance from a tub of fish, would he dive for the fish? And if he did so, would he retain the fish in his pouch from force of habit, hoping that his appetite might return?"

Everyone laughed. Even the waitress, waiting patiently with her pad, smiled vaguely.

"So," said Horstmann, "he's going to try it. He's going to place a tub of fish on the sidewalk below the lab window. Then he's going to tie a string around the leg of a pituitaryless pelican, and allow it to observe the tub of fish from the window sill. If all goes well, passers-by will be treated to the spectacle of a frustrated pelican swooping down from the third floor of the Science Building and then either looking sadly at the fish or grabbing

[19]

one, at which point it will be drawn up by the string."

The laughter amplified. Kate looked at Johnny. She loved to watch him laugh. All the blankness and austerity vanished from his face and it became young.

Then she saw Kurt's face. He was smiling, and his teeth were even and white and his eyes didn't smile at all. His brother looked merely startled. Kurt turned to him and explained something in German, at which Theodor nodded his brown head and laughed a little. But almost at once the patient, dogged look settled over his face again.

"What'll you have?" asked the waitress.

They ordered. "Bring my coffee now," Johnny commanded, as he always did, and a little silence fell.

"You mentioned Dean Calder," said Whittaker, to break the silence. "Is Kate a friend of his?"

"She's his secretary," said Johnny quietly.

The silence intensified. Theodor—Kate could not imagine anyone calling him Ted—looked swiftly at his brother and looked away. Hitch stared at her and then became absorbed in folding his paper napkin into a soldier's hat. Whittaker's face did not change.

"How marvelous," said Gladys Horstmann, a little too loudly. "The Dean's a wonderful guy."

Whittaker smiled. "Don't be so hearty, Gladys."

Kate decided to say what was in her mind. "You know, for some reason I can't understand I feel like an interloper. I know the other secretary was very popular with all of you, but that doesn't seem to explain the peculiar atmosphere I've run into."

She looked directly at Johnny as she finished speaking. He lowered his lids just as the waitress put a cup of coffee down in front of him. Without looking at Kate, he picked it up and drank.

[20]

It was Whittaker who spoke first. "I'll tell you what I think it is, Kate. It just happens that we at this table were probably more friendly with Garnet than anyone else in Medical School, and so when we learned from the Dean that she'd left we were each rather annoyed that she hadn't taken us into her confidence. It boils down to wounded pride more than anything else."

"You are right, of course," said Kurt. Kate couldn't tell from his polite, well-modulated voice whether he was being sarcastic, or perfectly sincere.

"I'll tell you all what I think," said Gladys, positively "I think that she met a man—a real, full-fledged, grown-up man, with money. I think he swept her off her feet. I think she'll pop back one day with a wow of a diamond wedding ring."

She looked at Hitch.

There was another silence, and the waitress came with their sandwiches. While she was serving them Kate stole a glance around at their faces. Hitch was a little pale; Kurt was staring at his sandwich as though he had never seen one before; Johnny was gulping coffee. His eyes met hers over the rim of the cup and then looked away.

Whittaker said, "Gladys, your thoughts are showing."

Then a small man in a big brown overcoat was suddenly at the table. He jerked out a chair with a grating noise, sat down violently, and grabbed a menu, beckoning imperiously at a waitress. Planting his chin in one hand, he looked at the menu with haggard eyes, looked dolefully up at the waitress and said, "I'll have a piece of lemon meringue pie, a pickled salmon sandwich and a cup of cocoa."

The waitress scribbled and went away.

Johnny said, "Kate, this is Dr. Uman. Dr. Uman, I'd like you to know Kathryn Farr, Dean Calder's new secretary."

Dr. Uman looked at Kate's nose and said, "Happy to know you." Then, before Kate could reply, he cast a swift and harassed look around the table and said, "Those raccoons are more trouble than they're worth. Now it's constipation." His eye settled on Gladys Horstmann with melancholy satisfaction and added, "They have to be walked."

Gladys looked stricken and the tension broke in laughter.

"Hello, Katy," said a suety voice just above Kate's left shoulder.

She looked up into the broad face of Sydney Vines. "Hello," she said, without enthusiasm, and turned away. Everyone was looking up at Vines, and it was odd to see the identical expression on the faces opposite her. It wavered between surprise, contempt and amusement.

"I'll tell you what I'm going to do for you, Kate," Vines said in a large voice. He drew up a chair from the next table and sat down just behind Kate's chair. "I'm going to take you on a Cook's Tour of the Medical School."

"You're out of luck, Vines," Johnny said flatly. "I'm taking Kate around."

As she gave Johnny a glance of relief Kurt Schwann stood up. "I find that I must go back to my Diptera," he said, his Heidelberg accent falling oddly on Kate's ears after the two broadly American voices.

"Your what?" asked Kate.

"Flies," said Whittaker. "He pulls their wings off."

Kurt raised a thin forefinger. "Always etherizing first, of course." He smiled, picked up his check, and left the table.

Kate turned to Johnny. "What *does* he do?"

"Genetical research."

Theodor Schwann spoke to her for the first time.

His accent was more pronounced than his brother's, and his voice was unexpectedly deep. "He hass a Rockefeller Fellowship," he said with unmistakable pride.

"That's right," agreed Johnny. "He's the most brilliant mind they've had around here for a long time." Kate tried to remember when his voice had been tinged with that same respect. She recalled almost at once. It was when he had spoken to her of his father, who had been a surgeon, and who had died long before she and Johnny met.

"You know," said Sydney Vines, so close to Kate's ear that it startled her, "it always makes me a little sick, the way bouquets are tossed at Schwann. Without the accent he'd just be one of the boys."

Kate saw Theodor Schwann's eyes grow larger. Blood darkened under his swarthy skin. But before he could gather his words Whittaker spoke. He spoke without heat, looking steadily at Vines out of his tan eyes. "You damned fool," he said. "That fat brain of yours is so full of ankles that there's no room there to respect a man who's doing more in science at twenty-six than you'll do in all your life."

"Wow!" said Vines, amused, and the breath stirred Kate's hair. He seemed unperturbed, but in a moment he got up, almost colliding with the waitress who was bringing Dr. Uman's lunch, and wandered off to another table where he slapped an acquaintance resoundingly on the back.

When the waitress had gone Dr. Uman looked up from his sandwich and said a peculiar thing. "I'm glad Kurt didn't hear that eloquent defense, Whittaker. He enjoys being hated by certain people, you know. And he doesn't like kindness."

"That iss right," Theodor nodded.

"Some of Kurt's poses annoy me like hell," said Whittaker, judicially. "But I admire him for being such a clever son-of-a-gun. Let's go, Theodor."

A moment later Dr. Uman picked up his pie and cocoa, and strolled to a near-by table where a big red-faced professor was arguing with a small, determined one.

"Let's go, Kate," suggested Johnny.

He picked up their checks and stood up. They said good-by and left Hitch and Horstmann sitting side by side at the big round table.

The end of the long line that was filing past the cashier's desk at the entrance was just beside the Medical table. She and Johnny joined the procession. It rather surprised her to hear Hitch say fiercely, "Why do you hate her so?"

Kate glanced over her shoulder. Hitch was half turned toward Horstmann, whose full pale mouth was closed in a thin line. She was stirring her coffee deliberately. She said, "I never hated Garnet, Hitch. But I'm a woman and so I'm the only person around here she didn't fool."

Johnny tugged at Kate's sleeve then, and she saw that the line had moved several feet forward. She and Johnny closed the gap and two giggling girls stepped into line behind them.

"Well," asked Johnny, who apparently hadn't heard Horstmann, "what do you think of 'em?"

"They're nice." And for something to say, "Horstmann's pelican story was good, if true."

"Poor Horsie," said Johnny. "The typical woman in science, Kate. Frustrated as the devil, but being a good sport about it. She'll plod along for years, and dabble in psychology on the side, and wind up marrying someone three inches shorter than she is."

"She'll marry Hitch, if she can."

Johnny smiled. "You don't miss a thing, do you?"

Outside, they walked toward the Science Building. "What's the matter with Kurt's brother?" she asked. "He has such a brown, silent face."

"Now there's a story. According to Kurt, Theodor was really going places, five or six years ago. Then his wife died. Cancer, I think. Theodor watched her die, and it wrecked him. Immediately after this Kurt and Theodor left Germany. Their family was strongly Imperialist, and they hated Hitler and what he was doing to their country, and especially what he was doing to free scientific thought. Well, Theodor's stayed with medicine, because it's all he has left except Kurt. He'll get his M.D. eventually, and he'll never amount to a thing."

"How tragic!"

"Yes," agreed Johnny equably. "Yes, it is." He looked past her at the brick facade of the Science Building. "Here we are. Do you really want me to take you through the joint?"

"I certainly do. If I'm going to work here, I'd like to know a little more about it."

But that wasn't the real reason. The real reason was that she couldn't bear to relinquish Johnny so soon.

So they turned into the doorway, and she noticed for the first time a queer face carved in the soapstone lintel, grinning down at them as they passed into the dark building.

THREE

THE FIRST FLOOR OF THE SCIENCE building had a chemical smell. They walked along a dark corridor, between shiny cream-colored walls accented by a shoulder-high band of brown and punctuated by tall brown doors topped with ground-glass upper panels, like the door to the Dean's office. Kate read, "Physiology Laboratory," "Organic Chemistry Laboratory," and then Johnny stopped and opened a door. He stood aside to let Kate enter, saying, "This is a sort of combination lab and lecture room. Not very interesting."

There were the usual dense rows of varnished tan lecture chairs with paddlelike arms, the usual blackboard along the front wall of the room, the usual altarlike stand for the professor's lecture notes.

Johnny pointed up at a rolled white screen at the top of the blackboard. "Most of our lectures are supplemented by lantern slides," he said.

Kate nodded, and looked around the walls at bright chromos, gaudy and a little foolish in their gilt frames. Van Leeuwenhoek; Galileo, leaning precariously out a very small window to point at a star. A gentleman with yellow hair and a red coat measuring his eye with calipers.

"Aren't they horrible?" laughed Johnny.

Kate laughed with him in the cool bright air under the high ceiling, as they walked toward the half-dozen rows of black lab tables with their Bunsen burner outlets of tarnished brass.

"Rotten equipment," confided Johnny, superciliously. "I'll be out at the County Hospital most of the time this year, thank God."

"Let's travel on," suggested Kate, quickly.

They traveled on to the rear of the building, and up a flight of stairs like the ones at the front. From the tower of the Philosophy Building next door, chimes sounded sweet and well remembered, ringing the hour.

Kate awoke from the smiling trance that the chimes had invoked to the realization that the smell here was different from that of the first floor. It was a sweetish, unpleasant smell, not like any she had ever known.

"Anatomy lab," announced Johnny, stopping beside a tall brown door not far from the Dean's office. "No one will be around. Work starts tomorrow."

He opened the door, and Kate stepped past him into a big square room. There were windows on two sides flooding it with a cold northeast light. Three skeletons were dangling from brown uprights. They were turning slowly to and fro in the breeze that came in through the open windows. The little wire springs at the jaw corners glittered as the light caught them, and the skulls were hinged so that the top of the cranium could be lifted like a lid.

The bones were not white, but a shiny yellow tan.

"Shellacked?" she asked Johnny, not able to take her eyes from them.

"Yes," said Johnny. "Saves wear and tear."

She nodded and walked farther into the room. The two walls that didn't have windows were covered with big white charts the size of bed sheets. Kate recognized only the vascular system, in red, white and blue. A foot of blackboard peeped out between two charts; she noticed irrelevantly that the chalk in the trough beneath was green.

The floor space was given to dissecting tables, sixteen of them. They were waist high, and their black tops were shallow V-shaped troughs. On several of them lay brown torsos, carven beyond resemblance to anything but meat, and in one case less than that. The sweetish smell was almost tastable now.

She turned to Johnny. "What is . . . ?"

"The smell? Glycerine and phenol, mostly. Preservative."

"Oh." In turning away from him she saw something that made her start. From a round crock against one wall protruded two skinny brown branches, each wrapped with white at the upper end. She was about to turn again to Johnny for elucidation when she realized what they were.

They were legs, the flesh shrunken against the bone, the feet wrapped in white damp bandages.

Johnny went over and moved one of the legs, peering down into the crock. She turned her head away.

"If this bothers you, we'll go," said Johnny, and she looked back to see him watching her with mild concern.

"Oh, it doesn't bother me at all." Her voice sounded high and shrill to her.

Johnny gave her a long look, and then they crossed the room to the east windows. The sunlight was bright beyond them. On the floor below the windows was a long row of white enamel pots about two feet deep. Johnny raised the lid from one and peered down. Kate came to his side and did likewise. She looked down at a head, the color and texture of tan clay, covered with sparse gray bristles of hair. The sweet smell of the glycerine was very strong indeed.

Johnny reached down with one big, long-fingered hand and lifted off the top of the head.

Kate stood staring, unable to move. Her gorge rose and she swallowed it.

"Cross-sections," said Johnny, in an emotionless voice. "The brain."

The brain was tan clay, too.

"I see," said Kate.

He replaced the top of the head, covered it carefully with a damp white cloth, put back the lid of the jar. They went on to the next.

Sliced hands, arms, legs. Cross-sections.

In the next pot, a sliced pelvis, the revealed organs shrunken together inside their hollow of bone and tissue.

"I think," said Kate, "that we'd better go."

Johnny replaced the lid of the last pot with a light clang and they went to the door. In order to make it less of a rout Kate forced herself to turn

[28]

in the doorway and take a last look at the room.

"It's funny to see it empty like this," remarked Johnny. "There are usually two men at every table."

And then Kate saw something that wasn't there. She saw young men in short white coats stooped above the black troughs of the tables, their intent eyes and hands prying, learning. Not conscious of the smell of glycerine, nor the death about them; conscious only of the unbelievable complexity of the human body which one day they would understand as a functioning whole.

She was glad she had seen that.

"You've got to meet Grizz," said Johnny. "Grizz is wonderful."

They went up the front stairs to the third floor, and along the corridor to a narrow rear staircase leading upward. Kate stopped to stare at a glass-topped case which contained some frazzled bird nests, and a stuffed pelican stretched out on its stomach.

"What," asked Kate, "are these for?"

Johnny shrugged and smiled. "No one knows. Been here for years. Probably Uman's responsible."

Kate laughed, and at the same time something in a far corner of her mind wondered why a dead stuffed bird should be not at all terrible, while a dead stuffed man . . .

They climbed the narrow cement stairs.

"It's sort of a penthouse," explained Johnny.

A hall led from the top of the stairs to a square room, smaller than the Anatomy laboratory, and filled with an intensification of the glycerine smell with which was coupled like an undertone an excretory odor from cages upon cages of white rats.

The only ventilation was from a door opened onto the sunny tar-papered roof. At the end of the room were two other doors, closed. At a battered table beside the door to the roof sat a small, plump, gray man in a soiled white jacket, who was listening to a little radio blare out: "Amapola, my pretty little flower, you're like a breath of spring, so sweet and heavenly. Amapola, you're . . ."

Whatever else Amapola was, they didn't learn, because Johnny yelled, "Hello, Grizz," and Grizz turned the radio down.

Grizz had wet blue eyes that looked as if they had melted at some time in the past, and only partly congealed again. The three-ply pouches beneath them seemed about to run down his face. His expression was amiable. On seeing Johnny, it became absolutely puckish.

"Hello, hello, hello," he said. "What can I do for you?"

"Got any fillings?" Johnny asked.

Grizz turned a moist and appreciative eye on Kate. "Listen to him!" he commanded. "You'd think that all I had to do was dig out fillings."

"Fillings?" asked Kate.

"Sure." He turned to Johnny. "Didn't you tell her?" He turned back to Kate. "I'm in charge of the cadavers. I embalm 'em when they come in from the morgue at the County Hospital." He winked at Kate, jerked his head at Johnny. "This your sweetheart? This your husband?" He shook his head solemnly from side to side, and before Kate could find an answer, went on: "Don't trust these medical boys. Don't trust 'em as far as you can throw a cat by its tail. You heard him. Fillings! Me!"

Johnny was laughing. Then he said gravely to Kate, "He sells the fillings to a Jew who deals in old gold."

Grizz wagged his head negatively. "Don't know what he's talking about. Pay no attention, my dear." His damp blue eyes brightened. He fumbled in his pocket and drew out a bunch of keys; selecting one key from the rest, he walked toward the two closed doors at the end of the room. Over his shoulder, he said to Kate, "Come on. I'll show you my cadavers. Ever see a cadaver?"

Kate looked at Johnny hesitantly.

"Come on," commanded Grizz, who had one of the doors open and was standing on the threshold. Kate walked slowly to the door. She hesitated, so that Johnny, who was just behind, bumped into her with an impatient little laugh.

"Come on in," said Grizz. "They won't hurt you. They're dead."

She followed him into a small, low-ceilinged room, lit by two high, tiny windows. The room contained four green-painted wooden vats, eight feet long, seven feet wide, and three feet deep. They were lidded. Grizz raised one of the lids and held it high.

The vat was literally packed with whitish-gray, stiff, dead, dead, dead bodies.

"Makes you think of sardines, doesn't it?" asked Grizz, cheerfully. Then he stooped over, picked up a chunk of brownish-gray meat, examined it, and flung it down onto the bodies, against which it thumped—dully.

"I'm going to be sick," said a voice in Kate's head.

She turned blindly toward the door, and as she reached it she heard the lid of the vat thud down. The smell of the rats was beautiful. She realized that she could literally taste, in the back of her throat, the thick, strange sweet smell of the little room behind her.

"She's all *right!*" she heard Grizz say to Johnny.

Kate looked longingly at the open door leading to the roof.

"Now I'll show you the embalming room," said Grizz.

[31]

"This isn't nearly as bad," said Johnny, reassuringly. "Those vats of cadavers got me too when I first saw them. And what got me worse was that awful, immortal smell."

"She's a girl to be proud of," said Grizz. "Guts."

"I think we'd better run along now," said Johnny to Grizz.

"Oh," said Grizz, disappointed. "Must you? But of course, if the little lady . . ."

That did it. Kate turned in her tracks and headed doggedly toward the door where Grizz was standing.

He beamed at her and put the key in the lock. "Got a new stiff this morning, Larson tells me." He looked sheepish. "I was kinda late. Awful headache . . ."

"With the money he gets for the fillings," explained Johnny, "Grizz buys Scotch."

Kate tried a weak smile, and stepped past Grizz, who was scowling up at Johnny and saying, "Ridiculous! Fillings! Scotch! *Tcha!*"

The cadaver lying on the long table just beside the door had been cleverly made of skin-colored wax by someone with a flair for detail. Gray bristles of sparse hair; gummily-shut eyes; soft brown freckles on a curiously stiff relaxed arm. Foreshortening emphasized the toed-out feet, like the feet of a person asleep on his back. But the sticky eyes were not a sleeper's eyes. And the nostrils were stuffed with white cotton.

Kate saw all this in a flicker of time. Then she turned her eyes away. They fell on a woman made of white marble; white marble on a wooden table against the rear wall, directly opposite the doorway where she was standing, with Johnny still teasing Grizz behind her.

The woman was young.

The woman was blonde.

She had long red fingernails.

"God!" whispered Johnny, suddenly. Grizz sucked in a gasp.

Kate stared up at Johnny, over her shoulder. His head was strained forward. His face was a slack white mask of unbelief and horror.

Hoarsely, Grizz said, "Larson didn't know her. Don't you see? Larson never saw her in his life!"

Abruptly, Kate realized that Garnet Dillon had come back.

FOUR

THE HEAD OF THE LOS ANGELES homicide squad paced and spoke at length, emitting a really unusual mixture of bad grammar and flawless logic.

Detective Richard Tuck sat and listened. While he followed perfectly the minutest ramifications of Gufferty's main thesis, and while a certain corner of his mind absently noted nine errors in grammar ranging from the mild one of a split infinitive to some staggering confusions of tense, his large, deliberate hand drew doodles on a scratch pad.

This habit of Tuck's was most disarming to suspects, who grew rigidly apprehensive when the big hand picked up a pencil and poised it over a pocket pad, and who relaxed and grew voluble on seeing that hand begin to draw lopsided daisies, ticktacktoes, and similar trivia. Suspects had no way of knowing that Richard Tuck was jotting down, in a private shorthand which he had amused himself for a week by inventing, some most pertinent comments about their testimony, all of which would be copied that evening in a small black loose-leaf notebook. Its pages changed with each case, slowly filling with fact after fact, a path of words leading almost inevitably from an initial act of violence through a maze of evidence to the portentous words, "We find the defendant guilty of murder in the first degree."

.". . . and that's the deal," finished Gufferty, pausing in his pacing to stand unhappy and stolid before Tuck's desk.

Tuck nodded, pressed too hard and broke his pencil point, flung the pencil aside. He looked around the familiar ugly office without seeing it, and then looked into the shrewd eyes of his superior. Neither man thought that the reversal of positions was odd, for Gufferty was as spendthrift of bodily effort as Tuck was chary of spending it. For several years he had paced out problems before Tuck's desk, finally coming to a stop and listening, short, and anxious, and bursting with arguments to the contrary, while Tuck spoke his thoughts.

"There's just one alternative that you haven't covered," said Tuck slowly, in his heavy, deliberate voice. "One man may be responsible for all five attacks."

Gufferty shook his head from side to side. "Five different weapons were used. A cleaver, a two-by-four, a baseball bat, a knife and a razor."

"And all five weapons were left beside the body," added Tuck, gently.

Gufferty's eyes grew blank with thought.

Tuck continued. "I've examined our records on similar attacks in the past five years. Statistically speaking, in less than half the cases the weapons were left behind." His voice became softer and very casual. "It would almost look as though someone were trying to have us believe that five different people are responsible for the attacks, wouldn't it?" He gave this a moment to sink in, his narrow brown eyes fixed on Gufferty's thoughtful face, and then added, "Which, if true, means that we are dealing with a very rare bird indeed—a homicidal maniac of considerable intelligence."

Gufferty made a rumbling sound of anguish in the back of his throat, turned, and went back into his own office as Tuck's phone rang.

"Tuck speaking."

"This is Ulysses Calder," said a quiet voice.

Calder. Calder. Of course.

"How can I help you?" asked Tuck. When a man calls a detective with whom he is acquainted, and calls him at the Homicide Bureau instead of his home, and speaks in a voice edged with strain, he does not want to talk about the weather, nor did Tuck see any point in such time-wasting amenities.

"Could you come to my office sometime today? We're at the start of a new semester out here, and that makes it rather hard for me to leave the campus."

"What's the trouble?"

Dean Calder's voice sounded very odd indeed when he said, "I don't know. Maybe nothing. Will you come?"

"I'll leave at once."

"And say, Tuck," said Dean Calder, and paused.

"Yes?"

"Could you come in a private capacity?"

"Certainly."

"Thank you!"

"Sure. Good-by."

Tuck replaced the receiver and looked thoughtfully at the doodles he had drawn a few minutes before. Then he stood up and went to an antique hatrack in the corner, taking from one of the pegs a dark gray fedora which he settled carefully on his long narrow head. As he went through the doorway leading to the main office he automatically stooped a trifle. Although this doorway was unusually high, some are not built to accommodate a man who is six feet five inches tall.

Gufferty was sitting at his big flat-topped desk,

scowling across at the colorfully flirtatious maiden on the large calendar beside the door that led to the echoing marble corridor outside.

With one hand on the knob of that door Tuck turned and said, "Surely you've noticed that the girls' purses were all missing. And furthermore you must remember that the Beagle girl and the Summers girl, before they died, both spoke of a tall man in a long black overcoat who grinned as he struck."

Gufferty growled again.

"Sit down," said Dean Calder. "It was good of you to come so quickly." He extended a pack of cigarettes, lit Tuck's and then his own. "I'm going to tell this chronologically. When you want me to fill in details, stop me."

Tuck nodded.

"Last Friday the secretary who had been with me for a year left unexpectedly. When I came in early Saturday morning, I found this note on my desk." He gave Tuck a folded sheet of typewriter paper.

Tuck saw that the note had been typed by an expert, and that the signature had been written in haste. It said:

DEAR DEAN CALDER:
I find it necessary to leave town for an indefinite length of time, and so am compelled to resign my job with you. Thanks for everything. The letter you left for me to type is in the top drawer, ready for you to sign.

Garnet Dillon.

"The signature, by the way, is certainly her own," the Dean said. Tuck nodded and went on reading.

"Not very explanatory, is it?" he said, handing it back to Calder.

The Dean shook his head. "And we were on very friendly terms. Businesslike, but friendly." He reached into the drawer and tossed a gold bracelet onto the blotter. "She left this behind her. It was her current favorite possession."

Tuck nodded. "I'd like to know a little more about her—what sort of person she was, you know."

Dean Calder considered the tip of his cigarette and then deliberately knocked the ash off into the heavy glass tray on the desk between them. "She was capable and self-sufficient. Her parents had died some years ago; she had no living relatives, and she had supported herself ever since. On the other hand, she enjoyed masculine attention and a good time as well as any other extremely pretty girl of twenty-two. 'Gay' is the best word I can think of to describe what might be called her extra-curricular personality. A week before she left I noticed a change, however. She made careless errors in her typing. She became solemn. By Friday, the day she left, it had reached a climax. When I spoke to her, she was only half there. I was sure that she was face to face with some crisis in her life. And while I know what young people think of interfering elders, I made up my mind that if by Monday there was no change for the better I would find out what was wrong and do what I could to help. Apparently I waited too long."

Tuck nodded.

"When I read that note last Saturday morning my first thought was that she had eloped with one of the students; there are several who seemed very fond of her. I think that all along I had believed her problem to be a love problem. She was the right age for it.

"However, she had gone and I was without a secretary. I called the school employment bureau

[37]

on Saturday, and this morning they sent me a young woman whom I hired at once.

"And this morning my elopement theory broke down because the three possible bridegrooms stopped in to see Garnet, and were apparently as astonished as I when I told them that she had gone.

"I had just returned from lunch today when in came Miss Farr, the new secretary, a medical student named John Greenwood, and Griswold, the chap who does our embalming. Greenwood had been taking Miss Farr on a tour of the Medical Building. A cadaver had come in this morning from the County Hospital, and the cadaver was Miss Dillon."

Tuck whistled a long, faint whistle.

"There was no sign of any violence. What had happened was plain. She had been picked up without identification, and had been taken to the County Hospital where she had died from pretty plain causes, not requiring a post-mortem examination. Then, following the usual procedure in such cases, she had been held at the hospital a couple of days, and then sent out to us for embalming. The only odd part was that we should have happened to be the next on the list. Otherwise, she would have gone to one of the other near-by medical schools, and unless someone came to identify her she would have been finally dissected."

"You say she was picked up without identification. Didn't she carry something that would identify her?"

"I wondered about that. She had a driver's license, but she couldn't have had it with her because then she would never have been sent here."

"Go on."

"I cautioned the three of them to say nothing to anyone, and sent Miss Farr home for the day because she was on the edge of a good old-fashioned faint. I questioned Griswold and found out that he had been late this morning, and that his new assistant, who had never seen Garnet, had brought the body up from the ambulance. It made no great difference except that Miss Farr and Greenwood would have been spared a nasty shock if Griswold had seen the body when it arrived in the ambulance.

"All right. Next I phoned the hospital to find what Garnet had died of. They checked their records and told me that she had been picked up at eleven Friday night in a small cafe near the station, suffering from a heart attack. And that's when I decided to call you."

"I don't understand," said Tuck.

"You remember that I told you she was suffering from depression for a week or so before she left? In her case it began with a sudden worry about her health; on Friday, a week before she died, she complained to me about a feeling of pressure in the region of her heart. I told her to go to bed earlier, drink less coffee and eat more. She asked me if I would mind examining her heart; her father had died of a heart attack, it seems, and she was worried. I told her that the fact that her father had had heart trouble would not necessarily mean that she had it, but she persisted. Since it was a simple matter for me to get out my stethoscope and humor her, and since there was the slim chance that there might be something wrong, I did what she asked."

With finality Dean Calder mashed out the glowing tip of his cigarette in the glass tray. "There was absolutely nothing wrong with her heart, Tuck. Nothing at all."

"Then the hospital was wrong in its diagnosis?"

"It was." A certain heat glowed under his clean skin. "If an autopsy after every death were required in this country, such things would not happen. But public sentiment is against it. So no one knows how many mistakes the doctors make."

He lit another cigarette, and in the flare of the match some of his inner heat subsided.

"So," said Tuck. "That leaves suicide or murder."

"I think the latter," said Dean Calder very quietly.

He dropped the wooden match into the big glass ashtray, and the small sound it made was loud in the room.

"I won't insult you by asking if you're going on a hunch of some sort," Tuck said slowly. "I know that you have a very good reason for what you just said."

Dean Calder made a small, deprecating gesture with the hand that held the cigarette. "Only this. And it's not much. Six months ago a professor, for no known reason, shot himself in the head. The first I knew of it was when I saw the headlines in the paper. I was sitting here and Garnet was sitting at that other desk over there, typing. I must have made some sort of involuntary exclamation because she asked, 'What's wrong?' and I looked up from my paper to see her watching me. I showed her the headline and said something about what a nasty thing it was, and then I got an amazing reaction.

"I don't know whether you know much about Garnet's generation; I do. They're not soft. I was ready for one of two reactions, either a perfectly controlled, 'Oh, how dreadful,' or a flippant remark. And since good taste was never one of Garnet's strong points, I think I half expected the wisecrack.

"Instead, she stared at the headline for a moment and then said, 'That's worse than murder!' I must have looked surprised, because she added,

'Or just as bad. Don't you see, Dean Calder? This man took the life God gave him. He had no right to do that. He'll be punished for it.'

"I said something to the effect that poor Harris was rather far beyond the long arm of the law by now, and in utter seriousness, she said, 'But not beyond the arm of God.'

"It interested me. That was something new. I drew her out. Tuck, the girl had a medieval mind. I had always known that she was in no sense an intellectual, but by heaven, she believed in a personal heaven and a personal hell, particularly the latter. I'm afraid I'm not making it clear to you, but I saw the girl's face and heard her voice, and I can no more conceive of her killing herself than I can conceive of her committing murder."

"You've made it clear," said Tuck, slowly. His voice grew softer. "This will be quite a problem. Bad girls die quite often, much more often than good little secretaries."

"I didn't say that she was necessarily good," said Dean Calder flatly.

"You said . . ."

"I said that she believed in a personal heaven and a personal hell. I said she was also rather stupid. But she wasn't good. To me, a good person is a person who conscientiously and intelligently does the right thing. A Garnet Dillon can be good only through fear, and her idea of right might not be right at all because she was not intelligent. I don't mean to split hairs, but I do want to tell you the truth."

"And you want to know the truth about her death."

"Exactly. I'm taking that responsibility myself because I belive that time is usually important in these matters, isn't it? And our President would waste a good deal of time looking for a nice, decent explanation."

Tuck reached for the phone. "I'm calling the Coroner's office," he said as he dialed. "The Coroner's ambulance is gray and there will be no siren. I'll have it come to the rear of the building."

The Dean nodded his head. "An autopsy's what we need," he agreed.

The Coroner's telephone rang, and rang again. Dean Calder struck a match. From the empty hallway on the other side of the closed brown door came the cheerful whistling of some passing student.

FIVE

FEEL BETTER NOW? Johnny asked.

Kate shivered. "Yes. Thank you."

The ocean broke and broke against the sand, three hundred feet below. One all-year bather was swimming out, a dot that barely seemed to move into that blue immensity.

"You kept shivering," Johnny said. "I had no idea what to do for you, and then I thought of bringing you here. I remembered that you always liked the sea."

This time she turned to him. She couldn't trust her voice to speak, so she tried to make her eyes tell him how kind he was. They must have done this overwell, because he dropped his gaze from them to his own hand, clasped carelessly around the steering wheel of his little car.

You strange, funny boy, she thought, her heart a little warmer.

"It must have been really worse for you than for me," she said. "After all you knew her."

"Yes."

She couldn't help it. "Were you very fond of her, Johnny?"

"Very."

Oh. What had Sydney Vines said? "Everyone

[42]

in pants around here was a little in love with her."

"What I'm worried about now is Kurt," Johnny confided.

"Kurt?"

He raised somber brown eyes to hers again. "Didn't you know that he was in love with her?"

With a shock, she remembered the puzzled German voice saying, "You see, we knew the former secretary rather well. She went away without saying good-by. We do not understand." And then, later—"Women!"

"That was a rotten thing to do!" she said aloud.

"To be in love with her? She wasn't *that* bad!" Johnny sounded puzzled and amused.

"No. I didn't mean that. I mean, it was rotten of her to go away like that. She might at least have told him."

Johnny was silent.

Johnny! thought Kate. Were you in love with her, too?

But that was one question she could never ask. So she said, instead, "Are you going to tell Kurt? It might be kinder, even if Dean Calder did ask us to say nothing to anyone."

Johnny seemed to think about that. Then he said, suddenly, "You know, I'm glad she didn't say good-by to him. That made him angry, and his anger may carry him past the worst of it."

"He'd have to be pretty mad for that."

"You don't know Kurt. He's the best friend I have, but that doesn't keep me from knowing that he's a complete egoist. He knows it, and admits it rather naively, which makes it not so bad. In fact, I sometimes wonder if Kurt isn't more modest than these very humble guys who know they're good and go around depreciating themselves."

"That's an interesting point. I don't know him well enough to say."

There was a silence. They both looked at the

sea. The swimmer was farther out, now, but it didn't seem much of an achievement from the top of the palisades.

"How is your mother?" asked Johnny suddenly, jerking Kate's mind away from a brooding return to the ugliness she had seen that day.

"Fine."

"Still in Arizona?"

"Yes. And still pretending she doesn't have to stay there."

"You know, even before I met your mother that vacation I knew she was going to be nice."

It startled Kate because it sounded like a compliment to her, too, and that was unlike Johnny. "Thanks. I rather like her myself."

Johnny ignored the flippancy. "You're a good person, Kate. I'm glad to be sitting here beside you." He laughed. "I was sure you'd married some opulent rancher by now."

"The only opulent rancher who wanted to marry me was unfortunately one that I didn't love in the least."

"Oh," said Johnny. "So it's love you want. I'm surprised at you, Kate! A person of your intelligence!"

"Still making fun of love? I imagined you'd outgrown that. How's *your* mother?"

"Fine. I saw her just before exams." .

There was another silence, and again Kate's mind drifted inexorably back over the day. The ambulance had picked Garnet Dillon up somewhere, dying. And no identification. And people with no identification were sometimes dissected by young men in white jackets. That much she understood, from what Johnny had told her. "But, Johnny!" she burst out. "How did she happen to be sent back to her own school?"

"That was chance."

"Oh. Of course." She brooded a minute. "But if

she'd been sent to another school? No one would have claimed her body because of that note she left the Dean. And then she would have been dissected?"

"Yes."

Nothing. Nothing left but bones, perhaps to swing grinning under a coat of shellac from an upright like a gallows in some anatomy laboratory.

She shivered, and her thoughts went on.

"It's getting cold," said Johnny. "Let's go back."

"Yes, let's." She could hear the abstraction in her own voice, through the absorbing hum of her thoughts.

He did something with the gearshift and then stopped.

"Kate!" He gave a short laugh. "Did you hear me? What's the matter?"

"Nothing. Nothing at all. My mind has a way of thinking in fiction now and then. I was thinking that the way Garnet Dillon died was a perfect way to commit a murder."

Johnny, with his foot on the starter, looked sideways at her, his eyebrows raised.

"I mean," she said doggedly, "the note she left was typewritten. Dean Calder told me so. All right. The murderer types that note so that no search will be made, removes any identification from her purse, poisons her. He so arranges it that when she dies she's alone. So she's taken to the hospital . . ."

"Not if she's dead, she isn't. She's taken to the city morgue. And by the way, that means she wasn't dead when the ambulance came."

"Morgue, hospital, what difference does it make? The point is the lack of identification, don't you see? And the letter to the Dean that would explain her absence and preclude any search for her."

[45]

"That's all dandy. But at both the morgue and the County Hospital autopsies are performed where the cause of death isn't plain."

"No autopsy this time."

"Then the cause of death was plain. Don't you see, Kate?"

"Yes. Still . . . there are poisons that don't seem like poisons, aren't there?"

"Several, including that old stand-by, the well-known South American drug which leaves no trace." Smiling, he shifted into reverse and backed slowly away from the edge of the cliff. A U-turn, and they were headed back toward Los Angeles.

"I wonder whether that note of the Dean's was signed . . ." Kate mused.

Johnny made an exasperated sound. "Kate! This is tragic enough without making a melodrama of it!"

"I know," said Kate, meekly. "But you know, I've had a queer feeling about this whole affair from the moment the Dean told me that she went away so suddenly."

"She did."

"Huh?"

Patiently, watching the wide ribbon of road ahead, Johnny said, "Kurt and I went over to Garnet's on Saturday morning. The landlady told us she had moved the night before. And just in case you're having visions of the murderer packing her things and slinking down the fire escape with them, the landlady also told us that Garnet turned in her key in person."

"Oh." They drove on in silence for a while, and then Kate said, "If the murderer knew she was going to leave, and knew that she had left that note, it would certainly have presented him with a grand opportunity, wouldn't it?"

"Listen, Kate," said Johnny. "I'm going to drive you to your apartment, and you're going to drink

[46]

a glass of hot milk and lie down for a while."

Kate laughed. "No. Drive me back to campus. I feel rather guilty, leaving like this on my first day. I want to see if Dean Calder needs me."

"You're sure you're all right? You still look sort of green around the gills."

"My gills," said Kate, "are green on purpose. It's terribly good this season."

"I shouldn't let you do this," Johnny said. "But I have a date with Beethoven."

"What!"

"My apartment's right across from the side door of the library. I can leave you to your duties, drive two blocks, and listen to his *Seventh*. You can make up stories about all this, Kate, because you never knew Garnet. I did. I need some good clean music, and maybe a drink."

"I've been dreadful. Please forgive me."

"You know perfectly well that I'd forgive you anything, so don't make those big mournful eyes at me. Where do you live, Kate? I want to come and see you soon."

She told him.

"Whew! I'm glad you decided to go back to the office. That's a long, long way from campus."

"I may get a place near school if I can find anything in the middle of the year."

"I think the little house next to Kurt's is empty," Johnny offered.

"You might," said Kate severely, "show a little more enthusiasm."

The Dean's office was locked. Kate turned away and hurried down the stairs, but she reached the street just in time to see Johnny's little green car swerve around the corner two blocks down University, where the huge pink library stood. So she waited for a moment in the shadow of the Science Building, deciding what to do. Then, abruptly, she turned the corner and started down

[47]

the side street toward a large stucco apartment building which looked big and clean in contrast to the musty old houses hemming the green grass and red brick of the campus.

Kate had never liked this part of town. The trees were as old as the houses, and some of them were dead. An old man in a faded blue shirt looked sourly up at her over the bright arc of water that fell from the nozzle of a garden hose upon his pocket handkerchief of lawn.

NO VACANCY, said a black and silver sign hanging beside the entrance of the apartment house.

> "This the land of lost content,
> I see it shining plain,
> The happy highway where I went,
> And may not come again,"

Kate thought, and smiled a little wryly to herself as she retraced her step to try again.

The landlady smiled a fixed, professional smile. "I have a lovely little apartment," she said. "Just lovely. This way, please."

With her keys jingling importantly she led Kate down the dark carpeted hall to a sign that said ELEVATOR.

As the little automatic elevator groaned upward, Kate looked at the initials that vandalistic students of other years had scrawled on its very varnished interior.

"Isn't that terrible?" demanded the landlady, in a voice which would have better suited a major catastrophe.

"Terri——" began Kate politely, and stopped, her eyes glued to two initials: G. D.

She shook her head impatiently, and the manager asked, "Anything wrong, dear?"

"No," said Kate firmly, as the elevator jolted to a stop.

The manager slid open the inner door, held it firmly in place with her posterior, and expertly shoved open the outer door. Kate passed through with a murmur of thanks, and the manager jingled after her down the third-floor hall, darting past in a moment to stab a key into the lock of a door.

"This is it, and it's a perfectly lovely apartment, dear."

It was exactly like a number of campus apartments Kate had known in the past. The tiny kitchen was painted a peculiar sour-apple green, the let-down bed hid during the daytime behind discreetly curtained french doors, and there was even the inevitable blotch of ink on the carpet beside the wobbly little writing table. But the sofa was chintz and gay; the wide west windows let the late sunlight fall in glowing squares on the floor, and looked out toward the library and the pointed tower of the Philosophy Building beyond.

Johnny's apartment house, only two blocks away, was on the same side of the street as this one. From the window she could see his green coupe parked out front.

"I'll take it," said Kate. "I'll move in tonight."

The manager's smile grew even wider, and in a gorgeous burst of volubility she assured Kate that it was a lovely apartment, that she was sure Kate would be very happy here, that the maid would come in every Thursday to clean, that it was a lovely apartment, and that she was sure Kate would be very happy here.

Kate sank wearily down onto the chintz sofa and lit a cigarette.

Not bad for one day. A new job and a new apartment. She looked around the room. Nothing to put away now except three boxes of gift sta-

[49]

tionery, a bottle of ink and a fountain pen that had seen its best days. I ought to write Mother. I'll do that tomorrow. Nine-thirty, I ought to eat something.

She put out her cigarette and went over to the desk.

All this junk will never go into that tiny drawer, she decided hopelessly, opening the shallow drawer with the vague notion that it might look bigger inside than it did from the outside.

Oh, she thought. The maid forgot to clear it out.

A small heap of pale blue stationery. Some envelopes. She could see three words scrawled on the top sheet. Three words in brown ink, ending in a blot.

". . . wherever I go . . ."

She opened the drawer wider, and a round brown monogram above two lines of hasty writing leaped out at her.

G. D.

Garnet Dillon.

She was quite conscious of standing for a timeless moment staring down into the drawer while she listened to her mind mumble to itself.

"Dead men's shoes. Her job. Her apartment. But that's how things are."

Then she picked up the top sheet of stationery and read what was written there.

". . . . can't stand it. This thing follows me wherever I go . . ." And then the blot.

She raised her head and looked into her own huge eyes staring out at her from the mirror above the desk. Her face was white against her black hair, and there was a smudge of dust on her nose.

Behind her the glow of lamplight, the gay chintz sofa, the wide windows looking out across the silent campus. But the cheerfulness of the lamplight had gone hollow, and the sofa was no longer gay, and the night was waiting outside the windows as it had waited for the other girl who had lived in this room.

SIX

THE APARTMENT HOUSE where Johnny lived was built around a patio. Kate stood there alone, with damp grass under her feet, a palm tree rustling above her head, and looked around at many doors and more lighted windows. Then, from an open second-story window to her left, the first bar of Beethoven's *Seventh* boomed into the darkness.

She smiled. She went to the door beneath the window and climbed the stairs, and did not have to look at the neatly lettered "John Greenwood" on the nameplate above the bell to know that this apartment was Johnny's. She rang, belatedly straightening her hair. In a moment the door was open, and Johnny was standing against a dimly lit room.

"Katie!" he said, surprised. "Come in."

She walked past him to face a roomful of people slouched comfortably with tall amber glasses of beer in their hands. Then, in the flicker of time that passed before they began saying "Hello," she realized that the smallness and dimness of the room had made a crowd out of three people: Gladys Horstmann, sitting on the sofa with her feet toed in just enough to spoil the effect of a well-tailored gray suit; Whittaker, looking gravely at Kate out of his light eyes; and Hitch straddling a small chair with his long tweed legs.

She answered their "Hello's," feeling embarrassed and foolish, and looked around for a place to sit.

"Take the big chair by the radio," called Johnny from the kitchen. "I'm pouring you some beer."

She did. The automatic record-player beside the

radio bombarded her eardrums with music. Gladys Horstmann shouted, "We're trying to get Johnny to go to the Hofbrau with us. Maybe you can do something with him. He's in one of his stubborn moods."

"What," asked Kate, "is the Hofbrau?"

"A German beer garden," said Whittaker. "Just the proper background for medical students, you see. Very Heidelberg. Pardon — Swiss, since Munich."

Gladys said, "Johnny should come."

"I'm broke," Johnny announced, coming out of the kitchen with a glass of beer which he handed down to Kate.

Hitch reached into his pocket, drew out a wallet and took out two one-dollar bills. "You can pay me back next week."

"That's Hitch," said Johnny in a side comment to Kate. "He'll loan you the shirt off his back. But he expects you to return it neatly laundered."

Hitch flushed, and Gladys Horstmann said calmly, "Shut your great flapping mouth, Greenwood, and take that money."

"Charming girl," said Johnny to Kate. "Like a Dresden figurine."

"Put back your dough, Hitch," said Gladys wearily. "I've got a suspicion that Johnny's not gonna join us."

Hitch obeyed and there was a little silence. Then Whittaker, his light eyes level on Johnny's face, said quietly, "Why don't you want to go, Greenwood?"

Johnny was slumped deep in a chair beside Kate's. He looked up at Whittaker out of shadowed eyes, and Kate suddenly knew that Johnny had waltzed at the Hofbrau with Garnet Dillon. She could see them dancing together, whirling under colored lights to gay music with a hint of sadness to it.

"I have a date with Kate," said Johnny.

"He has a date with Kate," repeated Whittaker to the ceiling.

"*You'd* like to go to the Hofbrau, wouldn't you, Kate?" asked Hitch.

"I never realized how popular Johnny was," Kate hedged.

"Why, hell," exploded Gladys, "the only reason we want him is because three's a crowd."

"And he knows the singer. He gets him to sing suggestive songs in German," added Whittaker.

Johnny looked at Kate. "Would you like to go, Kate?"

"I'm pretty tired, Johnny. I've just finished moving."

"On campus?" asked Johnny, quite eagerly.

She nodded and caught his eyes. "That tall building two blocks down the street," she said, trying to tell him what she could not say before these people who thought that Garnet Dillon was still alive.

His eyebrows went up.

"If you had a date with Kate," put in Gladys, shrewdly, "how come you didn't know she was moving?"

"I'm a creature of impulse," explained Kate

Gladys looked annoyed before she joined the laughter.

"Well," said Whittaker, peering at his wrist watch, "it's ten. And it boils down to this. Either we go to the Hofbrau by ourselves, or drink Johnny's beer here."

Johnny said, "Go on to the Hofbrau, for the love of Mike! What is all this, anyway? You've never tried to drag me along with you before."

"We've never had to drag you before," said Whittaker, his eyes on Johnny's again. "You were always way ahead of us, throwing confetti at yourself."

[53]

With a scraping and a low hum, the arm of the automatic victrola moved slowly back to the rim of the record it had just played and another record slid down the central pin with a clatter. Kate watched, fascinated. There was something horrible in the robotlike movement.

Then the doorbell rang.

"A few more of my buddies," said Johnny over his shoulder as he went to the door. "They've probably come to take me to the Grove."

Then his voice changed and he said, "Oh. Hello, Kurt."

While Johnny closed the door, Kurt walked to the center of the room. His thin face was very still and the slanted green eyes looked dull. For some reason Kate could not take her eyes from him.

"I'll get you some beer," said Johnny, and went into the kitchen.

And then Kurt, standing very straight in the center of the room, said, "I wonder if you know. She's dead."

"Who's dead?" asked Gladys promptly.

"Garnet," said Kurt.

The silence bulged with the music, going on and on, timeless and unheeding.

Kate's eyes went from Kurt to Johnny, standing in the door of the kitchen, and then to the other faces there in that dim little room. Everyone was staring at Kurt, and for a moment there was not a motion or a sound. Gladys Horstmann's full mouth, painted bright red for the evening, was a little open; looking up at Kurt, she was strangely like a votary before a shrine. Whittaker was unchanged, except that he seemed for a moment quite old. Hitch's blue eyes and his pink face and the sandy lock tumbling over his forehead were suffused with amazement. And all of them had lost the quality of youthfulness they had had that morning in the Student Union. Shock had made

[54]

their faces adult and a little hard; here and there a line showed that Kate had not seen before.

Then Hitch's eyes went wild and desolate and he shakily lowered his glass to the floor, carefully bending his blond head. Whittaker stood up and took a step toward Kurt. "How do you know she's dead?"

Kurt saw the half-poured glass of beer Johnny was holding. He went over and took it, and drank it down. Then he put the empty glass back into Johnny's hand and said, "Vines told me, just now. He went to the Dean's office after Miss Farr this afternoon. He heard the Dean talking to someone and listened outside the door because they were talking about Garnet. The Dean said he knew it wasn't suicide, and then the other man dialed a number on the phone and said, 'I'm calling the Coroner's office.'"

"Why did Vines tell *you* about this?" asked Kate.

Kurt turned his dull eyes toward her. He smiled. It was not a pleasant smile. "He wanted to see me writhe." Kurt stiffened. "He didn't."

"But," asked Gladys, who had changed her position and was leaning forward, "what did she die of? What's coming off here?"

"I don't know about that," said Kurt slowly. "But Vines thinks she was murdered."

"Murdered!" whispered Hitch.

"That's Vines' guess," said Whittaker quickly.

"The Dean's too, Vines thinks," Kurt replied.

"That's ridiculous!" said Gladys, angrily. "Vines thinks! The Dean thinks! What are the facts?"

Kate looked at Johnny. Again his eyes met hers at once. He shook his head slightly, and stepping forward, set the empty beer glass down beside the radio. For the first time, he seemed to become aware of the music, and switched off the record-player.

[55]

"This much seems plain to me," Johnny said. "You . . . we have learned of this because Vines listened to what he wasn't supposed to hear, which is typical of Vines. The Dean is apparently trying to find out the truth about Garnet's death as quietly as possible. I think we should all keep our mouths shut, and I think we should get hold of Vines and make him keep his mouth shut, too." He turned then to Kurt who was staring fixedly at a spot on the carpet. "Have you or Vines told anyone else?"

"No."

"All right. Then if any little rumors start floating around, one of us started them." His clear brown eyes went soberly from face to face.

Whittaker nodded. "Right as usual, Greenwood."

Johnny looked at the floor and said, "It's not necessary for me to bring up the fact that we all think a hell of a lot of the Dean . . . you don't have to talk about such things."

"And we all thought a lot of Garnet, too," said Hitch, in a low voice.

Gladys Horstmann looked at him quickly and then looked away.

"Oh, a great deal," said Kurt gravely. "All of us, am I not right, gentlemen?"

Smiling, Kurt walked stiffly to a vacant armchair beside Hitch. He leaned back in it, his long white hands on the end of its arms.

"I should like some more beer, Johnny," he said.

"Got any whisky?" asked Hitch. His voice was gray.

"Enough for one straight apiece. And then we've got to get hold of Vines."

As Johnny started toward the kitchen door, Kate called, "Wait a minute, Johnny!" He stopped, looking at her in surprise.

She took the folded sheet of blue stationery

from the big patch-pocket of her tan coat. She said, to all of them, "I moved to campus today, and I'm afraid I moved into Garnet Dillon's apartment." She handed the sheet of stationery to Johnny and said, "Is that her handwriting?"

His eyes on the paper, he nodded slowly, then raised his head. "Where did you find this?"

"In the drawer of the desk. The landlady forgot to clean it out. I don't know what to make of what's written there, Johnny. I hope someone else can."

"I can't." He passed it to Gladys, and went into the kitchen.

Gladys read it. She shook her head. "I don't like it," she said. Then she made a long reach and handed the note to Whittaker, saying in an attempt at lightness, "Here, master mind. You tell us."

Hitch leaned precariously sideways to look over Whittaker's shoulder. It was interesting to watch the difference in their faces as they read. Whittaker's was as blank as a sheet of paper; Hitch's changed from word to word.

"It's her handwriting," said Hitch. "She wrote me a note once on that same blue paper." He took the paper from Whittaker, stood up and started toward Kate. Then he veered abruptly, saying, "Oh, I forgot; Kurt hasn't seen it yet."

"Thank you," said Kurt, and raised one white hand from the arm of the chair to take the paper. He held it up in front of his face. Then he lowered it. Then he rose and handed the paper to Kate.

"I should advise you to take it to the Dean tomorrow," he said, and went back to his chair.

Kate put the paper into her pocket. She was disappointed. She had been sure that one of these people who had known Garnet Dillon so well would be able to make at least a guess as to the meaning of those hastily scrawled words. There

[57]

was something unnatural in their calm.

Unnatural! That was it.

SEVEN

SURE I REMEMBER HER!" said the red-haired counterman. "She come in"—he looked at the clock on the wall, whose hands stood at a quarter to eleven —"just about this time, last Friday night." He mopped the counter with a vigorous, circular motion.

"Alone?" asked Tuck.

"Yeah."

"Go on."

"Well, I was fillin' the coffeepot when she came in." With his thumb, he indicated the tall metal coffee-maker, its chrome glittering under the hard overhead lights. "I heard the door slam but I couldn't turn around just then. When I did, she was sittin' at the counter. Her face looked kinda queer, so I asked her if she'd missed her train, and she said 'Yes,' and I asked her what she was goin' ta have, and she said coffee, like it didn't matter much to her what she had."

"Was there any baggage?"

"No. She musta checked it. Women mostly do that, because they always have so darned much." He looked morosely at a fly circling above Tuck's coffee cup. "Where was I? . . . Oh, yeah. When she said 'Coffee,' like I told you, this guy who come in just after she did says, 'The same for me.'"

"What was this man like?"

"Him? Let's see. He was tall, and he had on a black felt hat and a black overcoat."

Tuck experienced a slight shock. A pattern began shaping itself in his mind. But he said, "And then?"

"Then I got their coffee and gave it to 'em. Then I had to go back to fix the coffeepot there. . . . It drips through, see, and you gotta run it off into a pan and pour it onto the grounds from the top. . . . And the next thing, this man says in a funny voice, 'This girl is ill!' I turned around, and there she was, slumped over with her face on the counter, real white, and her eyes shut. I didn't hafta look twice to know what was wrong. . . . My mom went that way two months ago—just fell over into her plate, and it was her heart. So I called the County Hospital and told 'em I had a gal here in the middle of a heart attack, and gave 'em the address. When I looked around, the guy was just goin' out the door, but his nickel was on the counter so I let him go. I didn't have no place to lay her down, so I hadda leave her there. If anyone hadda come in I woulda told 'em what was wrong, but no one did until the guys with a stretcher from the hospital. They got her on the stretcher and one of them says to me, 'Didn't she have a purse or something?' I said no; I was pretty excited, and they carried her off."

"And," asked Tuck, sensing a shade of doubt in the man's voice, "didn't she have a purse?"

The man's light eyes moved a fraction of an inch to the left of Tuck's gaze. "Now I think of it, I think maybe she did."

"Yes?" encouraged Tuck.

The man's eyes sought his. "Well, when she said she'd have coffee I think one of these purses made outta a black, velvety kind of leather was on the counter beside her, but I'm not sure, because most women lay their purses down on the counter like that, and I might be remembering from a lotta other times."

Tuck smiled to himself. As a witness this man was a rare find; he had stumbled on a basic principle of observation—that one can see only what one observes and one observes only things which are already in the mind, sometimes without any

[59]

outside stimulus whatever.

"But you think she may have had a black suede purse with her?"

"Suede. Yeah, that's it! And say, I think it had gold on it somewhere, but I'm not sure of that."

So, thought Tuck, if I can find that Garnet Dillon was in the habit of carrying a black suede purse with gold on it somewhere, it then looks as if there were a good reason for the man in the black overcoat to have left so abruptly.

The redheaded man began to wash some dishes stacked on a drainboard just out of sight below the counter, and with his ears full of this homely sound Tuck allowed his imagination a brief spree. This was always an interesting process to Tuck, for Reason, like a prudent friend, accompanied the reckless toper, urging him homeward, pointing out the fallacies of his flights of fancy as a good friend should.

Tuck's imagination said that it was plain that if the girl had had a black purse with gold on it, and the purse had vanished by the time the intern inquired after it, why then the counterman did not take it since then he would not have mentioned its possible presence to Tuck. And since no one else had been in the lunchroom except the man in the black overcoat, why then the man in the black overcoat must have taken the purse.

Reason agreed.

Now, argued Imagination, I grant that there are many men in black overcoats in Los Angeles, but there are not so many with a predilection for the purses of young women.

Reason agreed again.

Therefore it is not too far-fetched to assume that this man in the black overcoat who had taken the dying girl's purse *might* be the man in the black overcoat who has recently killed five young women in five different ways and then has stolen their pocketbooks.

Reason agreed dubiously that it was barely possible.

Imagination brooded.

There was no proof that the five murders had been committed by one man. That was a theory of Tuck's alone, borne out slenderly by the few facts he had sketched to Gufferty earlier that day. But accepting a single homicidal maniac as a possibility, and accepting for the moment the notion that this same man had sat one seat away from Garnet Dillon on the night she died, and that as she was dying he had stolen her purse and left, why then there were two possible alternatives.

The man in the black overcoat had found a sixth way of killing and had used it on Garnet Dillon.

Or Garnet Dillon had been poisoned by another murderer, and had happened to die one chair away from the man in the black overcoat.

Coincidence? Wow!

Of the first alternative, there was this to be said: Tuck knew of no poison which acted immediately and at the same time gave the symptoms of a fatal heart attack to an extent to fool even the greenest intern, even one prepared by the counterman's diagnosis to find a case of heart attack. Therefore the notion of the man in the black overcoat doctoring Garnet Dillon's coffee while the counterman's back was turned and her attention was directed elsewhere was out of the question. Which would mean that the paths of Garnet and the man in the black overcoat must have crossed before a quarter to eleven, Friday night, and under circumstances which would have allowed him to poison her, if he were to be considered even for a moment, and by the most giddy imagination, as her murderer.

And that their paths had or had not crossed before would be learned only by minute investigations. So, for the time being, that line of thought was a cul-de-sac.

As for the other alternative, that Garnet had been poisoned by someone else earlier in the day, why then the consternation of the man in the black overcoat was something that Tuck enjoyed thinking about.

What a beautiful situation! said Imagination. A psycopathic killer, who has murdered five young women for pleasure and for gain, prepares to drink an innocent cup of coffee at a drab, fly-ridden lunch counter, and lo, a sixth young woman drops dead one chair away! After the first alarm —when he said, "This girl is ill!"—must have come, to that twisted mind, a grim yet gleeful sense of the irony of the situation. And after that must have come an urgent desire to be elsewhere at once. And after that must have come the reckless, perhaps imperious urge to take the black purse on the counter; to turn even this near fiasco into a delightful joke against the god who had made him an alien from all men, slinking forever down the dark alleys of the world.

That's enough of that, said Reason. You're going too fast. Poison in her coffee! And you don't even know the results of the autopsy yet!

"More coffee?" asked the counterman.

Tuck looked down strangely at his cup, which he had emptied to the dregs during his internal dialogue, nodded, and closely watched the counterman fill it.

"By the way," he said, as the hot, steaming stuff was set before him with a thud. "Do you happen to remember what the man in the black overcoat looked like?"

"Looked like?" The counterman's face was blank. He shook his head slowly. "He was tall, and like I said, he had on this here black hat and coat, and . . ." His voice trailed off.

"Do you happen," asked Tuck, very casually,

"to remember his face?"

"Naw," said the counterman, and his stealthy hand appeared above the counter, grasping a fly-swatter, with which he very competently mashed a fly busy with a few grains of sugar. "It was just a face," he added, looking pleased at his victory.

Just a face. Well, thought Tuck, as he finished the last of the coffee, it's a good thing you don't know what sort of a mind may have been under that face, my friend. If you did, the face would like magic gain a scar, a leer, and a squint in the left eye, because witnesses, my friend, are witnesses, the world over.

He rose and dropped a dime to the counter.

"Only a nickel," said the counterman. "We don't charge for the second cup."

Tuck squeezed into the brown phone booth by the door. He slid the nickel the counterman had just returned to him into the slot, and dialed Dean Calder's home. A juiceless voice, which he took to belong to Mrs. Calder, asked him please to wait a moment, and then the Dean came to the phone.

"It's too soon for the autopsy results, I suppose," he said.

"I think it is. I didn't call to give you information but to ask for some. Did Miss Dillon own a black suede purse trimmed in gold?"

"Yes. It had a gold initial. She was fond of initials."

"Ah," said Tuck.

He dialed the Hall of Justice, asked for the Coroner's office, and then for Dr. Smith.

"H'lo," came the medical examiner's chronically dour voice, after a long pause.

"Tuck speaking, Doctor. Have you examined the Dillon girl's body yet? She came in late this afternoon."

"You guys never can wait, can you? You seem to think I can perform a complete autopsy the way

[63]

you carve up a Christmas turkey. No, I haven't finished. But I think I've found enough to keep you busy for a while. Here's the dope. She didn't die of any heart complication that I know about. Heart's as sound as a nut. But what a spleen! She had anemia, possibly leukemia. She didn't die of either of those. Here's what she did die of. I found traces of digitalis in the gastro-intestinal tract."

"Digitalis? But that's a medicine used for heart disease!"

"It is. It also has a poisonous cumulative effect."

"You mean," asked Tuck, his mind very busy, "that it takes more than one dose to kill?"

"That is the usual meaning of the words 'poisonous cumulative effect,'" snapped the medical examiner. "Now, one more item. She was . . ."

"And death by digitalis looks like death by heart failure?"

"How I hate that expression!" moaned the medical examiner. "All death involves heart failure! You might as well say a person died by dying!"

"What I mean," elaborated Tuck, "is that a person dying from the poisonous cumulative effect of digitalis might appear to have been the victim of a heart attack?"

"Yes. Without an autopsy, without a medical man there to observe the symptoms, yes. And even with an autopsy, digitalis would not necessarily be found in the system, because after assimilation it literally becomes part of the heart muscle. In this case, however, the girl died with digitalis in her intestine. It had not yet been assimilated into the blood stream. Just how much digitalis will cause death differs of course with different people; there is a case on record where two and one-half grains caused death, just to give you an idea. On the other hand, in digitalizing a heart patient a doctor often gives an initial dose of eight grains or so without ill effect, following this with repeated small doses. But in the case of a person with a perfectly normal heart, like this girl here, I would say that fifty grains, over a period of twelve to eighteen hours, would be the probable fatal dose. Death would follow in five days to two weeks. The symptoms are abdominal pains, slow heart rate, headache, chills, dilated pupils. But sometimes death comes without any symptoms whatever. Now, if there's nothing else . . ."

"Digitalis can be purchased at any drug counter, can't it? Without a doctor's prescription?"

"Yes. They usually slap a poison label on the vial, and they make you sign the poison book. Anything else?"

"It comes in little greenish pills, doesn't it?"

"Or capsules."

"How many grains each?"

"One and a half. Anything else?"

Tuck was thinking that Garnet Dillon must have swallowed about thirty digitalis pills, or capsules. Thirty.

". . . Because if there's nothing else," the medical examiner was saying. "I'd like to tell you that I also found that she was pregnant. About a month and a half. Good night!"

The sound of the receiver crashing onto its hook stunned Tuck's right ear. Slowly, he replaced his receiver, too.

Pregnant. Fifty grains, thirty tablets, over a period of twelve to eighteen hours.

No stranger did that.

As he walked away from the station toward his black sedan, his mind slowly masticated what it had just learned.

If Black Overcoat had never seen Garnet Dillon until she collapsed across the counter, why then Chance had stepped in and twisted the pattern a bit. And the thief had thieved, and so she had been one of the nameless bodies that find quietness at last in the antiseptic shelter of the County Hospital. And there Chance had stepped in again, and the body had been sent back to its own.

Tuck had a great respect for Chance. It never bothered him. It was a Puck, thumb to nose, mocking the pompous procession of cause and effect; Puck, running alongside, sometimes joining the procession to cause an effect, or prevent one. You had to respect an ethicless urchin who could change destinies.

But there was another side to the coin. Perhaps Black Overcoat and Garnet Dillon had not been strangers to each other. Digitalis. Fifty grains.

If the man in the black overcoat had known her, and had poisoned her, and had been present when she died in order to steal her purse, with its identifying driver's license, then he could not be the Black Overcoat with five murders and five purses to his discredit. Could he?

Tuck heard a train chuff slowly out of the station. The funeral donging of the bell was followed by a long hoot, mournful as a banshee's cry. He smiled at the drama in the sounds; scowled at the thought that another train had chuffed away like that, leaving behind a young woman already arrived at a different destination.

EIGHT

You know the old saying 'murder will out'?" asked Dean Calder. "It has. Oh. Pardon me. Miss Farr, this is Lieutenant Tuck. Tuck, Miss Farr, my new secretary."

"How do you do?" Kate said, and thought, Lord, but he's tall! He's the tallest man I've ever seen. Even his head is tall.

"My other secretary," Dean Calder was saying, looking at her, "used to like a cup of coffee at Chapel hour. I don't see why you shouldn't take the same prerogative."

"Thanks," said Kate aloud. And to herself, "The brush-off."

As she was getting her jacket from the cabinet above her desk Dean Calder went on to Tuck, "One of the medical students happened to be outside the door during our talk yesterday. He told what we said to another student, who told five more. But I don't think it will go any further. All of them, including the man who eavesdropped, came in a body this morning to assure me of that. Vines," he added thoughtfully, "seemed to have a black eye."

"Do you want me to take any mail?" Kate asked the Dean.

"Oh, yes. Thank you." He handed her several letters and a smile, and as she went out the door she heard him say, "They all were good friends of Garnet, so I . . ."

Tuck said, "Oh. All friends of the dead girl, I see."

He said this in a low, easy voice, as though it didn't matter a bit, but somehow Kate got the impression that it mattered quite a good deal.

"Hi," called a hearty voice, and Kate turned to see Gladys Horstmann bounding down the stairs that led to the third floor where the Biology laboratories were. "Going to the Union?"

When they were facing each other at a small brown table against the windows, their cokes in front of them, Gladys leaned conversationally forward and asked, "What do you know about psychopathic murderers?"

Kate was startled. This, coming from the tall, athletic creature with frank hazel eyes, was out of character. As though Johnny were to turn her suddenly and recite tender love poetry. "Not much," she said.

"I do. My brother is a psychiatrist, and we follow the really gory murders in the papers and try to guess the mania of the killer. They're mostly obviously paranoid, with just a few schizos."

"That must be loads and loads of fun for you and your brother," said Kate dryly.

The dryness escaped Gladys. "It sure is. There's been quite a wave of woman killings lately. But the odd thing is that none of the women have been raped, either before or after death. Apparently the killer got enough satisfaction out of plain murder."

"Sort of an epicure?" asked Kate.

Gladys slapped the table with the flat of her hand. "That's exactly the word I've been looking for! This man—I hold out for one killer, by the way—is a beast, no doubting that. But he's a tiger instead of the usual jackal." She smiled wholesomely and said, "We're none of us very far from the jungle. It's always right there under the skin, waiting to jump out."

"Now there," said Kate, "I disagree. That's a generality, and I don't know of any generalities that aren't also lies. Some people—this psychopathic killer of yours—are just what you said. Beasts. Revert to the jungle. But that doesn't apply generally."

Gladys seemed about to argue the point, and then capitulated. "O.K., O.K. You win!" She folded her arms on the edge of the table and leaned over them, her eyes fixed almost hypnotically on Kate's. In the cold north light falling across her face their hazel color broke down into tiny flecks of gold, of green, of brown. "I brought this up," she said softly, "because I think one of these birds did in our Garnet."

"That unfinished letter I found in the desk?"

"Yes. The Thing. The Thing that followed her. I don't think she left to get away from him, understand. I believe that her walk-out and her death are two separate threads of action. I believe just what I said yesterady morning, that she left to elope with a rich man. She probably mentioned this 'thing' as a fake excuse, to get sympathy from whoever that letter was intended for. And the Thing that had been following her followed again, and this time killed her."

"How?"

Gladys seemed taken aback. "How? They usually use a sharp knife or razor, or smash with something heavy."

"Then your theory's no good," said Kate, with a satisfaction that surprised her. "Because I saw her body. There wasn't a mark on it."

"You saw her . . . !" Horstmann began to clarion.

"Shut up!" whispered Kate, fiercely, looking around them. And then to Horstmann, "I can tell you this because you happen to know she's dead. The rest of the Student Union doesn't. And we've all given our word to Dean Calder to keep this quiet."

"Sure, sure," said Gladys. She whispered, "How did you happen to see the body?"

"It was sent here for dissection from the hospital."

Gladys jabbed wildly toward the ceiling with one index finger. "You mean she was upstairs in Griswold's . . . ?"

"Yes."

"Omigod," said Gladys. She scowled at her coke. She began to stir the ice around and around in the glass with her bent straw. Then she looked up. "I see what you mean. She must have been poisoned, and they missed it at the County."

"That's what I think."

There was a sudden clicking. It startled Kate, and then she realized that Gladys was clasping and unclasping the purse that lay in her lap. The

nervous gesture seemed out of place coming from
the big, square-shouldered girl.

"Poison . . ." Gladys mused. And added, "Of
course, it's not certain yet that she was murdered."

"No," agreed Kate.

"Poison . . ." Gladys said again. "Does that say
to you what it says to me?"

Kate's heart skipped; it was as though Gladys
had read her thoughts. But she said, "What do
you mean?"

"I mean that it looks as if Garnet had been
killed by someone who knew her." Her eyes narrowed. "Or wait. Does it . . . ?" Her eyes widened
suddenly, and she gave a mechanical smile at
someone behind Kate. Kate turned, and seeing a
girl she did not know, turned back again to
Gladys.

"What do you mean, 'Or does it'?"

Gladys looked at Kate, her eyes almost dreamy.
"I can see Garnet going into a bar for a drink,
let's say. She's left the old world behind and that
calls for celebration. She sits at a stool at the bar.
A man comes in and sits down beside her. The
man is the Thing in her letter, still following. Her
drink is in front of her. She's looking the other
way—maybe a good-looking boy is putting a
nickel in the juke box, or maybe she sees a girl
in a hat like hers. The Thing reaches past her
glass for a napkin or a pretzel. He drops poison
in her glass. He watches her die. He leaves." She
leaned forward. "How's that?"

"Not so good," said Kate. "I could believe it
more easily if she hadn't mentioned this 'thing' in
her letter. I find it rather improbable to picture a
degenerate stalking his prey. I always had the
idea that a homicidal maniac took what he could
get."

Gladys shook her head vigorously. "Not at all.

[70]

Look at Hickman. He had one object for his affections and only one."

"Well, but don't you see," said Kate, "that that brings you right back to what you're trying to get away from—that she was killed by someone who knew her?" She felt a shiver on her spine. "In fact, I think you're more in the soup than ever. You're not only saying that someone she knew is a murderer but also that he's a pervert of the most horrible sort."

Gladys' well-fleshed face showed a trace of pink, and Kate learned that her temper was short. Her irritation, it seemed to Kate, was due to a resentment at Kate's exhibiting any power of logic whatsoever.

"That's not at all what I mean," Gladys said. "All I meant to imply was that the killer—the Thing—had seen her before. Walking down campus. In the grocery store. And if you're wondering what a homicidal maniac was doing on campus, let me tell you that last semester there was gent who had a habit of waylaying coeds. He scared the entire Girls' Dorm out of their wits before he was caught. As a matter of fact, a campus with fifteen hundred girls bouncing along the grass is a logical hunting ground for guys with a lust for female blood."

"Granting that, I still think that the 'thing' she mentioned in that letter was a bogie in her own mind. Perhaps some regret she couldn't smother."

"You didn't know Garnet. She was short on conscience, honey. She knew the Bible verbatim, but she didn't seem to understand a word."

"How do you know that?" asked Kate.

"I don't like women who dangle hearts on a string."

"Oh," said Kate.

The pink was in Gladys' cheeks again.

Kate looked at the clock and grabbed her check.

[71]

She stood up and downed the last of her coke. It was as bitter as gall. She felt her whole face pucker up and saw Gladys smiling strangely at her.

"I dropped a quinine pill into it when you turned around," she said. "I hate to see a perfectly good theory go to the dogs."

NINE

PREGNANT!" EXCLAIMED DEAN CALDER. He lowered his blue eyes to his fine hands, busy turning a long yellow pencil over and over. "I see."

"Do you think she was the sort of girl for whom that might be an incentive to suicide?" Tuck asked him.

"I'm sorry, but I don't."

"What would she do?"

"I think," said Dean Calder carefully, "that she'd go to the child's father and demand a wedding ring."

"And if he refused?"

"She'd come to me."

"And you would . . . ?"

"See that she got the ring," said Dean Calder, grimly. His face lightened a little. "I've done that twice since I've been Dean here. I'm happy to say that both marriages are apparently highly successful. Kids now are afraid of marriage, most of 'em. Afraid of the extra responsibility, of children. I don't entirely blame them for that. But whenever I get a chance I ring in a word about my own marriage. I've been married since I was twenty-one. My wife has been ill for the last ten years. I wouldn't trade a day of my married life for all the 'freedom' the young men praise so highly." He coughed his embarrassment behind one hand. "Pardon the eloquence, Tuck. One of my favorite hobby-horses. Let's get back to the autopsy. The medical examiner found she'd been poisoned, of course?"

Tuck nodded. "He found digitalis in the gastro-intestinal tract."

The Dean's bright blue eyes widened. "He found ——But that means——" He paused, and during the pause his face resumed its normal expression. "It's hardly a layman's poison, is it?" he finished.

"Hardly. I'll be frank with you, Calder. The girl's condition, plus the fact that she was killed with digitalis, suggests something to me. It suggests that she may have been killed by one of the medical students who seemed so much in love with her."

The Dean nodded reluctantly.

"Would a medical student know the properties of digitalis? Would he know the fatal dose, the cumulative action of the drug? Would he know that death by digitalis could pass for death from a heart attack?"

The Dean nodded again.

"There's another reason for thinking that she was murdered by someone who knew her rather well," said Tuck. "And that's the fact that more than one dose of the digitalis must have been given in order to kill her."

"Oh, yes," agreed Calder. "Considerably more. And over a day's time, I should say."

"How?" Tuck asked.

"Garnet was a coffee addict," said Dean Calder slowly. "Strong black coffee, I might add."

"And strong black coffee would hide the taste of digitalis?"

"Student Union coffee," Dean Calder said, with a wraith of a smile, "would hide the taste of any-thing."

"Another reason for believing that the mur-derer was someone who knew her habits very well."

[73]

"Yes. Although I find it rather hard to envision this murderer deliberately and consistently dropping four or five digitalis tablets into each cup of coffee she drank. I believe that would be particularly difficult to do in the Student Union, where she took possibly four of her eight or ten cups a day, since she usually sat at the Medical table where there would be at least half a dozen close witnesses to such improbable dexterity."

"And how about the rest of her day's quota of coffee? Where did she drink that?"

The Dean's face froze at some recollection. "At home. In her apartment. I remember that she once told me that she always kept a large pot of coffee on her stove, Swedish fashion."

"And her men friends dropped in to see her, I suppose?"

"Often. Her apartment is on campus, and therefore very convenient."

Tuck said, "Thirty-five digitalis tablets in the coffeepot, five days to two weeks before she died. That's fifty-two and one-half grains of digitalis, with time to dissolve. And certain of being taken in ten or twelve small doses. And no risk to anyone except the victim, because no one else would drink enough of the stuff to cause the slightest harm."

Dean Calder's face showed that he was inwardly agreeing.

"This is a very clever fellow," Tuck said.

The frenzied clamor of an electric bell announcing the end of Chapel hour rubbed all Tuck's nerves the wrong way. Calder, inured to the sound, appeared not to notice it.

"Let's presume that you have hit upon the means the murderer used to administer the poison. The problem of learning who visited Garnet's apartment and poisoned the pot of coffee won't be an easy one. I know that several of the boys were frequent visitors. The murderer himself could admit that and certainly not incriminate himself by that admission alone. And, on the other hand, the murderer would surely have gone alone, in which case the only certain witness to his visit was Garnet herself. So, you see, he could also lie."

"You've analyzed it perfectly," admitted Tuck.

"There's something else that occurs to me," Calder went on. "Garnet died with digitalis in her intestine. That means that a fairly stiff dose was taken orally five or six hours before her death."

"But that wasn't the dose that killed her."

Dean Calder shook his head. "No. She had taken the fatal does not less than five days, and not more than two weeks, before her death. But she was given another dose from five to six hours before she died, otherwise the digitalis wouldn't have been found in her intestine. All right. She died at eleven-thirty, on her way to the hospital. Which means that between five-thirty and six-thirty she was given the dose that the medical examiner found. That ought to give you something fairly definite to go on."

"And now," said Tuck quietly, "I want to ask questions. I want to talk to those medical students who seemed so fond of her."

"Of course," said the Dean just as quietly. He rose and walked erectly to a narrow wooden card file atop one of the big green filing cases. His back to Tuck, he said, "These young men you're going to question happen to be three of the students who know that Garnet is dead." He drew three cards from the solid alphabetized mass within the file, and closed it. As he did so, the door to the office opened and Kathryn Farr came in, a trifle breathless, slipping off her green jacket which she hung away in a narrow cupboard behind her desk.

The Dean mused, hand to chin. "Let's see. You'll want a room. The office here is far too busy. Ah. There's a lecture room next door that will be vacant until late afternoon."

He went to Miss Farr, who had seated herself at her desk and was watching him out of intelligent eyes. "Here's the first of those odd jobs I spoke about, Miss Farr." He handed her the cards. "These are the section cards of three students whom Mr. Tuck is going to question. They tell you what room each student is in at each hour of the day. When Mr. Tuck is ready, you will bring these students to him, one by one, explaining to the professors that they are wanted by me, and then explaining privately to each student that he is going to be questioned about Miss Dillon. You will take them to the room next door where Mr. Tuck will be waiting." He turned to Tuck. "Is that satisfactory?"

"Perfectly," said Tuck. He was looking at Miss Farr as she glanced over the cards the Dean had just given her. It seemed to him that she looked longer at one card than at any of the others.

"I have a lecture," said Dean Calder, his hand on the knob of the door, "so I will leave you." He looked at Tuck and added, "You don't know how much I wish this were unnecessary." Then with a firming of his pale lips and a stiff little nod he went out into the corridor, filled now with the voices and footfalls of young men on their way to their ten-thirty classes.

"We'll have to give them time to get there," remarked Miss Farr.

Tuck agreed.

When the corridor was silent again Miss Farr rose and said, "I'm going now, if you're ready."

"Fine," Tuck said, and held the door for her, watching for a moment as she walked quickly toward the light streaming down the hall from the

[76]

window at its far end. Then he walked to the lecture room next door.

It was a corner room, bright with sunlight, filled with rows of varnished wooden lecture chairs. He walked past them to one of the windows and stood looking down at University Avenue. Raising his eyes, he followed to where it ended in a huge green public park, with a stadium where football was played in the fall.

He was thinking how different this world was from the world he knew, when he heard the door open and turned. Miss Farr was standing there, and just behind her a tall, white-jacketed young man with yellow hair and yellow eyebrows. He looked as though he were trying to appear completely at ease.

The small smile was on Miss Farr's mouth again. "Mr. Tuck," she said precisely, "this is Robert Hitchlock." Then she stepped backward past the blond boy and out the door, the faint smile lingering to show that the usual formalities of introduction were incongruous here.

"How do you do, sir," said Hitchlock, stepping forward, with his head held very high.

"How do you do," said Tuck. "Let's sit down." He reached out a long arm and swung a chair around for himself, and another, facing it, for Hitchlock. Hitchlock walked woodenly to it and sat down, his blue eyes squinting a little against the strong light.

"Dean Calder tells me that you're one of the people who know that Garnet Dillon is dead and that she may have been murdered."

"Schwann told us last night," said the young man earnestly. "Vines had just told him."

"And I understand that you were very fond of her."

"Yes." The pink chin was squared.

Tuck put on his best smile, and got out a pad,

[77]

which he laid on the arm of the lecture chair. Then he began to fill his pipe. "All right. Nothing to get huffy about."

Hitchlock relaxed a trifle, as Tuck had intended that he should. When he had his pipe going, he found a stubby pencil in his coat pocket, and asked, "Hitchlock, do you know any reason why Miss Dillon should have been murdered?"

"No, sir. Absolutely none. She was—very popular."

"There was no one at all who disliked her?"

There was a slight pause. "No one."

"When did you see her last?"

"Friday night. At the Hofbrau. That's a beer garden where we all go."

"You talked with her?"

"I said hello."

"Oh, you didn't go together?"

"No. She was with Kurt Schwann. He's in genetical research. They were having dinner at a little table on the dance floor. We were several tables back from the floor. We just waved at them at first, because it was very crowded. Then while we were waiting for the main course we went over and said hello."

"Who is 'we'?"

"Gladys Horstmann and Jeff Whittaker and me."

"What time was this?"

"About six-thirty."

"I see. Was Miss Dillon's behavior what you would consider normal for her? Don't draw any conclusions from what's happened since; just remember how she seemed to you that night."

Hitchlock considered. "Well, it was normal for her, yes. But I was surprised by it just the same."

"I'm afraid that's not quite clear."

Hitchlock looked at him soberly out of his blue eyes. "Well, I stopped in at the Dean's office to see her at lunch time Friday, right after my last exam. She was alone and she was crying. I didn't know what to do. I started to go away, but she lifted up her head and when she saw it was me she tried to smile. 'I've got the blues,' she said." He dropped his eyes in embarrassment. "I asked her to tell me what was the matter. She'd been acting funny for the last few days. She wouldn't hear when you spoke to her, and she drank gallons of coffee; it made her so nervous that her eyes were nothing but pupil. But she wouldn't tell me what was wrong. I asked her to go to lunch with me, but she was waiting for someone else." He tried to grin. "That's the way it usually was. She was usually waiting for someone else."

"Who?"

Hitchlock started at the abrupt question. Then he averted his eyes. "Usually it was Kurt Schwann," he said.

"Why were you surprised by her behavior at the Hofbrau?"

The student looked puzzled. "She was laughing and talking as though she'd never cried in her life."

Tuck stood up. "Thank you, Hitchlock. And say, we're still trying to keep all this under the hat, you know. So you won't . . . ?"

"I understand," said Hitchlock, with dignity.

When the door had closed after Hitchlock, Tuck jotted additional comments on the pad. Beside the names of Kurt Schwann, Gladys Horstmann and Whittaker, he placed a precise black question mark. On hearing footsteps approaching the door, he put the pad away.

Miss Farr, and another white jacket. A small one, this time, and above it a small, neat face with a firm cold jaw.

"Mr. Tuck," said Miss Farr, "Jeff Whittaker." She left.

Whittaker moved easily, as small men so often do. "I'm afraid I don't know much that will help you, Mr. Tuck," he said.

"Sit down anyway," Tuck suggested lightly.

Whittaker looked shrewdly at the window he would have to face, and sat down in the chair Hitchlock had vacated. Whittaker's composure was quite real; where Hitchlock's had stopped just below the skin, Whittaker's went clear through.

"I understand," said Tuck, "that you were quite fond of Miss Dillon."

"Quite. And fond is exactly the proper word."

"You weren't in love with her?"

Whittaker cocked his head to one side. "Well, perhaps just a little. But I still think 'fond' comes closer to the mark." The lines around his eyes grew sharper with otherwise imperceptible amusement.

"As you know, Whittaker, it's possible that Miss Dillon may have been murdered."

"So I understand."

"Do you know of any reason why?"

"No. None."

"Kurt Schwann and she were in love, weren't they?"

"She was in love with Kurt. Kurt was attracted by her; she was unusually lovely. He was amused by her; she had a pretty way of saying nothing. I'm not at all sure that he was in love with her."

"Do you have any idea of what their relations were?"

"If you mean had they ever slept together, I don't know. There was something cold and careful in Garnet. And Kurt isn't the hot-blooded type. He's rather impeccable. On the other hand, she was twenty-two, he is twenty-six, and normal people of those ages have certain impulses of which you know as much as I. And neither of them had families, so there was no leavening influence from

[80]

that direction. Kurt's brother doesn't count as family; he's more like a young brother than an older one."

"Kurt's brother—what did he think of Miss Dillon?"

"Not much. He once told me, in German, that she made him think of a statuette of the Lorelei made in Hoboken, New Jersey. I doubt if they've said more than ten words to each other."

"What's this brother like?"

"He's a sad son-of-a-gun who lost his wife and never got over it."

"Did you notice anything unusual in Miss Dillon's behavior when you saw her at the Hofbrau Friday night?"

For the first time, Whittaker hesitated a trifle. "Well, I'm not exactly sure. I may have seen wrong. When I first saw her it struck me that she was giving an imitation of herself. Her gaiety looked exaggerated. Then I passed that off as being the result of the atmosphere. Colored lights hiding behind artificial vines, waltz music on violins—you know the sort of thing I mean."

Tuck nodded.

"At about nine, when we were leaving—we being Hitchlock, a Miss Horstmann, and I—we passed by the dance floor. Garnet was waltzing with Kurt. I caught just a glimpse of her face over his shoulder, and I'll swear that there were tears in her eyes!"

"I see. Do you have any idea why she was crying?"

"No. None."

Tuck stood up, and Whittaker did likewise. "Thank you very much," Tuck said.

"Not at all." And Whittaker walked toward the door, entirely composed.

Again, as soon as the door closed, Tuck's stubby pencil began to write. And again it stopped just before the door was opened by the third of the young men who had known Garnet Dillon best.

"Mr. Tuck—John Greenwood," said Miss Farr, and closed the door.

A tall young man. Taller than Hitchlock, in spite of a scholarly stoop. A quiet young man, with wise eyes in a square, impassive face.

"I understand that you knew Garnet Dillon quite well," began Tuck, when Greenwood was slumped comfortably in the chair facing the window.

"Quite well, yes."

"And you were very fond of her."

"Yes."

Tuck put on his smile. "A little in love with her?"

"No."

"Oh! I understood . . ."

Greenwood shifted his position slightly and said with a touch of impatience, "Anyone who told you I was in love with her was wasting your time."

"I see. When did you see her last?"

Greenwood reflected.

Then: "I saw her last at five-thirty last Friday afternoon."

"At her apartment?" asked Tuck, smoothly.

"Yes."

"There was a reason for your visit?"

"Yes. I went to break a dinner date I had with her and—and a mutual friend."

"How long were you there?"

No change of expression. "About five minutes."

"Was anyone else there?"

"Yes. Kurt Schwann came in just after I did."

"He was the mutual friend you had the dinner date with, then."

"Yes."

"Was it usual for the three of you to go places together?"

[82]

"More or less. We enjoyed each other's company."

"Which of you would you say she liked best?"

A slight hesitation. "Kurt."

"They were in love?"

"Yes."

"Their relations were intimate?"

"I don't know."

"Oh, come now . . ."

The light brown eyes regarded him coldly. "I don't know."

"You know, of course, that she may have been murdered. Do you know any reason why she might have been?"

"No."

"When you saw her at five-thirty, would you say that there was anything odd in her behavior?"

Greenwood thought. "She seemed to be under a strain of some sort. She had been that way for about a week."

"Did you ask her what was wrong?"

"Yes. She said she didn't feel well." Greenwood shifted again. Then a change come over his face. It warmed. He smiled a little. "You've been asking me all the questions; now let me ask you a few. As you know, I was one of the people who found her body up in the embalming room. I've been very damned cricket about this, but I want to know what she died of, and where, and how, and all about it. If you say the word, I'll keep quiet, but I'm curious."

"She was poisoned, and she died in a little cafe near the Fifth Street station."

"What was the poison?"

"Digitalis."

His eyebrows went up. "That's a mighty odd choice."

"It is."

Greenwood stood up. "Well, do you want to

ask me anything more?"

"No. And thanks for your help."

"That's quite all right." Greenwood held out his hand, which Tuck took. It was a large, capable hand, and its brief firm pressure revealed to Tuck something about John Greenwood which he had not known before. John Greenwood was the most mature of the three young men he had questioned. In contrast Hitchlock seemed juvenile, and Whittaker just a shade superficial.

Tuck let Greenwood open the door. Then he called him.

"Where can I find Kurt Schwann?" he asked.

"His laboratory is on the third floor, in the other wing. You go up the stairs near the Dean's office and turn left, then you—" He gave an impatient laugh. "Perhaps you'd better let me take you up."

"Fine," said Tuck.

They met Miss Farr in the hall. She and Greenwood exchanged a greeting, and Tuck said, "I'll be back in a few minutes." They walked to the stairs and Tuck had the feeling that she was watching them go.

As they went along the third-floor corridor, near-by chimes rang the quarter-hour, four clear notes. Greenwood stopped at a door that said "Laboratory 310." He opened it, peering around the edge, then jerked his head to indicate that Tuck was to follow him.

A thin, dark man, also white-jacketed, was peering down the barrel of a microscope. His face was an ascetic's face and he gave the immediate impression of being as clean and sterile as the glittering beakers and test tubes with which he was surrounded.

John Greenwood introduced them and left.

"I understand you're in genetical research," commented Tuck, half sitting on the corner of the lab table.

"That is right," said Kurt Schwann, his eyes going with concern to a rack of cotton-stoppered test tubes one foot from Tuck's posterior. "Here— let me offer you a chair." He thrust forward the straightest, hardest chair Tuck had ever seen, and sat down on its twin, drawn up before the microscope. Then, very courteously, he asked, "What is it that you wish to know?"

The man's tone irritated Tuck. It was as though, beneath the outer courtesy, there lurked an insult.

"I want to know who killed Garnet Dillon—if she was killed," Tuck said.

A flicker of something halfway between pain and anger went across Kurt's face.

"I know nothing of that," he said.

Tuck allowed surprise to show on his face. "Oh, but I understood that you and she were very close friends."

"We were." There was a stress on the last word, as though that friendship were something very far in the past.

"Then you must surely know what no one else seems to know. You must know what it was that troubled her so for several days before she left."

"But I don't," stated Schwann firmly.

"Surely you asked her what was wrong?"

Schwann inclined his head. "I did. When I became insistent that she tell me, she said that it was nothing that concerned me. Naturally, I did not trouble her further."

"Did anyone hear her say that to you?"

"No."

"When did this happen?"

"Last Friday night at about five-thirty."

"Tell me about it. Tell me her exact words."

"Greenwood and Garnet and I had planned for some time to go to the Hofbrau . . ."

"I know all about the Hofbrau, so don't bother to stop to describe it," said Tuck.

Kurt inclined his head. "I live with my brother in a small, very old house facing the park. I remember that during the entire walk to Garnet's I thought only of her odd behavior of the last week; all sorts of wild thoughts occurred to me as to the cause of it. I tell you this so you will understand the mood I was in when I entered Garnet's apartment that night, and why things happened as they did.

"I was a half-block from the building where she lived when I saw Johnny get out of his car. I got up to the door of her apartment perhaps a minute after he did, and I had raised my hand to knock when I heard Johnny say: 'I'm not coming tonight, Garnet. I know that you have things to say to Kurt. A third person would be in the way.' I realized that Johnny was asking her to tell me what was wrong with her. It made me angry that someone else, even Johnny, should have to intercede for me with Garnet. I knocked at the door and she let me in. And I saw that Johnny had failed already, because she trying hard to be natural; she was pretending that nothing was wrong. We talked for a few moments of this and that, and she laughed a great deal and made a joke or two, and Johnny left and then all at once I heard myself saying, 'This is no good, Garnet. It doesn't fool me. For the love of God, tell me what's wrong with you! I deserve that.' And that was when she looked at me and said as though she was talking to a little boy asking questions that he had no right to ask, 'It doesn't concern you, Kurt.'"

Kurt Schwann's lips closed in a tight line as he remembered. "I have never been so humiliated in my life," he said in a low voice.

Tuck watched him, puzzled. He could smell a lie, and he would swear that all this was true. And he couldn't help feeling sorry for Kurt. This Garnet had picked his Achilles' heel with unerring

[86]

cruelty; she had gashed his pride with five words. If it was true that she had loved Kurt, it seemed a strange sort of love. A love that bordered on hate, and certainly did not deal in confidences.

"But you and she went on to the Hofbrau?"

"Yes. Johnny left us his car, as he frequently did, and Garnet and I went to the Hofbrau and had dinner together. She went on pretending, and I let her. After dinner we talked with friends for a moment, danced once, and had two steins of beer apiece. . . ."

"Did she leave the table at any time?" asked Tuck.

Kurt gave him a swift, sharp glance. "I was just coming to that."

Ah, thought Tuck.

"All through dinner she kept looking around her. I asked her whom she was expecting. She began to laugh. She laughed for a long time, hysterically. I almost went mad. When that was over, she laid her hand on my arm and said, 'Don't hate me. Let's have a happy time.'" Kurt smiled thinly. "So we went through the motions of having a happy time for two hours, and then she excused herself to me and left the table. I watched the dancers and wondered, and then began to realize that she'd been gone quite a while. Some more time passed and still she didn't return. I began to worry. I called a waitress and described Garnet and asked her to go and see if she was all right. She came back and said that no one of that description had been to the powder room. I asked to question the maid stationed there. The waitress led me to a door at the side of the building, which opened onto a narrow alley between the Hofbrau and the next building. To our right was the door of the ladies' room. To our left, far down the narrow walk, was the street, with people passing by. The waitress grinned up at me and said in German, 'It looks, my young sir, as though she went that way —' pointing to the street—'instead of this way.' "

The final ignominy, thought Tuck.

"The next morning," went on Kurt, "I brought Johnny his car and told him what had happened. The two of us went to Garnet's apartment. No one answered our knock. Then we went down to the landlady, and she told us that Garnet had moved away." He sat silent, reliving that moment behind slant green eyes that were fixed on a test tube. Then he looked at Tuck. "That is all I know," he said with finality.

Tuck stood up. "You've been very helpful." He looked around the small laboratory again. "What do you use that big refrigerator for?"

"To freeze fruit flies," said Kurt. "Low temperatures produce peculiar reactions in the chromosomes."

Tuck sat down again. "Would you mind very much telling me what you're doing? I'm really interested."

"Certainly," said Kurt, politely, and thought for a moment. Then he said, "As you perhaps know, Mendel's law of heredity is the working basis of most genetical research. Mendel was a monk who worked with garden peas, and he found out this: If a tall plant is crossed with a dwarf plant, the offspring are tall. In the next generation, however, the dwarf character reappears. So it must have been present in the genes of the preceding tall generation. Genes, by the way, are the determiners of inherited characters, for garden peas, for fruit flies, and for you and me, Mr. Tuck. To get back to the garden peas. Tallness, therefore, is a dominant character, dwarfness a recessive one. There is a definite ratio which governs the distribution of dominant and recessive characters. In this second generation, these grandchildren of the original pure tall and pure dwarf plants, one is tall and always breeds true, one is dwarf, and always breeds true, and two are tall, with the dwarf character as a recessive character, capable of again reappearing, according to definite ratio, in their children.

"This much is merely background. There is another side of the picture. Every once in a while an individual appears with a character for which there is no explanation. We call this individual a mutant, or 'sport.' Its appearance is purely accidental." He smiled, and Tuck noticed the extraordinary change that had come over his face as he talked about his work. All the lines of bitterness and uncertainty that had been there when he was talking of Garnet Dillon were gone, and in their place was youthful enthusiasm.

"I am trying to cause a directed mutation, Mr. Tuck," he said.

"I thought you said they were a matter of chance?"

"They are. But if they weren't . . ."

Feeling a little excited, Tuck said soberly, "Men would be like gods. They could create new forms out of the old."

Kurt Schwann smiled. "A rather striking way of putting it, Mr. Tuck. But—yes."

The quiet words startled Tuck. He said nothing.

"You will never see this, nor I, Mr. Tuck. But if, with intense heat, or intense cold, or chemical injection, or x-ray, I can break the predestined pattern of inherited characters, if I can cause a fly that on the basis of the Mendelian Law should have dark red eyes to have pink eyes, or white eyes, or no eyes, why then—" he stared at the test tube again—"why then, when you and I are dust, Mr. Tuck, a scientist may breed from the feeble-minded child of a feeble-minded mother—a normal child. And a new type of medicine will spring into being, a genetico-medicine, concerned not with the ills of the individual but with the inherited ills of the species known as man."

Tuck felt very much like gasping. And he was very glad that he had questioned Kurt Schwann about his work.

"Have you had any success with this idea of yours?" he asked.

"A little," said Schwann, carefully.

Tuck rose. "Good luck," he said.

Schwann stood up too. He was smiling. "Don't classify me as the mad scientist, please," he said. "And forget about the rather far-fetched picture of the future use of my discovery—should I ever make it. No one living can predict the use it would be put to. Sometimes it frightens me to think of it. When I think of the bombs that are dropping now, I wonder what men would do if they could cause directed mutations, and I think that they would perhaps create horrible monsters with which to kill each other in a new way."

Tuck left Kurt Schwann bent once more over his microscope, and walked past tall brown doors from behind which came the sound of professors' voices telling their wisdom to young men. It seemed to him that the morning's interviews assumed the aspect of a crescendo. First the ingenuous Hitchlock, then the composed Whittaker, then Greenwood, more mature and more capable than the other two, and finally Kurt Schwann, with his little fruit flies and his big idea. And for just a flicker of a moment it was absurd to think that one of these young men was a murderer. Then he remembered other murderers he had seen and spoken to. He sighed.

TEN

"While the Rose blows along the River Brink,
With old Khayyam the Ruby Vintage drink;
And when the Angel with his darker Draught
Draws up to Thee—take that, and do not shrink."

KATE CLOSED THE BOOK. Usually old Khayyam was rather a comfort with his cheerful and cynical hedonism, but tonight . . . "The Angel with his darker Draught." No—there was no comfort in that. She knew that the angel of whom Khayyam wrote in his quatrain was neither winged nor in white. It was a dark angel, its face lost in the shadow of a black hood. Death.

She looked around the room, and felt lonelier than she had ever felt in her life. She walked to the window and looked at the cold round moon. She looked at the clock. Eight. She wished that Gladys Horstmann would hurry.

Then, with a startling electric "Br-r-r-r!" that made her jump, a buzzer went off somewhere in the room. For a vague moment she thought of running for the fire-escape at the end of the outer hall, but realized in time that it was a summons by the manager to the telephone on the first floor.

The little elevator groaned slowly and sadly downward. She looked at the initials G. D. scratched on the wall.

"Listen," said Gladys Horstmann's bass voice, "I'm not going to that show with you tonight. Hitch came over."

"Oh," said Kate. "That's all right. I know how it is. I'll run over by myself."

"Thanks, pal," said Gladys. "See you tomorrow. 'By."

"Good-by."

Kate slowly replaced the receiver. She thought, I won't go back to that room.

It was a bright night, cold and clear. The trees' shadows were black in the moonlight, and the stars were made of ice. Kate blew an experimental huff of air ahead of her, but it didn't freeze.

That's sunny Southern California for you, she thought. The February night goes right through you and comes out the other side, but your breath doesn't freeze. It must be by special arrangement with the Chamber of Commerce.

When she passed Johnny's apartment she looked up at his window, and there was a light there. Her feet slowed by themselves but her will conquered them, and when she reached the wide stretch of University Avenue she was safe.

She watched her shadow lag and fall behind as she approached a street lamp and then leap ahead of her as she passed it, and wondered what Tuck had learned that day. What had Whittaker said at lunch yesterday in the Student Union? "It happens that we at this table knew Garnet best." She remembered last night in Johnny's room. What had been wrong with the picture? You couldn't expect people to jump up and tear their hair, even over the death of someone they had known and liked. People didn't do that any more; they labored to conceal what they felt most deeply. Still, there had been something wrong in that room. She was sure of that. She knew it in her bones.

The lights were on in the library of the Law Building, bright yellow squares in a black wall. And ahead were the dark trees of the park, and beyond them the great bulk of the Stadium, and beyond that, and a little to the left, the glaring sign on top of the theater just showing above the trees.

As she started to cross the side street that separated the campus from the public park, she heard symphony music. It was faint, but she could recognize a passage from the *Pastoral*. She crossed the street and looked back, and discovered then where it came from.

When Johnny had driven her to campus from the beach the day before, he had pointed out three squat little houses facing the park and dwarfed completely by the aspiring tower of the Philosophy Building. They were stubborn-looking little houses, and the owner was stubborn too. Years ago, when the University had owned more land than buildings, it had sold the former to build the latter. And now, when it needed land, the owner of the three houses was indulging in a perfectly legal form of banditry. So there they stayed. And Kurt lived in the middle of the three. And Kurt liked Beethoven, too.

She stood there in the sharp moonlight for a moment, listening to the music with half of a smile on her face. Then she remembered that she would have to hurry to catch the eight-thirty show, and turned and walked into the park.

Old trees growing near the walk touched branches above her head. Looking up, she saw the wild lacery of their leaves and twigs, black against the moon-bright sky. Then came the smell of roses.

Also by special arrangement with the Chamber of Commerce, she thought.

The cement path she was following ended in shallow steps leading down into a sunken garden a block wide and twice as long, filled with bed after bed of rose bushes. A wide walk went past the rose beds to the round fountain in the center, which it circled, continuing on the other side to end at shallow steps like those on which she was standing.

The garden of roses was more beautiful by night than by day. The red roses looked black, the paler ones white, and all of them were mysterious and strange, sleeping their wide flower sleep.

Entranced, she moved silently toward the fountain, whose liquid plume seemed to be less water than moonlight. The only sound was the sound of the fountain, catching itself in its wide shallow basin where lotus spread precise buds above the foolish dartings of small, quick fish.

She bent over the wide lip of the fountain to watch them. A drop of water struck a lotus bud and slid swiftly and gaily down its white wax bulge to oblivion in the dark pool.

The show. She'd miss the eight-thirty show, and have to come·in after the start of the picture. Leave the fountain, and see Joan Crawford. Leave all fountains behind her for something else less real.

Halfway to the steps at the other side of the garden, she turned for one more look.

Someone else was looking, too. Halfway between the fountain and the steps by which she had entered, a man was standing. He was wearing a long black overcoat, and a black hat brim hid all of his face but the chin in heavy shadow. He was standing motionless, watching. But he wasn't watching the fountain. He was watching her.

Not entirely unconscious of what she was doing, she backed three careful steps away. The man took three steps forward. He moved his right arm very slightly, and the moonlight gleamed cold on the bright blade of the short knife he was holding in his hand.

Suddenly she was screaming, screaming and running toward the steps, away from the man in black.

There was a stumble of footsteps ahead of her, and the beam of a flashlight cut through the moonlight and found her face. She made out the uniform of a night watchman, and a pale stare of alarm. Gasping, she clutched the good rough fabric of his sleeve, and then because she couldn't talk,

[94]

turned and pointed.

Beyond the bright plume of the fountain the path was empty in the moonlight, and the roses were sleeping their placid flower sleep.

ELEVEN

I WANT FROODY," SAID TUCK to Gufferty, who scowled absently up at him from the reports spread out on his huge desk and then scowled even more fiercely at the clock, which said just eight.

"I think he's gone home. FROODY!" A pause. "Yes, he's gone home."

"Did someone call me?" asked a sleepy voice from the doorway leading to the squad room.

Froody always made Tuck think of the Dormouse. He was small and fat and drowsy, and was constantly imposed upon.

Gufferty made a gesture which meant, "There you are, you've got Froody, so what the hell are you hanging around my desk for?" and Tuck dropped a fraternal arm across Froody's shoulders, which were roughly on the same level as Tuck's top vest button, and said, "Listen, old man, there's something you can do for me."

Froody winced slightly.

"You know and I know," said Tuck, "that you're a whizz at detail."

Froody sighed.

"What I want you to do is this. I want you to comb every drugstore in town, and get the names of anyone who bought digitalis in the last month. Start with the University section, and when you finish that, bring the list of names and addresses to me and I'll check it for the phoney I'm looking for. If there's nothing there, you'll try the downtown section, and so on."

"And so on," said Froody.

"You might start tonight," said Tuck.

Froody turned and made a mournful exit. From the rear he always made Tuck think of Queen Victoria. Tuck smiled, for he knew from previous experience that in just half the time in which anyone else could possibly do the job Froody would sleepily return with a neat list of the required information.

"What you been doin' all day?" asked Gufferty, his head still bent over the reports.

"I've kept busy," replied Tuck, and taking out his black notebook, stooped through the doorway leading to the inner office and his desk, reading his brief notations as he went.

The afternoon's questionees had corroborated the information given by the four boys in the morning. A waitress at the Hofbrau remembered how Garnet had left Kurt sitting alone at the table, and remembered taking him to the side door leading to the narrow alley. Her opinion was that Garnet had kept a late date with someone else. She thought it all very funny. Mrs. Nox, the manager of the apartment house where Garnet had lived, and whose talk had been redolent of a back fence in a small town, had taken a full hour to hint that Garnet had not been all she might have been, and to say that Garnet had given her the key to her apartment at ten Friday night, asking her to store in the basement her radio and several other items she had left there. The other items had been four sofa cushions and a suit box of old dresses. Mrs. Nox had also revealed that Garnet had departed in a yellow taxi, which Mrs. Nox deemed a reckless extravagance. The taxi driver had stated that he had been signaled by a blonde young woman standing in front of the Hofbrau at nine-thirty, had driven her to an apartment near the University where he had carried three suitcases and a hatbox to the taxi for her, and had

[96]

then taken her to the depot. Upon seeing Tuck's badge, the baggagemaster had allowed Tuck to examine Garnet's luggage, which had contained nothing of interest, and had told Tuck that she had given as her reason for checking it the fact that she had an hour to wait for her train. A ticket seller had remembered selling her a ticket to Grand Canyon at about ten-thirty that Friday evening; he remembered this because she had just missed a train bound there. Her change purse, he recalled, had contained a rather large roll of bills. A teller at the University branch of the First National Bank had obliged with the information that she had withdrawn all the money in her account just before closing time Friday.

Tuck sat down at his desk and considered these facts and those given him by the four young men that morning. Turning to a fresh page, he made a timetable of Garnet's actions prior to her disappearance and subsequent death.

Friday morning, February 1—Asked Dean Calder to examine her heart, which he did, finding nothing wrong.

Friday, February 8—Hitchlock found her at noon crying at her desk in the Dean's office.

Friday at three—She withdrew her money from the bank. (Therefore she had by that time made up her mind to go away.)

Friday at five-thirty—She left for the Hofbrau with Kurt Schwann, after spending a moment with John Greenwood who, according to Kurt, spent that moment hinting that she ought to tell Kurt what was wrong with her. This, still according to Kurt, she did not do.

Friday from six (about) to nine-thirty—Had dinner, and a dance, and some beer with Kurt Schwann at Hofbrau. Jeff Whittaker, Hitchlock, and a girl named Gladys Horstmann were also present. And they stopped at the table where Kurt and Garnet were sitting to say hello. They left before Garnet

[97]

did, and Whittaker says he saw her crying as she danced with Schwann. (Why?)

Friday at nine-thirty—Left Kurt Schwann sitting at the table, pretended she was going to the powder room, instead slipped out side door and down alley to street, where she signaled taxi. (Why the secrecy about her departure?)

Friday at ten—Gave key to her apartment to Mrs. Nox, left behind her a radio, some sofa cushions and some old clothes. Departed with three suitcases and a hat-box, which were already packed.

Friday at ten-thirty—Arrived at station, bought ticket to Grand Canyon, checked baggage.

Friday at ten forty-five—Went to lunch counter near station to wait for her train.

Friday at ten-fifty—Fell forward to counter in coma. A man in a black overcoat and hat, who entered when she did, called the counterman's attention to girl's condition; counterman phoned to County Hospital for an ambulance and gave his amateur diagnosis that the girl was a heart victim. While he was phoning, the man in the black overcoat left with the girl's purse.

Friday at eleven-thirty—Was taken in ambulance to hospital; died on the way. At hospital, her death passed as a heart attack. Being without identification, the body was held in the hospital morgue for two days, Saturday and Sunday, and then was sent to the University where she had worked, where it would have been embalmed, held for at least a month pending possible identification, and finally dissected, had not the body been at once recognized.

Tuck read through the neat timetable, and then marked a deliberate star between the first and second entries. The star stood for a mighty gap in his information.

He talked to himself about that gap. "Assuming that her anxiety about her heart was her first inkling that all was not well with her, I can assume that Friday, February 1, was the beginning of the chain of events that led to her murder. According to Dean Calder, her father had died of heart trouble, which was why she first thought of that as a possible explanation of her discomfort. All right. Then, finding that her heart was sound, she became convinced of her pregnancy. Maybe the anxiety about her heart was a subconscious smoke screen around her real fear—that she was with child. What then? Again according to Calder, she would have gone to the father of the child and demanded a wedding ring. And failing to get it, Calder thinks she would have appealed to him for justice. In many cases, of course, such an appeal, with its attendant revelation of frailty, would be the last thing to expect, but in this instance Dillon certainly knew that the Dean had twice before insisted on marriage in similar sad situations. And then Dean Calder was a doctor, and to most women a doctor is somewhat like a priest in that he is powerful in his ability to give aid, and thereafter silent about the need for aid.

"But she didn't go to Calder. Why?"

He reached out a long arm and pulled his desk phone to him. Simultaneously the other arm reached into the bottom drawer of his desk and emerged with a telephone book. He dialed Dean Calder's home.

"This is Tuck," he said when he heard the Dean's quiet voice at the other end of the line. "Tell me this. Was Miss Dillon friendly with anyone but medical students? Did she have any men friends that she had met before she came to work for you, for instance?"

"I believe not," Dean Calder answered. "She was from San Francisco, you see, and she'd only been in Los Angeles for a few days when I hired her. Why do you ask?"

"Suppose Miss Dillon had come to you and revealed her condition, but suppose the father was not a student in medical school, what would you have done then?"

"That," said Dean Calder, "would have been a little difficult. I would have gone to bat for her, of course, but my influence would have been considerably less. The reason is plain, I'm sure."

"Very plain," agreed Tuck.

He hung up thoughtfully. Everything pointed straight to Kurt Schwann. Not one young man but three had testified that it was he of whom Garnet had been most fond. He had certainly had the best opportunity to administer the final large dose of digitalis which was found in the intestine; they had been seated together at a small table during the last part of the crucial period five to six hours before her death. In fairness, three other people had also been there, but had been within poisoning distance, so to speak, only during the brief time they stood by the table saying their hellos. Greenwood had not had time to poison her at five-thirty. And of all the possible fathers of Garnet Dillon's child Schwann was the one over whom Garnet would have known Dean Calder's influence to be slight.

He opened his little black notebook to a list of phone numbers, and dialed John Greenwood's, which he had copied from his section card that morning. It was apparently a communal apartment-house phone, for the voice that answered said, "I'll buzz him," and after that there was a long wait that nearly exhausted even Tuck's patience. Then Greenwood's soft voice said " 'Lo."

"This is Lieutenant Tuck. I've got a thirty-two-dollar question for you, Greenwood. Did you suggest to Miss Dillon that she ought to tell Kurt Schwann what was wrong with her?"

Greenwood demanded, "What in the devil are you talking about?"

Tuck repeated the question.

"No," said Greenwood, promptly and rather

[100]

irascibly. "What gave you that idea?"

"I understood," said Tuck smoothly, an impersonal elation bright within him, "that during the few moments you were alone with Miss Dillon at five-thirty last Friday you had urged her to tell Schwann what ailed her."

Another silence. Then, in a tone that was both angry and supercilious, Greenwood said, "You know, you birds irritate the hell out of me. Why didn't you ask that in the first place? I'll tell you just what I said to Miss Dillon at five-thirty, as closely as I can remember. I said, first, that I wasn't coming to dinner with her and Kurt because finals had just about finished me, and all I wanted was twenty-four hours' sleep. Then I said, 'And anyway, you have things to say, you and Kurt. A third person would only be in the way.' Get that, Tuck? Now listen. Immediately after I said that there was a knock at the door and Kurt came in. He gave me a darned funny look, and when Garnet went into her dressing room for her coat and hat he said, 'Thanks, Johnny, for interfering.' I didn't get it. I would have asked him what he meant, but then Garnet came back, chattering something, and I left. It puzzled me all the way home, and finally I realized that Kurt—you must remember that Garnet's queer behavior of the last few days had puzzled him a lot—that Kurt had overheard what I said and had interpreted it as an unwelcome suggestion on my part that Garnet should tell him what her grief was. And that's perfectly logical, Tuck. Not knowing Kurt, you wouldn't know, as I know, how he would resent interference of any kind, even from a friend. And more than that, how he would resent the assumption on my part that I had more influence over Garnet than he did." There was a brief pause, and then John Greenwood said, "That's the deal, Tuck. Take it or leave it."

[101]

When Tuck replaced the receiver some of the elation had gone out of him.

"Still," he reflected, "Schwann can still be lying. There's only his word that he thought what he did, and what Greenwood thinks he did. And there is no witness to his statement that he asked Garnet what was wrong, and that she said it did not concern him. None at all." But he wasn't happy. Because it all came down to the old wheeze that if the story Kurt had told him that morning in his laboratory was a lie, why then Kurt was an excellent liar and a better actor, and neither seemed to go with a coldly factual mind absorbed with mutations and fruit flies. A good actor is necessarily a romantic; a romantic does not excel in science.

His phone rang. He killed the second ring dead and cocked his ear at the receiver. "Tuck speaking."

"This is Kathryn Farr," said a voice which had the high thin intonation shock gives to women's voices. "I think I've just seen the man who killed Garnet Dillon. I was crossing the park at the head of the campus this evening to go to the movies. I stopped and looked back and a man was following me. He had a knife. I screamed and ran. A watchman came, but when I turned around the man was gone. The watchman walked me to Kurt Schwann's house. He lives across from the park. I was afraid to go home alone. Kurt said I should call you."

With prescience of what was coming, Tuck asked quietly, "What did this man look like?"

"I didn't see his face because the shadow from his hat covered it. But he was wearing a long black overcoat."

A long black overcoat. Of course.

He hung up and stared at the functional black ugliness of the telephone. A thought which had scudded across his mind the night before came back to sit there like a raven. Black Overcoat was too gratuitously omni-present. He had been sitting next to Garnet when she began to die. He had taken her purse. And now he had appeared on campus, hungering after another young secretary. Under those circumstances, could he be someone who knew both Garnet Dillon and Kathryn Farr? He could.

Madness. A twist in the genes, a maladjustment far back in the chaos of childhood—a forgotten incident serving as a foundation for a toppling structure leaning always more perilously away from normality. Is madness confined to the slums? No. Rich man, poor man, beggar man, thief, doctor . . .

It was then that he became aware of a commotion in the outer office. Gufferty was speaking to someone in the reasoning voice which always heralded an outburst of splenic grandeur.

"This has got to stop," Gufferty was saying.

"THIS HAS GOT TO STOP!" Gufferty repeated.

Tuck smiled to himself and stood up. He knew that Gufferty's eyes were glaring and that his bald spot was growing red within the tousled circle of graying hair.

"Do you know what I read in the *Times* today?" Gufferty was rhetorically demanding. There was a loud rustle of newspaper. *"This* is what I read in the *Times* today. Listen. It's a letter to the editor, from a guy named Potts. Potts! He says: 'A man goes fifty miles an hour in a forty-mile zone, and a policeman drops down from the sky to nab him. In the last few months, five young women have been brutally killed, two of them giving a clear description of the killer, and what happens? Nothing. It seems to me that our police force ought to concentrate on the big fish, even if they have to let a few of the little fish go.'" There was the sound of newspaper being violently bunched together. "And you sit there and tell me he's been at it again!"

Tuck entered the outer office just in time to see Gufferty stuff a huge wad of newspaper into his wastebasket and viciously stamp it down with his foot. A small, alert detective named Kern was smiling. On seeing Tuck, he winked at him.

"Black Overcoat?" Tuck asked Kern, disregarding Gufferty's heavy breathing and icy glare.

"Yeah."

"When did it happen?"

"Monahan says he heard the one loud yell the woman gave at eight-fifteen—he took a peek at his watch while he was running toward the sound of the scream. She was out cold when he found her, but just before the ambulance got there she opened her one good eye and told him that what hit her was a long, grinning guy in a black overcoat."

"And," pursued Tuck, "where did it happen?"

"An alley just off North Broadway in the five-hundred block."

Eight-fifteen. Five-hundred block, North Broadway. Kathryn Farr had phoned him not more than five minutes ago. "I think I just saw the man who killed . . ."

He looked at the clock. It said eighty-thirty. That meant that it had been within a few minutes of eight-fifteen when Miss Far saw the man in the black overcoat. And University Park was approximately six miles from the five-hundred block, North Broadway.

He became aware that both Gufferty and Kern were watching him.

"What's the matter with *you?*" inquired Gufferty.

The friendliness of their relations permitted Tuck to tease Gufferty. It had become a habit with him. He said gravely, "Unless Black Overcoat has two bodies, which I doubt, he was not in University Park at eight-fifteen tonight. But at eight-fifteen tonight, in University Park, a young woman was followed by a man with a long black overcoat and a sharp knife."

"TWO OF THEM?" roared Gufferty, stricken.

"Two of them," said Tuck.

"Beat me, daddy," whispered Kern.

TWELVE

KATE HUNG UP THE RECEIVER and realized that she felt better. Some of the tension had ebbed out of her.

Kurt was calling, "Thank you, Mrs. Noonan, for the use of your telephone."

"Use it whenever you want," replied a pleasant voice from the rear of the house.

"A telephone is one of the many luxuries I can't afford," said Kurt, as he closed the front door of the little house next to his.

Their footsteps boomed hollowly down the three wooden steps of the porch and Kate said, "I'm afraid I'm being the world's worst nuisance, but I would rather be shot this minute than walk home alone."

"I have no intention that you shall," Kurt said calmly, and turned on the sidewalk toward his little house.

"But . . ." said Kate, halting.

Kurt looked down at her, smiling. "It made you feel better, didn't it, to tell the capable Mr. Tuck this thing that has happened to you?"

"Yes."

"I think a glass of wine would work still further wonders."

"Oh, really, I . . ."

"If you go home now," said Kurt patiently, taking her arm and gently forcing her into step beside him, "you will lie awake half the night staring at the ceiling, and then you will have bad dreams."

Kate laughed a little, and permitted herself to be urged. "You speak like an authority."

"I am."

Nothing more was said until they were going up the three wooden steps of Kurt's house, and then Kurt said quietly, "I think you are wrong in believing that the man who followed you in the park is the man who killed Garnet Dillon."

He opened the weather-beaten front door, and politely stood aside for Kate to precede him. From the kitchen came a rattling sound that was Theodor, still busy with the dinner dishes.

Kurt deftly took Kate's green jacket from her shoulders, and hung it in a dark closet beside the front door. Then he rubbed his long hands briskly together, for he had worn no overcoat, and said, with an easy gesture at a comfortable old leather armchair that was warmed to a rich brown by the lamp on the table beside it, "Now, if you will sit down for a moment . . ."

He vanished kitchenward, and Kate did as he had asked, looking about the room with real pleasure. It was a dimly lit, homely room that was not at all American. The row of fine old pewter beer mugs on the long mantel had something to do with this, as did three towering cases jammed with books most of which bore German or French titles. Nothing about the room was there for effect. Kate liked that. She relaxed more deeply into the big chair as Kurt returned with a tall-nicked wine bottle in one hand and a small tray bearing three glasses in the other.

"Theodor will join us in a few minutes," he said, setting the tray down on the table beside Kate's chair. "We take turns playing houseboy, you see, and this is his week for it."

The cork came out with a squeak, and in Continental fashion Kurt carefully poured a little of the deep red wine into his glass before filling hers. Then he filled his to the brim, corked the bottle and set it on the tray beside Theodor's glass, remarking, "In Germany, no one drinks water. Wine in the South, beer in the North, but *never* any water. Water is to wash in." He raised his glass an inch in a mute toast, and they both drank. "And those Germans," added Kurt, seating himself on a chair facing Kate, "are a healthy people, whatever else may be said against them."

"Why," asked Kate, "did you say that the man who followed me did not kill Garnet Dillon?"

Kurt looked down into the wine in his glass, and then up at Kate. "If she was killed, she was killed by the man she was about to run away with. In other circumstances her death would have been a matter of deep regret to me, but as it is I simply think about it as little as possible."

"Then you believe in Gladys Horstmann's theory—that she was leaving to marry a rich man."

Kurt looked down into his glass again. "I believe, as they say, that she may have something there."

Then Kate looked past Kurt's shoulder and saw Theodor standing just inside the doorway leading to the rear of the house, watching them out of his dark eyes. Kurt twisted in his chair and beckoned him forward.

"Miss Farr," he said, "you remember my brother Theodor, do you not?"

"Of course. Good evening, Theodor."

"Goot evening," murmured Theodor, almost inaudibly.

Kurt filled the other glass and handed it to him. Theodor immediately went to a chair in the far corner of the room, where he sat down, melting into the shadows.

"To speak of more pleasant subjects," said Kurt, holding the binding of an old leather-covered book toward Kate. "This is what I was reading when you rang my doorbell."

It was Goethe's *Faust*. Kurt turned pages lovingly. "This is a wonderful play. You are familiar with it?"

"Marlowe's *Faust* is more up my alley," Kate said. "I was an English major."

"Oh," said Kurt politely, dismissing Marlowe. "Still, the central idea of a man selling his soul to the devil for all knowledge is powerful in any language."

He read a few lines from the first of the book. Kate had never realized how beautiful the German language could be.

"You'll have to tell me what that means," she said, when he had finished. "I'm not a linguist."

"That means: 'I'm a master, even a doctor now. I have studied science, medicine, jurisprudence, even, alas, theology, and I know no more than I did when I began.'" There was something sad in his voice as he translated for her. Then he smiled. "I should not at all have minded living in an age when men had souls and there was a devil to sell them to."

The doorbell rang. Theodor, whom Kate had forgotten, put down his glass and opened the door on the second ring.

It was Dr. Uman. He made an odd picture there in the doorway, for he was swathed to the chin in his enormous brown overcoat below which showed, incongruously enough, white duck tennis trousers and a pair of large and dirty tennis shoes. His mouse-colored hair had certainly not been combed since Kate's first meeting with him the previous morning, and his eyes were just as harassed. He peeled off his coat and gave it to Theo-

[108]

dor, who hung it away where Kurt had put Kate's. Dr. Uman stood revealed in a heavily ribbed white tennis sweater. To Kurt, who had risen, he said, "Those rats. Griswold told me today there's no more room. I've got to have dozens more. Dozens and dozens," he enlarged, with a wild gleam in his sunken eyes.

"Miss Farr," said Kurt, with a faint smile on his lips, "you remember Dr. Uman . . ."

"How do you do," said Dr. Uman, bestowing upon her a vague glance in which there was not the slightest glimmer of recognition. "And so I was wondering, Schwann, if there might be room in your laboratory for a few cages of . . . we're dreadfully short of space, you know . . ."

"No," said Kurt firmly.

The bell rang again, and again Theodor rose to answer it.

"This seems to be my night for visitors," said Kurt to Kate, and went to the kitchen. Kate knew, without knowing how, that Johnny was standing on the other side of the front door.

". . . just have to put them on the roof, then," Uman was saying despondently, and then Johnny was in the room, looking especially tall beside little Theodor, who said something to him and took his overcoat, hanging it away with Dr. Uman's. Kurt returned with two more glasses.

"I'm jealous," said Johnny to Kurt after a rather surprised glance at Kate.

Kurt smiled, pouring wine.

". . . that roof's getting to look more like a zoo every day that passes." Dr. Uman was worrying to himself as he crossed the room to a comfortable chair. "For heaven's sake, sit down, Greenwood!"

Johnny laughed and sat down in the chair Kurt had been sitting in.

"As a matter of fact," said Kurt, handing him a glass and crossing the room to give Dr. Uman one,

[109]

"Miss Farr's visit was a matter of chance. A degenerate pursued her through the park with a knife, and this happened to be the nearest place of refuge."

Johnny's face sobered abruptly. "Is that true, Kate?"

"I'm afraid it is," All the eyes in the room were fixed upon her. "I feel dreadfully ridiculous, somehow."

"A degenerate," said Dr. Uman, looking at her with something like interest in his sunken eyes. "And with a knife."

"Vimen shoot nod valk alone at night," Theodor said unexpectedly from the shadowy corner where he had reseated himself.

"Tell me what happened," commanded Johnny. Kate did.

"Good God," Johnny said, quietly.

"Exactly," said Kurt, in a light tone.

But Johnny refused to be swerved from his serious mood. "Theodor is right, Kate. You shouldn't go about at night. Don't you read the papers?"

"Sure," said Kate. "Mad Mike, the man in black, slits girls' throats and rips 'em up the back."

Johnny's lips tightened. "It's not funny, Kate. One murder around here is enough."

"Quite enough," said Kurt quietly. Something in his voice made Kate glance over at him. He was looking down into his wine.

"Sorry," said Johnny, low and swiftly.

Then he added, "That reminds me of what I came to tell you, Kurt." He stood up. "I think I'll have a glass of water." Kate caught the suggestion in the look he gave Kurt; the two of them went into the kitchen. Her idle curiosity as to what the secret was soon melted before a sunny idea. "He's really fond of me," she said to herself. It was worth the terrible moment in the rose garden to know that.

In a few minutes they returned to the living room. Johnny was saying, ". . . thought you ought to know about it. I told him what I knew was the truth. Maybe he accepted it, maybe he didn't."

"You are a good friend," Kurt said.

"Forget it." Johnny turned toward Kate. "I'm going to take you home. I think you've had about enough for one day."

Although he seemed somewhat abstracted, Kurt said, "Come again, both of you." And to Kate alone, "Miss Farr, you realize that you have broken the ice between us. I shall return your call."

"Look at him!" laughed Johnny, shrugging into his overcoat, which the watchful Theodor had disentombed from the closet beside the front door. "Cutting my throat right in front of my face!"

"I never cut throats," Kurt said gravely. "Too messy."

They all laughed, and then Theodor was holding Kate's green jacket for her.

"Vimen shoot nod valk alone at night," he said, solemnly.

Then she and Johnny backed through the doorway, saying good nights as they backed, and Theodor closed the door.

They didn't say anything for a while, walking down University Avenue under the round cold moon with their two dissimilar shadows long ahead of them until a street lamp pushed them swiftly back. Once Kate looked into Johnny's face. It was expressionless.

She was thinking reflectively what an enigma every human being is to every other human being, when Johnny said: "It frightened me horribly, what almost happened to you, Kate. I didn't know I could be so frightened by anything."

She could think of absolutely nothing to say, so they walked on in silence.

[111]

When they reached the entrance to Kate's apartment house, she turned to Johnny to say good night. And quite easily, quite naturally, his arms went out around her, and he bent and kissed her lips.

Kate closed her eyes, half expecting to hear a shrill, derisive whistle from one of the cars parked along the curb. But they were lucky. His lips left hers, and she opened her eyes. He was staring down at her as though he was seeing her for the first time.

With an uncertain laugh he kissed her again. Her arms were half pinioned to her sides by his embrace, but they went blindly out toward him, clasping him around the hips. She slipped her cold hands into the big patch-pockets of his brown overcoat.

Her right hand closed on a knife.

Stunned, and with sickening horror mounting from her stomach to her brain, she felt gingerly along the edge of the blade. Then, with a whimper, she tore herself free and sped up the steps to the door. As she shoved it violently open she looked back and saw him watching her dumbly, moonlight bright on his face.

THIRTEEN

SHE FUMBLED FOR THE LIGHT switch beside the door of her apartment, her thoughts a chaos. Some half-conscious desire for a return to normality made her go to her small radio and turn it on; after a blank moment the tag-line of a comic's joke fell flatly into the room, followed by an inhuman roar of laughter. She turned the radio off.

Shakily, she lit a cigarette, while one thought repeated itself in her brain like the variations on a theme in a symphony. "Why the knife? Why the knife in Johnny's pocket?"

[112]

And like counterpoint, the dim, wishful thought, "There's some perfectly logical explanation." The man in the park couldn't have been Johnny, for that would mean that Johnny, hard-working, hard-playing, music-loving Johnny, whom she had known for six years, was a maniac. It was unthinkable.

There was a loud, firm knocking at her door. As she crossed the room she thought with relief, it's Johnny. He's realized what made me run away, and he's come to explain.

But it wasn't Johnny. It was Lieutenant Tuck, towering above her, looking down at her from coffee-colored eyes in a long tan face.

"The landlady was locking the downstairs door," he remarked casually. "I made it in the nick of time."

Determined to be just as casual, Kate replied, "She always locks it at nine-thirty, I understand. Mrs. Nox takes the morals of the students here very seriously. She seems to dwell in the happy belief that nothing naughty could possibly happen *before* half past nine. Won't you sit down?"

"Thank you." Tuck lowered his lengthy bulk into a small occasional chair beside the little desk, on the edge of which he rested his arm momentarily, jerking it away as the desk tilted dangerously under its weight. Kate sat down on the sofa, her hands quietly folded in her lap, and waited for him to begin.

"I've come," said Tuck, "for a more particularized description of the man who followed you in the park."

Kate frowned. "This is a little difficult, Mr. Tuck. You see, I'm rather nearsighted, and I only saw him for a moment before my feet started running in the opposite direction. He had on a dark overcoat and a dark hat. The brim hid his face. I'm afraid that's the best description I can give."

[113]

"On the phone," said Tuck easily, "you mentioned a *black* overcoat and hat."

Damn! thought Kate, realizing that something deep in her mind had shown where her thoughts had so recently been running. She said smoothly, forcing a smile, "But you see, I've had time to think it over, Mr. Tuck, and I realize now that at night all cats are black."

"The saying goes, 'At night all cats are gray,' " corrected Tuck, absently. "But I see what you mean. Would you say that this man was very tall?"

Kate thought for a moment. "How tall?"

"Would you say he was as tall as I am?"

"No. And I'm very sure of that. There was nothing to scale him against, of course; he was standing in the middle of a wide walk, in the center of the garden. But I'm sure that if he'd been nearly as tall as you the brief image of him I have in my mind would include the idea of tallness. Do you see what I mean?"

"I do. Your reasoning is very valid. So our picture becomes a trifle clearer. We have now a man in a dark overcoat and hat, not much over average height."

Suddenly Kate sat up straight. "Wait a minute! Something's clicking in my head! I seem to remember that the Man in the Black Overcoat of tabloid fame, whom of course I imagined this to be, was described as an unusually tall man."

"Yes," said Tuck.

His uncommunicativeness angered her a little. "Mr. Tuck, I'm doing my best to help you. Perhaps if you would tell me what you're getting at, I could help you more."

A swift tightening of all the muscles of Tuck's face, a tightening of his lantern jaw, showed that he had reached some decision. In contrast to the alert look of the face his voice was very easy as he said, "If anyone concerned with this mess might be said to be a disinterested party, you are that person, Miss Farr. I am going to take you into my confidence, if I have your solemn promise that nothing I say will be repeated to anyone."

"You have my promise."

Something in Tuck's face showed her that he held no illusions about such promises. Therefore it was necessary to him, she decided, that she know what he had to tell her.

"Your guess was right, Miss Farr. The man who followed you was not Black Overcoat of tabloid fame." He paused a moment to rearrange his thoughts, and the slow pumping of her heart seemed to her to fill the room. "But I think he may have been the man who killed Garnet Dillon."

"Yes?" said Kate, and felt her fingers making absurd pleatings in her skirt. She forced them to lie still in her lap again.

"As you and Greenwood may have deduced from the fact that her corpse reached the little room upstairs, and from the fact that I at once appeared asking all sorts of questions, her death was such that it appeared to be a natural one, which means poison."

Kate nodded.

"Black Overcoat doesn't use poison," said Tuck.

"Black Overcoat," countered Kate, "is as mad as a hatter. If you can predict what a lunatic will do, you're in the wrong profession, Mr. Tuck. You should be a psychiatrist." She smiled as pleasantly as he had done.

"You're smart," Tuck said. "And you're right. I knew it wasn't Black Overcoat, because at the moment you saw the man with the knife the genuine Black Ovrecoat slugged a girl six miles away. She gave an unmistakable description of him before . . ."

". . . she died," finished a voice in Kate's mind. She kept to the point. "But how do you know

[115]

which is the real Black Overcoat?"

"Which girl is dead?"

"Of course."

"And so Black Overcoat steps out of the picture, and someone else steps in."

"Not a very nice person," Kate managed to say, her mind full of the knife she had found in Johnny's pocket.

"No," said Tuck slowly. "Not a very nice person."

There was a brief silence.

"Miss Farr," said Tuck's even voice, "tell me the names of the people you showed that note of Garnet Dillon's. That note in which she mentioned the thing that followed her."

"Didn't Dean Calder tell you?"

"He told me only that you had showed it to a half-dozen people, and later named three."

"Gladys Horstmann, Jeff Whittaker, Robert Hitchlock, John Greenwood, and Kurt Schwann," said Kate.

"Quite a list," Tuck commented dryly.

"Let me get this straight," commanded Kate. "You think that the person who killed Garnet saw that note and got the idea of capitalizing on the Thing, of using him as a red herring."

"That's one possibility that occurred to me."

"Then," said Kate slowly, "one of the people who saw that note may have murdered Garnet Dillon."

"Yes."

Kate remembered the unnatural atmosphere she had felt last night in Johnny's room. If Tuck was right it was now explained.

"But why was she murdered?" asked Kate.

"She was going to have a child."

The room whirled. She stared at Tuck for what seemed like a long, long time before she heard herself saying, "Aren't you thinking in terms of *An*

[116]

American Tragedy? Isn't that a little out of date?"

Tuck rose. "I've found that tragedy has no regard for dates. Oedipus is with us, and Hamlet. And Jack the Ripper and Neill Cream. Read the papers, Miss Farr, and see if I'm not right."

Kate closed the door after Tuck and sagged against it, drawing strength from its support. She realized that never in her life had she spent two such days as the last two. She felt as though she would like to go to sleep and sleep for a long time. Looking at the clock, she thought, The reaction set in at five minutes to ten. I think I'll have a glass of hot milk.

That made her think of Johnny, and the picture of him as she had last seen him, tall and astonished in the moonlight, flashed across her mind. Tall and astonished. Tall . . . !

With a dizzying headiness, she realized that Johnny, knife or no knife, could never have been the man who stood staring after her in the rose garden. For Johnny was tall, even with his stoop. Standing stiff and straight, as the man in the garden had stood, he would be easily six feet two.

The weariness left her like magic. She felt fresh, exhilarated. She began worrying about what Johnny was thinking. She had not been a good friend. She had jumped at a hideous conclusion.

High and clear from below her window came a whistle. She cocked her head and listened. The sound resolved itself into the first bars of Beethoven's *Fifth*.

She ran across the room and flung the window wide, leaning out into the cold bright night.

Three stories below, and therefore much foreshortened, Johnny was looking up, his head tilted back, his lips whistling for her. On seeing her he stopped and said, very naturally, "The front door's locked."

"Yes," said Kate foolishly. "Yes, it is."

"Come down a minute," said Johnny.

"Yes, Johnny," said Kate.

She grabbed her door key. She didn't wait for the elevator. She ran down the stairs. He was waiting on the front steps.

His face was very serious, looking down at her. "I know what you must have felt, finding that knife in my pocket," he said. "Although you don't seem to realize it, you had a shock tonight that would have floored an ordinary woman. At the time I didn't know what to make of what you did. When you tore away from me and ran into the house, I was stymied. I went home and went through the pockets of my coat as I always do, and found the knife. I got a glimpse of what hit you."

"Believe me, Johnny, as soon as I had time to think coherently, I knew there was some perfectly ordinary explanation for the knife."

Johnny's brows drew together. "There is," he said. "But it's not so ordinary. This isn't my overcoat. It's Dr Uman's."

FOURTEEN

Who the hell is dr. uman?" wondered Tuck. He opened the door of his black sedan, jack-knifed his length through the opening, and demanded of the two startled faces that jerked toward him, "Who is Dr. Uman?"

John Greenwood's eyebrows rose. Kathryn Farr smiled slightly. "How very ubiquitous of you, Mr. Tuck," she said.

"Yes. Who is Dr. Uman?"

Then Greenwood smiled. "A very Suspicious Character," he said sepulchrally.

Kathryn Farr giggled suddenly.

"Who is he?" demanded Tuck, patiently. "How do you happen to be wearing his overcoat?"

[118]

"He's a professor in Biology. He's quite smart, and quite screwy," said Greenwood. "I happen to be wearing his overcoat because we were both at Kurt Schwann's just now, and the room was dark and my overcoat is brown too."

"Does this Uman usually carry knives in his pocket?" asked Tuck.

Greenwood apparently considered the question. "He might," he said. He grinned. "Offhand I would say that Dr. Uman might carry anything in his pocket."

"Did this Uman know Garnet Dillon?" asked Tuck.

"Yes," said Johnny.

"Do you suppose he's still at Schwann's?"

"Could be."

"Good. I'll ask you to show me the way, Greenwood." He turned to Kate. "Good night. We don't want to look like a posse."

"O.K." She smiled. "Somehow I can't imagine Dr. Uman . . . And anyway, he has on white pants."

"Good night," said Tuck, and got into the car.

Greenwood said, "Good night, Katie. Drink some hot milk."

She laughed, and turned toward the front door as Tuck switched on the ignition and stepped on the starter.

"Turn left on University," commanded Johnny, slamming the door.

"Why all the hilarity over Uman?" Tuck asked.

"When you see him, you'll understand. It's hard to take him seriously, although he's doing some remarkable work with the pituitaries and thyroids of smaller animals."

"That's swell," said Tuck, turning into University. "How tall is he?"

"About average, or a little shorter. Say five eight."

"Didn't his coat feel rather tight?"

Greenwood stretched out an arm. The sleeve came well past his wrist. "For some strange reason," he said, "Dr. Uman wears his clothes three sizes too big. That's just one of his many peculiarities."

"Let's see that knife," said Tuck. "I suppose you've handled it?"

"Smudged hell out of it," agreed Greenwood, handing it to him.

It was a perfectly ordinary kitchen knife, very sharp. Tuck gave it back to Greenwood, who put it in the pocket of Uman's overcoat.

They drove on in silence for a few minutes and then Greenwood said, "Turn right, and it's the middle of those three small houses."

Tuck parked. The front windows were lighted. "I guess he's still here," Greenwood commented. "I might as well get my own coat."

Kurt Schwann answered the door. He looked surprised to see Greenwood, and still more surprised to see Tuck looming up in the rear.

"Come in," he said, politely.

Uman looked up from his chair without interest. "I thought you went home once," he said to Greenwood. And to Tuck, when Kurt Schwann had performed the necessary introduction, "How do you do. Detective, huh? What a time you must have with disguises. Or isn't that done any more?"

"I've come back for my overcoat," said Johnny as he took off Uman's. "Theodor gave me yours by mistake."

"Oh?" said Uman, supremely disinterested, and to Kurt, with vigor, "Where was I? Oh, yes. Everyone knows that there is a definite connection between the working of the thyroid and the pituitary, and my point is that . . ."

"Speaking of points," said Tuck, picking up Uman's overcoat which Greenwood had laid across a chair before going to the closet for his own, "how do you happen to have this knife in your pocket?"

He produced the knife as he spoke, and Kurt looked at it sharply, and then at Uman, an odd expression on his thin face.

"Was that in my pocket?" said Uman, blinking at it vaguely. And then he looked swiftly up at Tuck, the vagueness leaving his face, and shrewdness taking its place. "Whoa! Just a minute!" He stood up. "I never saw that knife before! I have no more idea of how it could have got in the pocket of my overcoat than you do!"

"Think back," urged Tuck gently, and handed him the knife, handle first.

Uman looked at it, shook his head, and laid it on the table beside the empty wine bottle.

"I know what you're thinking," he said morosely. "Miss What's-her-name and the man in the park. I assure you that I have better things to do than follow young women for any reason whatsoever, let alone the reason that goes with that knife." And he turned to Kurt and spoke fervently in German, a language that Tuck did not understand.

When he stopped, Kurt Schwann said, "He says that the whole idea is preposterous, anyone could have put the knife in the pocket of that coat, and that any—ah—so-and-so should know that Biology professors are too busy to indulge in strange quests by moonlight."

"What do you mean, anyone could have put that knife in the pocket of your coat?" asked Tuck of Uman.

Uman gave him a baleful look, and then sighed resignedly. "Look. I have two overcoats. One, I keep at home. One, I keep in the biology office. The one I keep in the Biology office is this one here."

"Why do you keep one in the Biology office?"

"Look. Sometimes I work in my laboratory until late at night. It is cold when I leave to walk home. So I have the coat there to put on if I didn't wear the other one in the morning. Clear?" He answered himself. "Clear as glass."

"That's right," said Kurt, looking obscurely relieved. "In fact that coat in the Biology office is rather a joke. It hangs on a hatrack in the corner, and occasionally Dr. Uman becomes so absorbed in a problem that he absent-mindedly puts it on when he goes out to lunch, regardless of the temperature."

"I see," said Tuck. And to Uman, "Then I take it you worked in your laboratory tonight."

Uman shook his head negatively several times. "You take it wrong. I went home, had my dinner, and then left to come here and discuss a problem with Kurt. I did not wear my other overcoat. It was very cold. So when I passed the Science Building, I went up to the office and got this one."

"Then the Science Building is not locked at night?" asked Tuck.

Dr. Uman looked at him as if he suspected him of purposely misunderstanding. "The Science Building *is* locked at night!" He added, in a more moderate tone, "I have a key."

"And," asked Tuck, "who else has keys?"

Dr. Uman made a broad, impatient gesture. "*Everyone* has keys!"

"Not quite everyone," said Kurt. "Officially, there is a key for each office. Actually, about every professor has a key, as well as Fellows, like myself." He smiled. "A great many keys," he conceded.

"Yes," said Tuck. "And of course, everyone knows that you keep the overcoat in your office, Dr. Uman?"

"Everyone," said Uman, with the spacious gesture.

"I'm going home," Greenwood said, from the door. He had on his own overcoat.

"I'll give you a lift," Tuck offered, and picked up the knife from the table. He turned to Kurt. "Where's your brother?"

"He has gone to bed. Do you wish to question him about anything?"

"No. Has he been in all evening?"

"All evening," said Kurt, decidedly.

"I'll tell you something," Dr. Uman said suddenly. "Someone had worn my coat before I put it on tonight. When I put it on, it was still warm."

"Ah," said Tuck.

He let Greenwood off at his apartment house, and then continued two blocks down the street to Kathryn Farr's.

Parking, he walked up the driveway of the private house next door as he had seen Greenwood do a half-hour before. He whistled.

In a moment a window went up on the third floor, and Kathryn Farr's head peered out.

"Oh," she said. "It's you."

"You'll have to let me in," called Tuck. "I've got to ask some more questions."

As she drew in her head, he heard a young male voice within the darkened first-floor apartment outside which he was standing say dryly, "That girl has charm! Two in one night!" A deeper but equally dry voice replied, "Betcha the next one has a guitar."

He smiled to himself, and walked toward the street. When Kathryn Farr came to the downstairs door, wearing a house coat and several curlers, he asked, "Do you mind if I come up? This is rather public."

"I don't mind if Mrs. Nox doesn't," she said, wearily.

As she spoke, that lady thrust a head covered

with a peculiarly nauseating purple hair net through her narrowly opened door and demanded, *"What* is going on here?" Tuck came into the lighted hallway. "Oh. I beg your pardon, Lieutenant Tuck."

"Official business," said Tuck solemnly. "Won't wait."

"I understand perfectly," she replied, with worldly mysteriousness. She started to close the door, and then opened it again. "Have you discovered anything?" she whispered.

"Very little, Mrs. Nox," Tuck whispered back. Disappointedly, Mrs. Nox closed her door.

When they were seated, each at one end of the chintz sofa, Tuck said, "I'm going to ask you for particulars again. Tell me, from when you had crossed the street to the park to the moment you first saw the gentleman in the overcoat, was there time for someone to have seen you, gone to the top floor of the Science Building, come down, and followed you part way across the rose garden?"

"No, I don't think so. Now tell me why someone went up to the top floor of the Science Building."

He told her about Dr. Uman's well-known dark-brown overcoat, and the abundance of keys.

"I see," she mused. "Aside from the fact that Dr. Uman believes his overcoat to have been warm when he put it on tonight, there is still that knife I found in the pocket to suggest that the coat someone put on to scare the daylights out of me was Dr. Uman's."

"That's right. And that leads to several interesting questions. First, why was Dr. Uman's overcoat chosen?"

Before he could go on, Kate Farr said, "I think I can answer that. It was a very dark brown, and it was available."

"And I think we can accept that. So then we are face to face with the fact that whoever wore it did not own a dark overcoat. And did have a key to the Science Building."

"Of course, there's always this angle. That the knife was planted in the pocket of Dr. Uman's overcoat to throw suspicion on him and away from the real masquerader."

"I eliminated that notion as soon as it occurred to me. Do you know why? Because of the way you and Greenwood laughed at the idea of Uman being the masquerader. The person who followed you must have known Dr. Uman, since he knew about the overcoat. He would certainly have chosen a more likely suspect than the notoriously eccentric professor whose very name provokes laughter."

"So then we come back to the theory that Dr. Uman's available overcoat was used because the masquerader did not have a dark overcoat of his own. Say, I like the term 'masquerader,' don't you? It has a nice, macabre quality."

"I think the man who followed you has a nice, macabre quality."

"And you have no idea who he is?" probed Kate.

"No," said Tuck. "Now, please tell me the people who knew that you were going to an eight-thirty movie across the park tonight." His pad was out, his pencil poised in readiness.

"Why," said Kate Farr in bafflement, "no one knew. No one, that is, except Gladys Horstmann." As soon as the words were out, she sat staring at him, her mouth a little open.

"I've heard of her before," said Tuck. "Tell me about her."

"She's large"—Kate made a troubled gesture with one hand—"and wholesome, and a Fellow in Biology—Uman's assistant, as a matter of fact . . ." Her voice trailed off, and she brushed one small hand wearily over her frown. "I don't quite understand this. . . . Perhaps it's because I'm so darned tired . . ."

[125]

"Look," said Tuck, leaning forward. "You said that you didn't think the person who followed you would have had time, after seeing you enter the park, to go up, get the overcoat from the Biology office, come down, and appear when he did."

"I'm sure there wasn't time," said Kate, watching him.

"And remember, not only would he have to get the coat, but the knife as well."

"The knife! Of course!"

"It's just a kitchen knife, available at any five-and-ten, but surely you can see that the knife argues premeditation."

"Yes," said Kate, a little grimly, "I do see." As though making some sort of decision, she leaned suddenly toward him. "Mr. Tuck. I said that Gladys Horstmann was wholesome. I should have said that she looks wholesome. She's the sort of person you'd type-cast for captain of a girls' hockey team. What she's like underneath, I can't say for sure because I've known her only since yesterday morning. But I can tell you this. Like a good many people of my age, she's gone hog-wild for behavioristic psychology. She . . . she revels in the untidy action of certain psychotics. And she tried this morning to convince me that this tabloid Black Overcoat could have poisoned Garnet Dillon. She dropped quinine into my coke at Chapel hour to prove her absurd theory that this degenerate could have sat down at a bar beside Garnet, poisoned her, and watched her die."

"Ah," said Tuck. "And how did she know that Miss Dillon had been poisoned?"

"I told her about Garnet Dillon's body being sent here and that I had seen it, and that she hadn't been stabbed, beaten or shot to death," said Kate. "She deduced the rest herself."

"And now you're pointing out to me that the type of mentality that would think up the quinine trick would be apt to think up the masquerade."

"I'm throwing that in extra," Kate said. "That's a guess. But I'm not guessing when I tell you that Gladys Horstmann knew what show I was going to tonight. In fact, she made the date herself this afternoon. She phoned at eight to break it because Bob Hitchlock had dropped over. She's in love with Hitch."

"Where does she live?"

"On Twenty-ninth. About six blocks from campus."

"Does she have a car?"

"Her brother has."

"Of course, she might have told someone else that you and she were going to cross the park a little after eight this evening. Or were you planning to go in her car?"

"We were going to walk." Kate shivered. "I don't like this. I don't like it at all. Wait a minute! If Garnet Dillon's . . . I'm embarrassed . . . If her condition was the motive for the murder, why then Gladys Horstmann isn't the murderer. Masculinity in a woman goes just so far. So then why would she put on that óvercoat and follow me across the park, if she did?" She frowned, and then continued speaking, more to herself than to Tuck. "Let's see . . . the person who followed me wanted to make me think it was Black Overcoat. Yes. And it would seem that that person would also be the murderer. But Gladys isn't the murderer. So if she followed me, the reason was . . . to protect the murderer. And that would be . . ."

She suddenly sat up very straight, her eyes wide and shocked.

"Hitch!"

FIFTEEN

Tuck walked along university toward the Science Building, staring out over the heads of approaching students, aware of occasional head-turnings and utterly unconcerned.

He was saying to himself, "There are two general types of women. Women with purely feminine minds, and women with somewhat masculine minds. I'm taking a gamble that this Horstmann has a somewhat masculine mind. I'm wasting my time if she isn't susceptible to logic, if she's the frilly sort who says, 'I don't care if you did find my fingerprints all over the gun, I didn't kill him, so there!'"

He found the Biology office without much trouble, using Schwann's laboratory as a starting point, and opened the door onto a south room full of sunlight, empty of anyone except a large, broad-shouldered young woman who was reading at a desk that faced the door. The sunlight was kind to her dull hair, cut almost as short as a man's and swept back from her broad plain face. On hearing him enter the office, she tore her eyes from the book, looked up and with a pleasant smile asked, "What can I do for you?" He noticed with satisfaction that her voice was quite deep.

Miss Horstmann?" he asked.

She nodded.

Deliberately, he drew up a chair so that he faced her. "My name's Tuck. I'm investigating Miss Dillon's death."

Her face did not change, but her eyes narrowed by a hair's width.

He drew out a pad and pencil. "I'd like the names of any people you may have told about your movie date with Miss Farr last evening."

Gladys Horstmann's short eyelashes flickered. She looked at the pad and the poised pencil. "I

[128]

don't believe I told anyone," she said, easily.

" 'Don't believe' isn't good enough."

"All right. I didn't tell anyone."

Tuck carefully stowed away pad and pencil in his inner breast pocket. He clasped his hands around one knee. "Neither did Miss Farr," he said. He reached into the side pocket of his overcoat. "So I'll give you back your knife," he added, and laid it on the desk beside the book she had been reading. He saw that it was *Lizzie Borden*.

"What's coming off here?" she asked, with every evidence of astonishment.

Tuck sighed ostentatiously. "Miss Horstmann, you disappoint me. I gave you credit for a more masculine intellect. Now I'll have to ask some more questions. How did you spend last evening from seven-thirty on?"

"Let's see. We finished dinner—my brother and I—at about seven-thirty. I washed the dishes, and my brother dried them, until about ten to eight. Then some pals of his came over to play poker. Just before eight Bob Hitchlock came in, so I phoned Kate Farr to tell her I wouldn't be able to make the show with her. When I hung up I found that Bob was going to play poker too. I don't care much for it, so I—I went to my room to read. At about ten-thirty, Bob had lost all the money he had—he always does—and so he stopped. We went to a drive-in and had a malt, and then he drove me home and I went to bed."

Tuck had taken out his pad and was making rapid notations calculated to impress. Now he lifted the pencil from the pad, stared reflectively at the eraser, and said, "You didn't leave the house between eight and ten-thirty?"

"I drove to the drugstore just after Bob came. We were out of cigarettes."

Tuck nodded, wrote, and said, "I imagine that you returned home at about eight-thirty, after you

[129]

drove to the Science Building, got Dr. Uman's overcoat, drove to the edge of the park, waited in your car for Miss Farr, and spectacularly followed her into the rose garden. I imagine that you got the knife from the kitchen drawer at home. And it was your brother's hat, wasn't it?"

Gladys Horstmann looked steadily at him, and then gave a loud, explosive laugh. "All right, so I scared the whey out of dear little Kate. Bring on the handcuffs!"

"No handcuffs. No handcuffs at all," Tuck said mildly. "Just a few more questions. Nothing ever happens without a reason, you know. And I'm rather interested in your reason for that masquerade."

Gladys spread out a square hand on the desk and looked at it. "There were two reasons. First, I really do believe that a psychopath killed Garnet Dillon, although I perhaps went a little far trying to convince someone else. Second, Kate Farr gives me a pain!"

"Oh," said Tuck. "She gives you a pain."

"She's one of those goody-goodies," said Gladys, dispassionately, "who go around insisting that human beings are made up of sugar and spice and everything nice, as well as Sweetness and Light. I told her a simple psychological truth this morning, that the veneer of civilized ways is plenty thin and that it cracks pretty often. That's why the nice man next door suddenly shoots his wife; that's why . . . "

"Lizzie Borden took an ax . . ." finished Tuck.

Gladys Horstmann did not smile." Exactly," she said. "And Kate Farr threw up her hands in holy horror. Said I was generalizing. Said that everyone was very damned nice indeed, except for a few psychotics who were very damned bad. It got my goat, Mr. Tuck. She's probably told you that I put a quinine pill in her coke; I did that to prove that

[130]

a psychopath could have murdered Garnet. I did it to prove that poison could be a psychopathic killer's weapon, given the right time and place for using it. Last night—well, last night, when I decided I couldn't be bothered playing poker with the boys and was wondering what to do with myself until Hitch lost enough so he'd have to stop playing, well, the idea just popped into my head, full blown. It was in the nature of a sudden upsurge from the unconscious; undoubtedly I'd been cherishing a desire to give Kate Farr's holy smugness a nudge all day, and then when I found myself with an opportunity to give that nudge, the unknown desire showed itself above the level of consciousness."

"The only thing I have against psychology," observed Tuck, "is its wordiness. Go on."

Gladys Horstmann looked surprised. "That's all," she said.

"If Kate Farr gives you such a pain, why did you make a date to go to the movies with her?"

Gladys shook her head. "You don't understand. I don't dislike Kate. She's rather pleasant company. And I felt that I owed her an overture after my gag with the quinine. But at the same time, she gives me a pain."

"Go on," said Tuck.

"Stop saying 'Go on'!" Gladys snapped. "There's nothing more to say. I hung up the phone. I thought, 'Gee, she'll have to walk clear across the park alone.' Then came my big idea, and in a flash I thought of the knife I'd washed, and my brother's black hat, and Dr. Uman's dark-brown overcoat." She added, "Don't say 'Go on,' because that's all there is to it."

"If that's all there is to it, then I think you should consult a psychiatrist, Miss Horstmann."

She frowned at him.

"Because you're not sane."

Her voice thinned. "I'm perfectly sane."

He nodded. "I think so too. That's why I think there was another reason for that absurd masquerade. Now I'm going to talk some psychology at *you*. A sane person may do something absurd, but he does it for a sane reason. I quite believe your innocent motive in asking Kate Farr to go to the movies with you, because if there's one plain fact about this park business it's that it was cooked up on the spur of the moment. Mature thought would have discarded it as ridiculous. Therefore, something happened last night, at about eight o'clock. It gave you the imaginative notion to convince Miss Farr that a maniac was loose on campus; ergo: that the same maniac may have done in Garnet Dillon." Very softly, he asked, "What happened last night to make you think Hitchlock killed Garnet Dillon?"

She looked at him out of stone eyes. "Nothing. Absolutely nothing."

After an equally ceramic glance, he stood up to go.

He opened the door of the Dean's office onto the clatter of a typewriter. Sleep had erased last night's weariness from Kathryn Farr's face; she looked abstractedly up from her notes.

"I want Hitchlock," Tuck said, without preface.

As directly, she replied, "He went down to the Union about five minutes ago with Johnny. John Greenwood, that is. They're probably at the Medical table." The typewriter burst into chattering again, then she stopped. "How are you getting on?"

"I'm not."

She smiled as though she knew he was evading her question, and went on typing.

The Student Union reminded him of his own college days, fifteen years before. The coeds wore their hair in swinging bobs now, instead of

[132]

cropped short, and there were fewer blondes. Waistlines had crept from the hips to the waist, and there was less rah-rah. But the atmosphere was somehow the same. He walked past the crowded brown tables and chairs and felt very old.

On seeing Hitchlock's yellow head, he wedged himself between chair backs, and tapped the tweed shoulder.

The surprise on the pink face changed to discomfiture as Greenwood said, "Looks like the law wants you, Hitch," and added negligently, "How are you, Tuck? Care for some coffee? It's rotten, but strong."

"Thanks," Tuck declined. "I'd rather have a talk with Hitchlock, here. Hitchlock, where can we be alone?"

Hitchlock stood up abruptly. "We could go upstairs to the Student Lounge. It's about the size of Grand Central Station, and usually pretty empty."

"Swell," said Tuck.

The other people at the table, among them Whittaker and Schwann, who had been watching without being quite conscious that they were doing so, suddenly began talking. Tuck followed Hitchlock to the cashier's desk.

As he reached it, Hitch moaned, "Oh, hell. I forgot my check." And to the cashier's fixed, polite smile, "Look. I forgot my check. I had a cup of coffee."

"I guess I can trust you," she said, and deftly slid his nickel across the desk and into the drawer of the cash register.

"Who wouldn't trust a face like that?" Tuck asked Tuck.

He followed Hitchlock back around a corner, into a dark inner hall of the building, and up a flight of cement stairs.

Hitchlock had told the truth. The Student Lounge *was* approximately as large as the Grand Central Station. It was also empty, with the trifling exception of six students leaning around a grand piano upon which an elaborately nonchalant chap was playing "St. Louis Blues," and two intense conversations on two of the gargantuan sofas.

They crossed the thick carpet to an unoccupied sofa facing the fireless fireplace over which hung a portrait of a severe old gentleman in a black gown and a white beard.

Hitchlock sat down in a corner of the sofa, cocking one leg over the other. His effort at nonchalance missed fire.

"Why is everything so big?" Tuck asked, in order to have a moment to examine Hitchlock minus the white coat. His angular young body could not completely eradicate the labors of the excellent tailor who had made his gray-blue sport coat, and his shoes, although scuffed and stained with acids from the chemistry lab, were the best shoes Tuck had seen for quite a long time.

"There's money here," he said to himself, while Hitchlock fumbled out something to the effect that big things were supposed to be impressive.

Then Tuck leaned forward and asked quietly, "Hitchlock, why does Gladys Horstmann think you killed Garnet Dillon?"

The cocked foot thudded to the carpet, and Hitchlock sat up very straight. An expression of utter astonishment grew slowly on his face and stayed there. In contrast to the subdued look he normally wore, it was as though his face had come sharply into focus. Then he shook his head dully from side to side, like a man recovering from a physical blow. "I don't believe you," he said. The pink face went slowly out of focus again. "This is one of those tricks I've read about." Deliberately, he cocked his leg, looking straight into Tuck's eyes.

"Gladys Horstmann thinks you killed Garnet Dillon," said Tuck.

"Wait a minute," commanded Hitchlock. His lips were thinned a trifle, his pink cheeks were pinker. "Are you saying that Gladys Horstmann *told* you that I killed Garnet?"

"No. I'm saying that she thinks you did."

"Mr. Tuck, put it to me straight."

"Fair enough," Tuck said, equably, and told how Gladys Horstmann had borrowed Uman's overcoat and staged the episode in the park.

To his surprise, Hitch burst out laughing. He threw his head back against the sofa and laughed at the ceiling for a full minute. Then he sobered, and blew his nose.

" 'Scuse it," he said, putting away his handkerchief. "But it's so like Horsie. She's such a nut. If she'd keep her mind on biology, she might get somewhere. But science isn't dramatic enough for most women, and Gladys is no exception. She dabbles in psychology on the side. It's sort of a wonderful never-never land to her. Anything can happen there. Her brother's not bad, but he's nuts too." Then the lingering smile vanished and his yellow brows drew together. "But I don't see what this has to do with the business about Horsie thinking I . . . I killed Garnet."

"The reasons she gave me, when I accused her of the masquerade, were not convincing. I think that she did it to protect you. I believe that something happened after you walked into her house last night which made her think you might be the murderer. What was it, Hitchlock?"

Hitchlock shook his head. "I don't know." He cast a shy, strained look at Tuck. "The whole idea is so absurd, somehow. I . . . I don't even

[135]

know how Garnet died, or why, or where. It's the first time I've hidden my head in the sand for a long while." He gave a short laugh and looked attentively at the scuffed toe of his shoe. "When I was a kid I was always hiding from things I didn't like the looks of. Medicine jerks you out of that. But here I am, reverting to type." He looked up at Tuck. "How did she die?"

"She was poisoned. Her death passed at the County Hospital as a heart attack. There was no identification, so the body was sent out to a medical school. It happened to be sent here."

Hitchlock's eyes were blue marbles. "Here!"

Tuck nodded.

"And Horsie knew this?"

Tuck nodded again.

"Let me get this straight, Mr. Tuck. Gladys knew that Garnet's body had been picked up unidentified?"

"Yes."

Slowly, the cocked leg dropped to the floor, and Hitch straightened.

"Now I get it," he said with a nod.

He reached into his hip pocket for his wallet, saying as he did so: "Gladys hates to see me lose at poker. I always lose. Last night, just as I started to play, she swiped my wallet. I caught her as she was taking a fiver out. She said that she was going to put it aside for me for a rainy day. It made me as mad as the devil—she's awfully darned domineering—but I turned back to the game." His wallet was open now, and he was prying down into a mass of papers and bills.

"She must have seen this," he said, and held out a small card enclosed in a clear celluloid case.

Tuck took it. It was Garnet Dillon's driver's license.

[136]

"You're wondering where I got it, of course," said Hitchlock resolutely, "so I'll tell you. When Gladys and Whittaker and I left the Hofbrau last Friday night I found they wanted to see a show I'd already seen. I told them to go ahead, that I'd wait for them at the Hofbrau with Kurt and Garnet. But when I got back, the waitress was clearing their table. She lifted up a beer-mug, and I saw this under it. Garnet used it to prove she was twenty-one. I told the waitress it belonged to a friend of mine and tucked it away, intending to give it to Garnet when I saw her, but I never saw her again."

He forced a laugh. "Looks bad for me, doesn't it?"

Tuck wondered about that, looking into Hitchlock's ingenious face.

SIXTEEN

"You are my own,
Life's only sensation.
I am alone,
Without your inspiration.
So I pray to stars above, while I hold you tight,
'Don't let her say good night tonight!' "

THE DOLEFUL-VOICED SINGER expertly tapered off the last note of his song, then beamed and bowed into the glare of a spotlight and moderate applause. When he had trotted briskly back to his saxophone, the watchful band leader tapped a new tempo on the air with an imperious baton, the spotlight died, and the first couple glided across the shining dance floor.

Johnny turned to Kate. "Every time I come to a place like this I wonder why I did it."

A small, uncontrollable anger stirred inside Kate, born, she knew, of the fact that after warmly urging her to accept this date when he

came into the office that morning with Hitch, he
had not noticed her new black date dress and
hat, and had subsequently behaved like a resigned
aristocrat on his way to the guillotine.

"Why did you want to come here, Kate?" he
asked.

She looked at the bright scarlet of the punch
for which this place was famous, and then looked
straight at him and said levelly, "Because we
used to come here in the dear dead days beyond
recall. I thought that it might make us a little
less like two strangers exchanging polite comments on the weather."

He returned her gaze for a moment and then
said, "Would you like a Scotch-and-soda?"

"There is nothing," said Kate, "that I want
more than a Scotch-and-soda."

He beckoned a white-jacketed waiter. "Take
this grizzly gruel away," he commanded quietly,
with a large gesture at the pitcher of punch, "and
bring two Scotch-and-sodas."

The waiter nodded, started to write the order
on his pad, and then paused and glanced dubiously at Kate.

"Is the lady twenty-one?" he asked.

"I'm twenty-four," said Kate. "Take a closer
look at the circles under my eyes."

The waiter smiled perfunctorily and turned his
gaze on Johnny.

"Carries her years nicely, doesn't she?" beamed
Johnny.

The waiter smiled again, and went away, re-
turning in a moment in the suave wake of the
headwaiter.

The headwaiter bent over Johnny. "If the lady
would just show us something to indicate her
age . . . " he murmured.

"Do you have your birth certificate about you?"
Johnny asked Kate.

[138]

"Oddly enough, no. And I don't drive a car. But I'm still twenty-four."

Johnny looked up at the headwaiter with a lovely grin. "Do I look twenty-five?" he asked.

"Yes, sir."

Johnny indicated Kate with another large gesture. "She's a year younger than I am," he said. Then, as though that settled everything, "Care to dance, Katie?"

"Yes."

He rose, the waiter drew back her chair, and in a moment they were one of the crowd of dancing couples.

In a few minutes something vaguely familiar about the music touched Kate's mind. "Isn't that Tchaikovsky?" she asked.

"It is. And that faint, whirring sound you hear is Tchaikovsky turning over in his grave." He gave a sigh. "Shall we sit down?" he asked hopefully.

"Why not?"

Two Scotch-and-sodas were at their table when they returned. Kate laughed. "I believe," she said reflectively, "that what I've always liked best about you is the neat way you get what you want."

He picked up his glass. "You're wrong there. Well, Katie, here's to two strangers."

"Two strangers," she echoed.

The singer was at it again. Now the refrain was "Tonight we love."

" 'Tonight we love,' " Johnny said to Kate. " 'You are my own, life's only sensation.' Ugh!"

"Ugh," agreed Kate.

"Sex," observed Johnny, looking over the floor at the clot of dancers swaying at the feet of the singer, "is in a pretty bad way. Tawdry little songs, aimed at adolescents . . . "

"I love 'tawdry,' " commented Kate.

" . . . And slick movies," continued Johnny, "full of sexy characters whimsically at odds until the last half of the last reel."

"I think you're looking at the surface, Johnny."

He gave her a blank stare.

Kate found herself frowning at her Scotch-and-soda and saying, "When I think of love, I think of 'Let me not to the marriage of true minds admit impediments. Love is not love which alters when it alteration finds, or bends with the remover to remove.' "

"Shakespeare," said Johnny, softly.

"And I think of this, too:

" 'Take of this grain, which in my garden grows
        And grows for you;
    Make bread of it; and that repose
        And peace, which everywhere
    With so much earnestness you do pursue
        Is only there.' "

His eyebrows were a question.

"And I think of, 'But, soft! what light through yonder window breaks? It is the east, and Juliet is the sun . . .' "

" ' . . . Arise, fair sun, and kill the envious moon that is already sick and pale with grief,' " said Johnny slowly.

"Johnny! You surprise me!"

"But it was never that way for us," Johnny said, looking at her out of somber brown eyes. "From the moment I met you, it was never that way for us."

"Are you going to look me in the eye and tell me you remember the moment you met me?"

He looked down into his glass. "Joel had told me of his wonderful friend who wrote poetry. Knowing Joel, you know that he made me expect a cross between Sappho and Elizabeth Barrett Browning. When he took me over to

[140]

meet you, you were living at the Girls' Dormitory. It was a Saturday, just before dinner. We waited downstairs while the girl at the desk buzzed your room, in a big awful place—plush, like a hotel lobby. Then you came down. You were frowning, and you didn't have any lipstick on. You said hello, and shook my hand. That was when you were working on Saturdays in the Campus Shop of a department store. You said your feet hurt. I looked down, and you had on slippers. Huge, comfortable slippers, lined with lambs' wool." He laughed. "No balconies for us, Kate. And there was another time I particularly remember. We had come home from a dance the fraternity gave, and we were standing on that wide terrace in front of the dorm. In spite of the garden furniture it had atmosphere; I think it was the flagstones, and the urns, and the fact that it was very late and you had on a blue taffeta dress that swished when you walked. I was saying good night. You were looking up at me, and you looked very sweet. Then some girl with a front room yelled, 'Kiss her and get it over with! I want my sleep!' I was just about to tell you that I was in love with you."

A pulse throbbed inside Kate, near her heart or perhaps a trifle nearer her stomach.

The singer began to sing again. This time it was to the effect that "There's nothing left to do but say good-by."

"Shall we?" asked Johnny.

The pulse inside Kate throbbed again, sickeningly.

"Shall we say good-by to this place?" he asked. She nodded.

As he beckoned the waiter, she found herself saying, "You didn't notice my new dress."

"Oh, but I did. It's not your kind of dress,

[141]

Kate. It's a wise dress, and you're sweet. I liked that blue taffeta thing much better."

"Frank, aren't you?"

"To you, yes. I'd have told anyone else that it looked like a million dollars."

"Oh."

"Choose another place, Kate," he said, as he laid a bill on the waiter's obsequiously extended tray.

"I warn you, I'll probably be nostalgic again."

"Be nostalgic."

"I choose the observatory." She felt her lips curve in a grin. "Or don't you remember?"

He looked at her intently. His face was almost sad. "Why is it," he asked, "that women go around cherishing the idea that men can forget so easily? I remember, Kate. I remember. I've remembered you a good many times during these last two years."

The observatory, with its great round dome flanked by two smaller domes, seemed to hang out over the glittering lights of the sprawling city of Los Angeles. Kate got out of the car and stood looking at them, and the splendor of the scene moved her so deeply that she said, "Cheap jewels. Rhinestones."

They walked together along a wide cement space toward the three domes, one shade darker than the dark and starry sky. They came to a white statue, with the faces of scientists who had pursued the truth out beyond the stars looking in profile across the night. A small steady wind was blowing in from the west. She took off her hat and let her hair flow with it.

"Copernicus," said Johnny, pointing upward. "The guy who changed the universe."

She felt a low laugh in her throat.

His eyes moved from the stone face of Copernicus to the sky beyond.

"Look, Kate. The Big Dipper. **And Orion.** And the Little Dipper, too. It's funny **how you** never see the stars in the city."

The low laugh left Kate's lips for the second time.

He turned to her. "I love you, Kate."

This was it, then. The Moment. Take it, take it. "I love you, too, Johnny."

They kissed.

When they drew away from each other at last, he looked down at her, with enchantment fading from his face, and said, "It'll be three years before I'm finished with medical school and my internship."

Looking up at him, so wise, so young, so very solemn, she felt years older than he. "Yes, dear," she said. "Shall we talk about that later?"

He laughed a little, and they put their arms around each other and walked to the wall that overlooked the city. They stood there a while, their elbows on the wall, quite satisfied to say nothing. Then Johnny broke the silence.

"Katie," he said, with something very like awe in his voice, "look at those damned stars!"

The wind from the west stirred in Kate's hair. She thought, I shall remember this until the day I die.

And then, absurdly, she felt cold tears spill over onto her cheeks.

In a moment she heard Johnny say, "You're crying." She glanced up and saw his face peering down into hers. She turned her head away. He put the fingers of one hand against her cheek and turned her face toward him again. "There's nothing to cry about," he said with an uncertain smile on his lips.

She felt obliged to say something light. "I can cry for no reason at all."

With one finger he wiped the tears from her

cheeks, intently, carefully, gently.

"This is our moment," she blurted.

He nodded, gravely.

Putting his arm about her waist, he said, "I'll take you home. It's late."

As they crossed the wide windswept place to his car, another little car arrived, its headlights blinding their eyes for a moment. The car's radio was playing, "You are my own, life's only sensation. I am alone without your inspiration. . . . "

They looked at each other and burst out laughing.

SEVENTEEN

AND DO YOU KNOW WHAT he pulled out of his wallet?" asked Tuck. "He pulled out the girl's driver's license. Then he looked at me like an overgrown choir boy and said, 'I guess this looks bad, doesn't it?'"

Brigit Estees boomed the heel of her oxford against the side of Tuck's desk, on whose wide top she had casually deposited her hundred and fifty pounds of healthy womanhood. The sound was loud under the hard lights of the empty squad room. Brigit frowned. Brigit's shrewd eyes crossed slightly as she concentrated on a lock of auburn hair that had fallen over her forehead; she blew it out of the way. Then she looked down at Tuck.

"You know what you have, of course," she said, calmly. "You have a story-book case. And you've been spoiled for this sort of thing by the fact that the usual homicide is a Negro cutting another Negro's throat in the presence of twelve witnesses. What does Gufferty say?"

"Gufferty says it's my baby. Gufferty says the Coroner's inquest is coming up in two days. Gufferty says I'm getting nowhere fast."

Brigit smiled, then sobered. "There are several little angles about this murder that puzzle me badly. One is: Why digitalis? Why choose a poison whose fatal dose varies greatly, which means that the killer had to give her a whopping big amount to be sure she would die?"

"If you only knew how often I've asked myself that question! I've mulled over the properties of the drug, and the only points that strike me as being even vaguely significant are these: There is a time lapse of from five to thirteen days between the time a fatal amount is taken into the body, and death. The symptoms are not of a painful and therefore not of an alarming nature; not infrequently they're absent altogether. And it is easily obtainable."

"I can't see of what value the five-to-thirteen-day time lapse before death could be. The symptom part is logical—naturally it would be to the murderer's advantage if the murderee didn't become aware that she was being poisoned. But I can't quite see why the fact that it's easily obtainable should matter if you're on the right track and someone connected with the medical school is the murderer. Don't forget that there's a Chemistry lab in any medical school, chock full of poisons to be had for the swiping. How about this heart-attack angle? Could the murderer have chosen digitalis because it resulted in a death that simulated heart attack?"

"I can't see how. He surely couldn't have known under what circumstances she was going to die. He couldn't have known that Joe the red-haired counterman was going to be present, all primed by the death of his mother to plant the idea of a heart attack in the interns' minds. For all he knew, she might have had all the usual symptoms and then some, right under the eyes of Dean Calder. No. That doesn't work."

"Then in addition to the lack of painful symptoms, the only significant property of digitalis is that time lapse of five to thirteen days before death. Say, wait a minute . . . !"

"I think I know what your going to say," said Tuck.

"Suppose he knew she was going away? Then that time lapse becomes vital, because he could poison her *less* than five days before her departure and be certain that she wouldn't die until she was miles away from anyone who knew her! Yes! And he stole the driver's license from her purse so she wouldn't be identified and sent back."

"Then why did she die before she left town?"

"Well, yes, that. Still, you'll admit it was pretty close. If she hadn't missed her train . . . And wait! That date she'd had with Kurt Schwann! The poisoner didn't know she was going to keep that!"

"Still, what bothers me is the fact that it would have been so much easier to poison her a day or two before she planned to leave, instead of cutting it so fine."

"I can think of several pretty logical reasons to explain that. She changed her mind about when she was going. He wasn't certain of having a later opportunity . . . "

"Guessing isn't going to get us anywhere."

"I don't care," said Brigit doggedly. "I like it."

"You like it."

"Yes. Three's just enough of a glimpse of chance stepping in and mucking up the nasty foresight of this killer to make the whole thing ring true to me."

"Bless you, Brigit! You believe in chance too!"

"Why not? If I'd happened to grow up with less freckles and more eyelashes and smaller feet, I'd be the mother of five kids now instead of a

[146]

lousy policewoman."

They laughed.

"There's something else that bothers me," said Tuck. "Why that final dose between five-thirty and six-thirty on the night she died?"

"He wanted to be sure," said Brigit sagely. "Maybe he'd already given her fifty grains. He slipped that in for good measure, so nothing could go wrong. It seems to me that all you have to do is find out who was within arm's length of her on Friday, between five-thirty and six-thirty, and there's your man!"

"I already know that."

"You already . . . !"

"Yes. At five-thirty she was alone with Greenwood; from six to six-thirty she was at the Hofbrau having dinner with Kurt Schwann. Also present were Hitchlock and Whittaker, and for good measure, Gladys Horstmann. At six-thirty, these three people stood congenially around the table where Dillon was, saying hello." He grinned. "With your memory for names, you have by now recalled that the chief suspects are Greenwood, Schwann, Hitchlock, and Whittaker."

"Well, at least Horstmann's out. You've got something to be thankful for. And speaking of Horstmann's manifest innocence brings us smack up against the motive for the murder, and a nasty little backstairs motive it is, too. Boy meets girl. Whoops—child. Girl won't do away with child, so boy does away with both of 'em. But that's not enough. There has to be a motive for the motive. I mean, right now as we sit here a good many lads are learning that their sweethearts are with child. How many of them are going to solve the problem by murdering her? Not many. Granted that in this case there was no other way out, that the girl's mania against suicide would certainly go hand in hand with a disinclination for murdering the child at an abortionist's, and that the boy wouldn't or couldn't marry her. *Why* wouldn't or couldn't he marry her? Why did an apparently decent young student commit such a hideous crime? There must be a staggering reason there. That's what you should look for."

Tuck found his head wagging like a mandarin's as she spoke, and stopped it. "I spent the better part of this afternoon trying to find that reason. Here's what I found, chiefly from Dean Calder who makes it his business to know all about the backgrounds of his boys. Hitchlock comes of a wealthy old Los Angeles family. His mother is a bit of a matriarch, and has him well under her thumb. However, there's no reason, says Calder, to believe that she would object to his marrying an attractive woman of his choice."

Brigit raised her forefinger aloft. "*But* maybe she did just that. And maybe his fear of her is psychotic; there have been such cases."

"Maybe. Whittaker, who by the way is considerably older than the other boys—he's on the verge of thirty—has a small private income, and absolutely no one to say him yea or nay. His only living relatives are two elderly aunts in Boston. When he turned up at medical school, simply because he was sure medicine would never leave him time to be bored, he had just terminated a mess of a marriage. But he's not making any alimony payments, because the girl was very rich. And apparently the marriage left no scars; Calder believes he has too good a sense of humor for that. He's been heard to make remarks about the infelicity of the monastic life and would probably have welcomed a chance to marry Garnet, because there is no doubt that he was very fond of her."

Again Brigit's forefinger went up. "*But*, sup-

[148]

pose he's still nuts about his first wife, and suppose he learned that she wanted him to come back to him, after learning that Garnet and he were well on their way to the alter . . . "

"Oh, Brigit," Tuck mourned. "You disappoint me."

Brigit said doggedly, "I'm trying to show you that big forces can be at work under a surface that looks as innocent as . . . as lollipops. Have you ever seen a limestone cavern? Stalagmites and stalactites? Rivers beneath the ground did that. And people are the same. Rivers beneath the surface can channel out big dark caves, with queer twisted ideas hanging around the place."

"I'll grant you your big dark caves. Can I go on?"

"Oh, by all means," Brigit said sweetly, her eyes bright with her triumph.

"John Greenwood has no father and a very lovely mother with whom he gets along in a friendly, civilized way. There's enough income from property her husband left to see him nicely through medical school. Calder has no doubt in the world that if Greenwood suddenly told her he was going to marry, she would say, 'How nice. You must bring her over to dinner some-time soon.' Greenwood himself was the Golden Boy of the Pi K A house as an undergraduate, but buckled down to work when he started medi-cal school and has been pulling down a nice, steady, straight B average ever since, which just can't be done with one eye on a girl's ankle." He paused elaborately for Brigit to make her com-ment.

"These nice, sober boys," she mused. "I be-lieve you said that Garnet was a frivolous little thing?"

"I get it," said Tuck. "He saw a long life of silly giggles over the toast ahead of him, and

[149]

so killed her off."

"And then, of course, there would be the problem of supporting a wife and going to medical school at the same time . . . " said Brigit, delicately.

"That angle's no good. Calder is sure that Garnet Dillon would have preferred to work after marriage. She had a rather empty head, and solitude would have driven her mad. She was just smart enough to know that. And she liked 'nice things.' "

"Carry on," said Brigit.

"And then," said Tuck, "there's Kurt Schwann." He paused, to give himself time enough to paint an unprejudiced picture. "This afternoon I talked to Uman, the head of the Biology Department, about him. He's very poor, Brigit. His fellowship carries a minute salary, just enough to feed and house him. His brother is a little better off, being the elder son, he inherited enough money from the father's estate to see him through medical school. But Kurt hasn't a sou. Or should I say 'mark'?"

"Ah-ha," said Brigit.

"Wait until you hear the rest. Just before Thanksgiving, he applied for an assistant professorship in Biology which carries a quite decent salary, and which would allow him time to carry on with his research. The appointment was confirmed on the Monday of the week Dillon died. He starts teaching next September."

"But you still think he's your man, don't you?"

"We've all bowed down and worshiped before the shrine of science for so long, Brigit! We've made scientists a race apart. Horror films for dozens of years have made us accept the idea that a scientist will kill for the great god science (when he isn't injecting peculiar substances into bosomy ladies who are always, you remember, strapped to a sort of vast ironing board.) But I don't know. I wonder whether in actual life a scientist feels differently toward his profession than a good salesman or an artist. Let's be fair. Could you imagine a young salesman killing a woman he should marry because she might cramp his style?"

"Of course, there's the matter of opportunity . . . And there's the fact that by all reports Kurt was the guy of her choice."

"But no proof, Brigit," said Tuck, wearily.

"It looks a little as though you're going to have to get all the suspects together in the approved style, build up a terrifically wordy case against one of them, and then shout, 'You might as well confess, So-and-so!' "

Tuck smiled wearily. "And unless I had proof, he could laugh in my face and say, 'Prove it!' Which, if he's as smart as our murderer, is exactly what he'd do."

"Yeah," said Brigit, gloomily.

"I've been looking for you," said an equally gloomy voice from the doorway. Tuck looked up and saw Froody waddling toward him, pawing in his breast pocket with one pudgy hand. He dropped a folded sheaf of papers onto the desk in front of Tuck. "There's a list of every blooming soul who bought digitalis during the past month at any drug counter around the University. Alphabetized. *And* the date of purchase. You may be interested to know that the average monthly turnover of digitalis at any one of the big cut-rates is twenty sales a month. There are six cut-rate drugstores in the University section, and four small private places. And remember, you said *you'd* check the list!"

"Oh, absolutely. Thanks loads, Froody."

"Any time. Any odd job." Froody said sadly. Before he turned away he nodded toward the list in Tuck's big hands. "I got phone numbers from the book wherever I could. You'll hafta go out after the others. Do you want I should start on the downtown drugstores right away? Or do you want to check first?"

"You'd better start right away," suggested Tuck, cheerfully.

Exuding Dormousishness, Froody moved toward the door.

"Chin up, Froody," called Brigit, who had jumped down from the desk and was bending over Tuck's shoulder, her eyes going avidly down the first page of Froody's list.

"Yah!" said Froody, and left.

Smiling a little, Tuck turned his attention to the list, just as Brigit's forefinger jabbed past his cheek and lit on a name near the bottom of the page.

"Hey!" she yelled.

Tuck looked at the name.

"Ulysses Calder, 412 Oak St., PL 4500."

The date of purchase was Friday, February first.

And that was one week before Garnet Dillon died.

Brigit shook Tuck's shoulder roughly, jerking him out of a waking dream where kaleidoscopic thought fragments whirled dizzily.

"Why not?" she demanded.

EIGHTEEN

BRIGIT SWUNG HERSELF TO THE DESK; again her heel boomed hollowly against its side. Then she stopped booming and leaned forward. "It fits. There are two sides to this mess that have puzzled me. One is, why didn't Garnet Dillon tell the Dean who the proud papa was? The other is, why, if Kurt was the father of her child—and moreover had refused to make an honest woman of her—did she keep that date at the Hofbrau with him? Both of these questions are answered if the Dean was the proud papa. Answer number one. She *did* tell the Dean about the child. The Dean, of course, didn't tell you that. Instead, he built himself up as the Great White Father by saying how puzzled he was that Dillon *hadn't* told him her trouble so he could help her. Answer number two. There was no reason for her not to keep the date with Kurt, so long as he wasn't the father of her child. You've been told that she was fond of him, she certainly had decided to leave town, having drawn all her money out of the bank at three that afternoon, and she wanted to see him once more before she left forever. And then his story that she said, 'This doesn't concern you, Kurt,' begins to look very much like the truth. Also, even the coffeepot disappears . . . the Dean could have handed her the digitalis, in another box, of course, told her how to take it, and told her that it was something to calm her nerves, or eliminate the child or . . . "

"She wouldn't have agreed to that."

"Who says she wouldn't? Who told you all that tale about her horror of suicide and murder? The Dean did!"

Tuck found himself smiling. "If he had killed her, why would he tell me that? He could just have easily told me that she had once tried to kill herself! That she had strongly expressed herself in favor of suicide, under certain circumstances! In fact, if Dean Calder killed her, why did he call me at all? The hospital had diagnosed her death as a heart attack. He was safe."

Brigit deflated. "Yeah. There's that." Then she inflated again. "Wait a minute! *He knew she couldn't have died of a heart attack*. Not only because he had poisoned her, but because her heart was O.K. All right, what if someone else, one of the lads who was so fond of her, also knew that her heart was O.K.? What if one of them had gone to the President of the school and said, 'This looks

[153]

fishy to me. Let's have an autopsy'? It certainly would have looked like a possibility to me, if I'd been in Calder's shoes when the body bounced back!"

"So he called me, told me it looked to him like murder. So the first thing I did, of course, was suggest an autopsy. As he knew I would do."

"Yeah but wait! He gave you most of the information you're working on. And having called you, he knew he could do just that. He knew you'd turn to him for information! And what does he do? From what you've told me, the first thing he did was to plant in your mind that she was a gay gal, with a few of the lads nuts about her. He showed you that note she left—typewritten, you'll remember—which established his story that she'd told him nothing at all, that he was as much in the dark as you. And whose word have you that the signature's in her handwriting? Dean Calder's! And I'll bet you any money in the world that he got in a word or two about how happy his marriage is!"

Tuck grinned wryly. "You have me there."

"Ah-ha!" crowed Brigit.

Tuck said, "Now let me talk a while. You say that if Calder had killed her, the first thing he would do on realizing that her body had boomeranged would be to call me, establishing his innocence by doing so, and enabling himself to direct my thinking more or less by means of what information he gave me. I say that as soon as he phoned the hospital and found that her death had passed as a heart attack, he would go to the President of the university, tell him the sad story, offer to take charge of the girl's funeral, in view of her lack of relatives. Even if someone *did* happen to know that her heart was sound, even if that someone *did* come to him, or to the President with that information, what harm could that do Calder? He could look very surprised, and heartily agree that

[154]

an autopsy should take place. He would still be the logical person for the detective handling the case to come to for information; he could still misinform him. So what did it gain him to ring in me right from scratch?"

"You're a pal of his."

"That's putting it rather strongly. He's a friend of my father; I've met him about three times. And here's something else, and don't pull that dark caves stuff on me. Dean Calder is a highly respected man. A great many young men look up to him. He's fond of those young men. Even presuming that he's not fond of his wife any longer, even presuming that he went mad over Dillon, I cannot believe that he would have descended to a backstairs affair with her."

"You like him; I never saw him. I'm looking at all this from a highly objective viewpoint. I'm looking at the facts, not at the people involved. And I say that a good many middle-aged, respectable men have gone dippy as loons over pretty young blondes, and you know it!"

Tuck glanced down at the list Froody had given him, and picked up the telephone. "Before we hang him, let's see what he has to say." He dialed PL 4500. After the sixth ring, he replaced the receiver. "No one home."

"And another thing," pounced Brigit. "Who would know better than Calder how to administer the digitalis? And who bought it, anyway?"

"He bought it under his own name. Don't forget that. And at a drugstore near the campus."

"One week before she died," said Brigit. She clapped a hand across her mouth. "Oh, Lord! Poor Froody!"

Across Tuck's mind flashed the picture of a dumpy figure wild-goose-chasing through fluorescent-lighted drugstores. He and Brigit burst out laughing at the same moment.

[155]

Tuck reached campus the next morning at the start of the nine-o'clock class. Cold sunlight was brilliant on the green of the grass, the weathered red of the buildings, the colorful figures of the hurrying students. He found a parking place for his sober black sedan between a beige convertible and a shabby old coupe, and got out to walk the block to the Science Building.

As he reached the entrance, he saw across the street a group of students laughing up at a window above him. He stepped to the curb and looked up too.

A skeleton was grinning out into the sunlight. Invisible thread held one arm in a lackadaisical wave, and the skull was topped by a bright orange rooter's cap.

He smiled to himself. And even as he smiled, he thought in a swift flash that somewhere inside that building, walking among the young mockers who fixed that bony arm in its salute, there was another sort of person whom he must find.

Going into the building, he found himself face to face with Hitchlock, coming out.

"Have you seen it?" asked Hitchlock, pointing briefly upward.

Tuck nodded.

"First-year men," confided Hitchlock loftily. "They'll get that ground out of them in short order."

"All right, gentlemen," bellowed a voice from the open window where the skeleton was. Clear in the morning air they could hear a scurry of heavy feet, a scraping of lecture chairs.

"Get out your pens," commanded the bellow. And then, heavily laden with sarcasm, "Since you are so interested in the human skeleton, I'm going to give you a little pop quiz. All about the skeleton, gentlemen. You have just ten minutes to make a complete list of the bones of the human frame."

[156]

Someone groaned.

"You see what I mean," smiled Hitch, and stepped past Tuck into the bright morning.

Dean Calder was at his desk, and Kathryn Farr was at hers, sealing envelopes.

"Well! Good morning," said Calder.

On seeing Tuck Kathryn Farr bounced to her feet, smiling. "If you'll give me the keys, Dean Calder, I'll go and get your mail. That'll save you from sending me down for coffee." She seemed to be in good spirits, Tuck noticed.

Calder's bright blue eyes twinkled, but he said gravely, "An excellent idea, Miss Farr." She went to his desk, and he extracted a ring of keys from his pocket and handed it across to her. With a swirl of her plaid skirt she was gone.

"I take it that there's a new development, Mr. Tuck. Sit down. Cigarette?"

Tuck sat down, shaking his head. "Dean Calder, you bought some digitalis on Friday, February first. I want to know more about that."

As soon as Tuck said "digitalis," Calder's eyes widened so that white showed around the blue iris. Then he clapped his hand to his forehead. Then he opened the drawers of his desk one by one, searching through the contents with restrained anxiety. When the drawers were all closed again, he sat up very straight in his chair, an odd look on his face. The look turned into a pinched smile as he said, "I imagine you had a bad moment when you learned that."

Tuck nodded, and Calder reached abstractedly for a cigarette from the ever-present pack on his desk. "I believe I told you that my wife is ill? She has heart disease, Tuck. Myocarditis. She's been using digitalis for years. I've been buying it for her for about that long."

"You didn't mention having purchased this digitalis when I told you digitalis was the poison used

[157]

. . ." suggested Tuck, carefully.

"Your father once said that you have an unusual knowledge of psychology, Tuck," said
Calder, around the cigarette he was lighting with
very steady hands. He expelled a puff of smoke
and again smiled that pinched smile. "I'm glad of
that, because I believe my explanation will make
sense to you, as it might not to many people." His
eyes were clear and wise, looking into Tuck's. "I
believe you will concede that an act repeated
often enough becomes habitual? Every Friday I
buy a week's supply of digitalis for my wife. I buy
it either at the Campus Drugstore during lunch
hour, or at our corner pharmacy on my way home.
When you mentioned digitalis as the poison that
killed Garnet, I thought first of my wife's ill
health; the name of the drug was, you will realize,
bitterly familiar to me. But I made no more connection between the particular purchase of which
we are speaking and the fact that Garnet died a
week after that purchase than I made between her
death and the fact that I had fish balls for lunch
on that day, another Friday habit."

Tuck nodded slowly. "I can see that," he said.

"I'm sorry I didn't make that connection, Tuck.
Had I done so, it might have meant a short cut
in your investigation. Because I find that the digitalis is gone."

Tuck merely stared.

"Here's the story. On Friday, February first,
after having eaten my fish balls, I walked down to
the Campus Drugstore and bought three vials of
digitalis. I came back here, and then I recalled that
my wife had expressed a preference for capsules
rather than pills; it comes in both forms. I took the
package from my coat pocket, unwrapped it, and
saw to my dissatisfaction that the vial contained
pills. I put the vials on my desk, in a prominent
place so that I would not forget to take them back

[158]

and exchange them. I did forget. My wife, knowing that we were in the first throes of final exams out here, said nothing; I imagine that she sent out to a drugstore, rather than bother me. I didn't think of that digitalis again until today. And now I find that those three vials are gone, Tuck. And I didn't take them."

"How many pills are in each vial?" asked Tuck.

"Twelve. One and one-half grains each."

Tuck made a rapid mental calculation. Evidently Calder did the same, for at the same moment, they both said, "Fifty-four grains."

"Let's go over this carefully," said Calder. "Garnet died on Friday, February eighth. Allowing the briefest possible lapse of time between the fatal dose and death, which is five days, she must have been poisoned before the preceding Monday. The digitalis was on my desk Friday, February first, at one o'clock. It must have been stolen on either Friday or Saturday, in order to allow Sunday for the poison to be administered in a series of small doses. And Friday the first—this is narrowing down nicely, Tuck—no one came into this office. No one, that is, who could possibly have any connection with this grim business. I was here all afternoon, correcting papers from a morning exam. Furthermore, no one could have come in after I left, because I was the last to leave and I locked the door, and the only key is in my pocket. Or was, until I gave that bunch of keys to Miss Farr just now."

"Where was Miss Dillon?"

"She left at four. She had an appointment of some sort. Now, let's see where that takes us."

"It takes us to the fact that the digitalis must have been taken from your desk on Saturday."

"Quite right. And I believe I can help you here, Tuck. No one knew that I had bought that digitalis. The person who took it saw it on my desk, realized that it would be of use to him, put it in his pocket—and that was that. The only possible reason I can assign for anyone coming into this office, in view of the fact that I am rarely here on Saturday, was to see Miss Dillon, who was always here until noon. Very well. At the risk of seeming discursive, I must say something which I believe to be important. Final examinations began on Friday, February first, the same day I bought the digitalis which has disappeared. If you remember your own college days at all, you remember how infinitely precious time becomes to students during finals week. No one loses a moment that could be spent absorbing one new fact or clarifying an old one. Because of this, I am certain that the man who came into my office on Saturday and took that digitalis had a final examination on Saturday morning. Otherwise, we have the improbable picture of a student losing valuable time by making a special trip to the building simply to talk to a pretty girl. And even in the case of an extremely pretty girl like Garnet, I can't believe that. On the other hand, a student already in the building might easily, after having taken his exam, stop for a word or two with Garnet to relieve the tension."

"I remember, and I think you've got something. But wait a minute. If the digitalis was stolen, it was stolen in order to poison Miss Dillon. Which means that the person who stole it knew about her unfortunate condition. Wouldn't that make a special trip to campus perfectly plausible? He wouldn't have come to chat with a pretty girl then. He'd have come to discuss a matter of vital importance to both of them."

"Wouldn't that discussion have taken place when she first told him of her condition? And that couldn't have been more than a day or so before, remember, because if there's one thing we can be certain of, it's that Garnet's discovery that she

[160]

was pregnant coincided with the first of that odd behavior of hers. And as the person who saw her most steadily, I can say that the first inkling of her mental condition was on the morning of Friday, the first, when she asked me to examine her heart. So the child's father must have learned that he was the child's father sometime Friday or Saturday. If he learned of it on Saturday, he still stopped by for a chat."

"That's logical," agreed Tuck.

"If he learned it on Friday, his trip to the office could have been only to exchange a few reassuring words with her, or to make an appointment to discuss the matter further. And again I say he must have been on campus, must have had an exam that morning, for otherwise he could just as well have telephoned, or seen her at her apartment in the afternoon."

"I agree," said Tuck.

Dean Calder stood up and went to the case where the section cards were kept and again extracted three cards. Then he went back to his desk, and from the top drawer he took out a mimeographed sheet of paper. "Here are the section cards of our three young men. Here is the final exam schedule. As you can see, the date of each exam is listed beside each class. By comparing the two, you can find who had an exam on Saturday morning."

As Tuck folded the section cards inside the exam schedule and put them away in his inner breast pocket, Calder said, "I have felt like a Judas ever since this miserable business began. I want you to understand that I am fond of all three of these young men. I am also fond of truth and justice. So if a despicable murder has been committed, I certainly cannot shield the murderer."

"There's one other possibility that occurs to me," mused Tuck. "Garnet may have taken the digitalis herself. A fit of depression, you know, and the knowledge that here was a way out."

"No. I still say that she wasn't capable of suicide. And in addition to that, she didn't know arsenic from aspirin. She wouldn't have known that digitalis was a poison, nor the fatal dose."

"That's that," said Tuck. "Well, I've learned something this morning. Until now, this murderer has been a bit on the Borgia side. But it begins to look as though the notion of murder occurred to him when he saw that digitalis on your desk. And we get a different sort of person altogether, and a different sort of crime. Digitalis was used only because it was available. The motive must have been there, but the means came into his hands accidentally. If you hadn't bought that digitalis, Dean Calder, Garnet Dillon might still be alive."

"An unpleasant thought," said Dean Calder quietly.

A cool draft from the corridor ruffled the papers on the Dean's desk as Kathryn Farr opened the door and briskly crossed the office with Dean Calder's mail and the keys he had given her. "We seem to have a skeleton in the closet, Dean Calder," she smiled. "Right now, it's waving out the window of the Anatomy lab. It gave me quite a start."

"That happens every semester, Miss Farr," he said. "I sometimes wonder when the boys will think up something new. Excuse me for a moment." Putting the keys away in his pocket, he sorted through his mail. One long white envelope interested him especially. He tore it open. Then he showed it to Tuck.

Tuck saw the first large-type line: "From the people of the state of California, Greetings."

"Coroner's inquest," Tuck nodded. "You'll have to identify the body, in view of the absence of relatives, and tell the Coroner's jury what you told me about Garnet's sound heart and her repugnance to suicide. With the inquest, of course, the whole thing comes out. The reporters will love it because it involves a pretty girl. It will make page one in spite of the war."

Calder nodded. Then he said, "Miss Farr, will you call the President's office? Do your best to make an appointment for me sometime today. Tell him it's about a matter of greatest importance."

Over the clicking of the telephone dial, Tuck said to Calder, "And the Coroner's verdict will be murder by a person or persons unknown."

He was wrong.

A brief tussle with the exam schedule and the section cards of Robert Hitchlock, John Greenwood, and Jeff Whittaker won Tuck the information that Robert Hitchlock, John Greenwood, and Jeff Whittaker had all taken exams on the morning of Saturday, February second.

"Oh, yes, I always work here in the lab on Saturday," said Kurt Schwann, looking politely puzzled as to the point of the question.

"Then I suppose you were here Saturday before last. February second."

"It's odd that you asked that," said Schwann, "because I wasn't here that morning. You see, I had dinner the preceding evening with a friend at Cal Tech, and as our discussion of spontaneous generation lasted until early in the morning, I spent the night with him and did not return here until Saturday afternoon at about two."

Spontaneous generation, thought Tuck.

"I am well acquainted with Dean Calder," said the pharmacist at the Campus Drugstore, an angelic old gentleman in a soiled white coat. "For

[163]

years he's been buying digitalis here. His wife has heart trouble, you know."

"I know," said Tuck.

Mrs. Nox's apartment was still dark, and still smelled of furniture polish.

Mrs. Nox's shapeless legs were crossed precisely at the ankles, and her knees were decently invisible beneath pink cauliflowers rampant on a deep blue ground. "Friday, the first of February," she mused. Suddenly, she lurched forward in her chair; one heavy arm shot down and the plump fingers picked up an invisible something from the rug, which she disposed of in the large abalone shell which was serving Tuck for an ash tray. "Now I remember!" she said.

"That was the night she came in with a bottle of whisky. At least I thought it was, by the shape of the package. I met her as she came in the front door. Her rent was due; usually she gave it to me in the morning before she left for work but this time she forgot, so I met her to remind her. She was awfully late that day. It must have been close to eight when she got home. Usually she got home about five-thirty. She looked simply terrible, Mr. Tuck." She repeated, with considerable satisfaction, "Terrible! White as a sheet, as though she'd been drawn through a knothole. I could see she wanted to pass me by with just a nod, so I said, real cheerfully, 'My, I never knew you to work as late as this. You look all tuckered out.'

" 'I am,' she said in a tired sort of way, and tried to pass me.

"I stepped in front of her, and said, 'My dear, if you'll take a word of advice from an older woman, don't let your employer take advantage of you like this. Once is the first time, but if you're not careful, it'll be happening again.'

" 'Oh,' she said, 'I haven't been working all this

[164]

time. I left early, in fact. I had an appointment.'

"It was then that I saw the shape of this bottle she had in her arm. 'May I ask what's in that bottle?' I asked.

" 'Medicine,' she said, looking me straight in the eye, and smiling. It was a queer, sassy smile, and you can be sure I wouldn't have left it at that, but just at that moment down the stairs came Miss Landis in 205 yelling that gas was escaping from her stove; she's scarcely a lady, Mr. Tuck, always shouting everything at the top of her lungs, and the telephone started ringing, so Miss Dillon got away."

"What a shame," soothed Tuck. "She didn't say any more about this appointment?"

"No. And listen, Mr. Tuck. It *was* whisky. I'm sure of it because I went up to her apartment an hour later to get her rent, and as soon as she opened the door I smelled it *distinctly*. After she gave me the money, I said, 'Miss Dillon, you've been drinking.' " Here Mrs. Nox paused in slight confusion.

"And what did she say?"

"She said, 'Mrs. Nox, that is none of your business,' and shut the door."

"Tsk, tsk, tsk," said Tuck.

"I think," offered Mrs. Nox, "that she became Dead Drunk. There was a phone call for her from Pasadena at nine-thirty, and I buzzed three times and she didn't answer." Mrs. Nox made an effort at judicial fairness. "If course, she *may* have gone out. I was listening to 'Ask Me Some More,' and I wouldn't have heard her."

"Do you happen to know who the phone call was from?"

"I do. He didn't leave any name but I recognized the voice in a minute. It was that German boy. Kurt Schwann."

"How about the next day, Saturday, the second?

I'm anxious to find out what visitors she had."

Mrs. Nox looked sad. "I'm afraid I won't be able to help you much there, Mr. Tuck. I had my neuralgia all day and most of Sunday, and I wasn't up to caring who went in or out. Shooting pains, you know, all up the side of the head . . ."

"Damon and Pythias!" Tuck said, changing words in midstream.

"However," went on Mrs. Nox, "I can tell you this. She went out with a man at dinner time. I didn't see them, because I just simply couldn't move, but I heard him mention her name."

"You didn't recognize the voice?"

"No, I didn't."

"Do you remember what he said?"

"Something about dinner. That she'd feel better after dinner. Something like that."

"Would you recognize the voice if you heard it again?"

Mrs. Nox sounded very dubious. "I don't think so. I was in a daze with the pain of my neuralgia. Have you ever had neuralgia, Mr. Tuck?"

"No."

For fifteen minutes Tuck listened to a discourse on the varied agonies of neuralgia, and when he made his escape, possessed the maddening information that without much doubt the man who walked past Mrs. Nox's door with Garnet Dillon at dinner time on the evening of Saturday, the second of February, had murdered her.

NINETEEN

So NOW YOU HAVE SOME IDEA, Mother Dear, why this letter is so late. It's a very horrible mess, isn't it? And she was so young. Not a day older than I am. Tuck doesn't seem to be getting along very fast, although it's hard to tell with a person like Tuck. His long face has a way of looking perfectly blank no matter what happens. When he told me the sordid motive behind all this, he might have been making a comment about the weather. I almost wish he hadn't told me, because I find myself looking at one or another of the boys around here, and wondering . . . Kurt Schwann was in love with her, according to Johnny, and he should know if anyone does. And yet I find it very hard to imagine him capable of such a crime. There's one fact, though, that goes a little against him, and that's his lack of curiosity about it all. Yet in a way, that's understandable. I am quite sure that Kurt is the sort of person who weeps alone. Does that make sense? What I mean is that his enormous pride would make him always fearful of showing his feelings; it's not always fair to accuse a person like that of being hard. I'm sure Tuck suspects Kurt; he questioned him up in his lab after he had pumped Johnny and Hitchlock and Whittaker. Johnny told me so. But of course Tuck knows that Kurt is too clever a person to be tricked or browbeaten into an admission of any kind. I like Kurt rather better than I did at first; he was very sweet to me after that business in the park, and I can't imagine him having an illegitimate child with Garnet Dillon. I think his pride goes with a rather high standard of personal conduct, and that doesn't jibe with the other. In fact, from what I've heard about Garnet, I don't see how they got together at all. She seems to have been a rather ordinary young person, a sort of perpetual moth, enjoying not getting her wings singed. Which she did. But then, most of what I know about Garnet comes from Sydney Vines, a fat white slug of a boy with glittering eyeglasses. And quite obviously, Garnet gave Sydney the brushoff, for which he hates her thoroughly. He's an elbowmassager, and it takes a considerable amount of dexterity to avoid his plump paw. I believe that he's a victim of an inferiority complex; he knows that women can't stand him, and covers it up with an assured manner and amusing babble. I dislike him thoroughly."

Kate put down her pen, and limbered her aching wrist, scanning the last of nine closely written pages as she did so.

Then the door to the office burst open, and Dr. Barnum surged through, a battered folder under one arm. Kate smiled to herself in anticipation. Even in the short time she had been there, she had learned that huge, red-faced Dr. Barnum was never dull.

"God, but those new men are dumb," he bellowed. "D-U-M-B, dumb! I've seen more intelligent expressions on hopeless idiots! They're so stupid that . . ." He paused, and with a rapidly wagging hand erased what he'd just said. A look of fierce cunning came over his vast face. "No! I take it all back! They're not dumb! They're malicious. That's it! They sit there, baiting me, seeing them, so help me, every mother's son-of-a——"

"Ahem!" said Dean Calder.

Dr. Barnum turned on him like an adder. "And they're up to something, Calder. There's a ringleader with a face like a shrewd orangoutang who urges them on. You remember the time the first-year man stole the cadaver one night and hung it from the tree outside the President's office? There'll be something like that, so help me!"

Calder said philosophically, "The young men never change, Dr. Barnum. All we can do is let them put their foot in it and then be severe. And try hard not to recall our own student days."

"*You* can be philosophical about it. *You* don't have to teach 'em," said Dr. Barnum, with a lack of respect which did not annoy Dean Calder in the least.

With some of the red fading out of his face Dr. Barnum turned to Kate and said in a fairly normal voice, "Miss Farr, I'd be very much obliged if you'd retype these lecture notes for me. They're so thumb-marked and gooey and smudged that I can't read 'em."

"Certainly," agreed Kate, extending her hand

for the dog-eared folder. "When do you want them?"

"No hurry," said Dr. Barnum largely. "I have to teach these cretins the A B C's of physiology before they're ready for this stuff."

With a helpless wave of one hand, he tore the door open, squeezed himself out into the corridor.

"May I give you a word of advice, Miss Farr?" asked Dean Calder. "I know Dr. Barnum. He told you there's no hurry, but he'll be in at nine in the morning for those notes and be sulky when he finds they aren't all ready for him."

"Thanks. I'll fox him."

When Dean Calder, his white jacket replaced with a gray coat, was ready to leave, she was still a good dozen pages from the end of her task.

"I think I'll have a bite of dinner and come back tonight," she said.

"Nonsense. It's not that important. I certainly didn't mean to suggest that you should use your own time to finish this. Let Barnum wait."

"I haven't a thing to do tonight, Dean Calder. And I'm really interested. I remember enough from the science courses I took under protest so that is isn't quite Greek to me. I'm learning something new with each page."

Dean Calder smiled down at her. He had a very nice smile. "My dear, I trust you will not take it as flattery if I tell you that I believe you're a person who learns something from everything. It's a nice way to be. Life stays interesting."

She was quite flustered, and could only say, "Thank you."

He placed the ring of keys on her desk. "Don't forget to lock the door. Some extremely private data about the students is filed in this office. Last year I had to expel two boys who couldn't resist the temptation to find what their professors thought about their chances to get their M.D.'s."

"I won't," promised Kate, and dropped the keys into her purse.

She typed until she realized that her nose was a scant foot from Dr. Barnum's notes in the dimness of the room. Looking at her watch, she saw that it was five-thirty, and luxuriously relieved her tired back by stretching her arms wide above her head. There was a click, and the door opened. Sydney Vines came in.

"Hi," he said.

"Hi."

He strolled to the center of the room, his moon face turned toward her. Even in the dimness, his suit was too green and too tweedy.

"I went to my locker to change my coat, and what did I hear? Music, darling, absolutely music. Your typewriter. So I said to myself, 'Why don't I ask Kathryn Farr to have dinner with me?' and Myself answered, 'Why not, indeed?' Have dinner with me, Kate?"

"Sorry. I can't."

He seated himself negligently on one corner of her desk. "Kate, how does it feel to be wearing dead men's shoes?"

"Fine," said Kate. "I've got callouses on all my finer sensibilities."

He giggled. "Oh, yes. Tell me another. Seriously, though, what do you think about it all?"

"Not much. I didn't know Garnet, and I don't know much of anyone else around here, so I just mind my business and let Tuck figure it out."

"Tuck," mused Vines. "I think he's a fool."

Not out of any particular fondness for Tuck but rather because of her lack of fondness for Vines, she found herself disagreeing with him. "I think he's a rather smart chap, myself. Naturally, he's handicapped by having to handle a dirty mess with kid gloves." And then, although

[170]

she had been about to cover her typewriter and get something to eat, she began to type. To her intense annoyance, Vines sat stolidly on the corner of her desk, watching her with a small, unpleasant smile.

I'm letting him get under my skin, she thought.

Abruptly, she centered the carriage, and covered the machine. Humming a little tune quite as though Vines wasn't there, she opened the narrow cupboard and got out her coat. Vines slipped off the desk and stood waiting for her. She took a great deal of time, putting on fresh lipstick in the little mirror on the cupboard door.

"I used to watch Garnet do that," said Vines abruptly.

"Did you?" commented Kate with elaborate lack of interest, while inside she felt a queer little flutter, realizing that this mirror she was peering into was Garnet's mirror, tacked up, probably, by Garnet's own red fingernailed hands.

Sydney Vines followed her out the door. She was full of a thwarted anger as they walked in silence together down the darkening corridor, because she didn't feel like cooking supper in her apartment and it looked as though she would have to, unless she wanted to eat dinner at a cafe table across from Vines' white face.

To her surprise, Vines said, "Well, so long," when they reached the entrance of the Science Building, and went briskly off in the opposite direction.

She decided to walk down to Mrs. Pratt's Nook, rather than dine in the cheerless vastness of the Student Union. She had just entered, and had just been slightly warmed by Mrs. Pratt's never-failing beam of welcome, when she saw Hitch-lock spooning up soup in one of the small booths. Mrs. Pratt's Nook was full, and rather than wait for a table she slipped in opposite him. He looked up with his mouth open for a cracker, and the unfailing pinkness deepened in his cheeks.

"Hello!"

"Hello, Hitch. Do you mind my moving in on you?"

"Heck, no. Glad for some company. They've got baked hash tonight. It's usually pretty good."

When the student waiter had taken her order and Hitch's soup plate, she leaned back and looked at Hitch, who looked at his green doily.

"Let's make a bargain," she said. "I won't start talking about the murder if you won't."

"That's swell with me," he said fervently. "I haven't been able to think about anything else. Tuck thinks I did it."

"What?"

Hitch nodded solemnly. "I picked up her driver's license from a table in the Hofbrau, the night she died. She'd forgotten it. Tuck found out about it. The connection isn't hard to make. Anyone can see that it would have been to the murderer's advantage for her to have been unidentified." He gave a short laugh. "Only the whole thing is: I didn't kill her."

"Stop me if I'm wrong, but wasn't she having dinner with Kurt that night?" asked Kate, slowly.

Hitchlock's eyes got very wide. "Gee! I never thought of that."

Oh, you didn't! thought Kate. Then you're very dull, my lad. Much too dull ever to have reached your third year in medical school.

But she said, "I thought we weren't going to talk about the murder."

"Right," said Hitch firmly, and the student waiter appeared balancing her soup and his hash on a muscular arm.

When she paid her check and stepped out onto University Avenue, the street lamps were on.

She tied her tan coat about her and started up to the Science Building. The library was ablaze beyond the bare branches of sycamore trees, and by contrast the Science Building, as she neared it, seemed very dark.

Not quite dark, though. There was a light on in Dean Calder's office. As she stared up at it, she remembered that she had forgotten to lock the door.

She rushed to the big double entrance door, peering through its heavy glass into the black lower corridor as she tried the latch. No, the janitor had locked it. She fumbled in her purse for the keys the Dean had given her, found the right one after several tries, and laboriously shoved open one side of the door. It closed swiftly behind her, with a final, vicious click, and she stood inside the empty building full of the unpleasant realization that she hadn't the slightest notion how to turn on the lights.

"There's something about an empty building," she remarked to herself, "that gives me gooseflesh. Now why is that? Empty buildings are no worse than full ones, except that they're so darned empty."

Grinning in derision at the incoherance of her own thoughts, she squared her shoulders and marched down the lower corridor to the stairs.

"There's someone behind me!" a voice in her mind said, as she mounted them. She forced herself to count to five, and then she turned casually around. Her eyes, growing accustomed to lack of light, saw only darkness there.

Running up the second half of the flight, she remembered how unafraid she had been when she walked into the dark park two nights before.

Dean Calder was right, she thought dryly. I learn something from everything.

Three steps from the head of the stairs she

stopped dead. No light showed through the square of glass in the door to the Dean's office.

She thought, Maybe I imagined it. Maybe it was a reflection from the Law Building.

Quickly, she went to the door and tried it. It opened. As she felt on the wall beside the door for the light switch, she remembered that it was behind the door, which meant that she had to close herself into the office to turn on the light.

She did that very quickly, before she had time to think. Then, blinking at the sudden glare, she looked around the familiar, ugly room.

Her typewriter was uncovered.

As she methodically put on the oilcloth cover and absently picked up her letter to her mother from the desk, she was thinking that there was no possible doubt in her mind that she had covered her typewriter before she left for dinner.

She set the catch that locked the door, and with a last long look around the office, turned the light off, and went out.

The long row of overhead hall lights was on.

"Hey!" she called. "Who's there?"

Utter silence.

"You'll have to turn off the lights," she called. "I don't know where the switch is."

Then she saw that the door to the Anatomy laboratory was partly open. The lights were burning inside.

Curious, and beginning to be angry at the senselessness of what was happening to her, she strode very briskly toward the door of the Anatomy laboratory, wondering what she would say if she were faced by a grinning crew of first-year men.

She opened the door and peered in. The big room was empty. She was glad to see that whatever lay on several of the dissecting tables had been covered with long white cloths.

Just like shrouds, her mind said.

She stepped into the laboratory, and looked around for the light switch. It was beside another entrance to the lab, at the far end of the room. She had not noticed this other door on her previous visit because it was covered by a chart. It was also locked, apparently for keeps. She switched off the light, and in utter blackness started back to the door by which she had entered.

It was shut.

The light from the hall fell through the frosted glass panel onto the square desk just inside the door.

There was something on the desk that hadn't been there when she came in. She stopped, paralyzed, when she saw what it was. It was a head. A human head, resting on the base of the severed neck.

It was staring straight at her.

She found herself giving a yell of primordial horror.

She put her hand over her mouth; then she dropped her arm limply to her side and started slowly toward the door. As she neared the head certain unpleasant details leaped out at her with terrible clarity. The eyes were fixed on her in the pale stare of death. They caught and held some of the light falling in from the hall, so that they did not seem nearly so dead as alive. Alive in a dead head. Such a big dead head. The man must have been a giant.

I have to pass it to get to the door. I have to pass it to get to the door. I have to pass it to get to the door.

She passed it quickly, not taking her eyes from the head.

The door was locked.

She wanted to scream again, she felt a scream welling up inside her, but she didn't scream.

[175]

She opened her purse with shaking hands and took out Dean Calder's keys.

Let's see. If this door is like the door to the Dean's office, you can lock it by pushing in a little button in the middle of the knob, but once you've locked it you have to unlock it with the key. And the keyhole's in the middle of the button.

Creepingly conscious of the head just behind her, she stooped and barely made out the keyhole.

The hall lights went out.

She swung around, her back to the door, her eyes going around the room. Beyond the windows, the sky was faintly luminous. And the head was a round mass against that luminosity. She could see the intricate curvings of one bloodless ear.

Resolutely, she turned back to the lock, and fumbled key after key into it. The fifth key fitted. She swung open the door.

The corridor was much blacker than the room.

"Well," she asked herself, "what can I do? I can scream, and someone may or may not hear me, and if they do, what will I say? Please carry me home, I've been scared by a head?"

With a feeling that was very near kin to the sensation, partly epidermal and partly visceral, that precedes a leap into cold water or over a chasm, she leaped out into the hall and stumbled rapidly down the stairs. The building was as silent as Cheops' tomb.

When she had reached the lamp-lighted street, she breathed again. The door to the building clicked solemnly shut behind her.

"There's something there that doesn't like me," she whispered. "And I don't think it's first-year men."

TWENTY

TUCK STRODE ALONG THE MARBLE corridor of the City Hall, hoping that Brigit Estees had not left for dinner. When he entered the outer office of the homicide squad, Gufferty looked up from his desk. His face took on an unconvincing look of surprise and awe. "Well, well, well, if it isn't Sherlock Holmes," he said. "Nice to see you!"

"Excuse me if I don't laugh," said Tuck.

"Why shouldn't I? I excuse everything else you do." He scowled. "But I'm getting impatient with you, Philo Vance. Since you've been working on the Case of the Beautiful Blonde, a society woman shot her husband and a Filipino named Mendez knifed somebody who made a crack at him. As long as you're on the city pay roll, you've gotta be here when I need you. That's all."

"Tuck?" called a woman's voice. Brigit Estees appeared in the doorway leading to the squad room. "Where have you been, anyway?"

She was wearing a cheap red satin evening dress, over which was slung a tan sport coat. Her face was heavily made up, and an improbably large and perfect artificial gardenia adorned one side of her auburn head.

"It's Sadie Thompson!" Tuck marveled.

She came eagerly toward him. "Listen! I've got a wonderful idea. And you're part of it."

A wariness began to seep through Tuck.

"You know this Black Overcoat fellow?"

"We've never been formally introduced, but I've heard tell."

"Cut the schamltz and listen. I've done a little work with a map of the city, and I've found out that every one of these attacks happened within an area of ten blocks. I've gone over the reports and found that he has a liking for dark alleys."

Tuck closed his eyes. "So you're all dressed up

to play decoy. You're going to stroll past one of the dark alleys in that ten-block area, and if you're lucky he'll pop out and bash you. Oh, what a wonderful, wonderful idea."

"He's not going to bash me, because you're going to be hiding in a parked car, all ready to wing him as soon as he shows."

"Lord, grant me patience," murmured Tuck.

Brigit's famous temper caught fire. "I'll remind you of who got Coster and the Rake woman! Me. Me, disguised! You were at a concert that night, I recall, while I was getting evidence on one of the biggest vice rings in town!"

"That's right," Gufferty said.

Tuck turned on him. "But she knew where she could find them. In this case, she might have to work this gag a dozen times and still not get a tumble from this fellow!"

"That's right," purred Gufferty.

"You mean I'm in on it?"

"Yup."

"Now listen," Brigit commanded, opening the marked map which she drew from her scarlet purse. "There's the spot. I'm going to show at eleven. The alley's at one side of a deserted warehouse; you can't miss it. Use your head about parking. The idea is to look like an empty car. You'll probably have to squat down in the back seat."

"I probably will," sighed Tuck.

Gloom reigned in Tuck's soul as he crouched on the floor of his car, one eye glued to the lower corner of the open back window. The deserted warehouse was no less deserted than the entire neighborhood, a place of vacant lots, sprouting grass and billboards; and ramshackle flats with an occasional bare electric bulb throwing pallid radiance through a dirty window. Far down the street the clanging bulk of a streetcar came

[178]

nearer, and from behind the red neon of a beer parlor a hill-billy tune tumbled faintly and cheaply into the night.

Tuck had parked thirty feet from the alley. Several other cars left to the mercy of the night air made his unnoticeable. The corner where the trolley car would stop was thirty feet ahead of him, bright under the lonely glare of an arc light.

He looked at his watch. Eleven. And Brigit was always prompt. It was her virtue and her vice.

When the streetcar ground to a halt, she got off and wove unsteadily to the curb. She looked at her wrist watch, the prearranged signal that she was ready. Then she waggled tipsily toward the dark mouth of the alley.

Tuck felt himself tense, like a wound spring. He suddenly realized that Brigit was extremely brave, and that he was very fond of her.

Exactly at the entrance to the alley Brigit stooped, her back to that black maw from which death might leap, and straightened the seam of her stocking.

Tuck rose to one knee, and the steady muzzle of his automatic poked an inch into the night.

Nothing happened.

Brigit took as long as she could over the stocking, and then straightened and waggled down to the beer parlor. Tuck watched until she was safe inside, waited fifteen minutes, and then climbed over into the driver's seat, started the car, U-turned and drove down to the beer hall, parking across the street.

Inside the noisy, flat-smelling cafe, he gave a good imitation of a man who was no gentleman picking up a lady who was no lady.

They tried the same general plan at two more likely alleys, with the same result.

Brigit was undaunted. "We'll try again tomorrow night," she said.

[179]

TWENTY-ONE

A LETTER CAME FOR TUCK in the morning mail. The address on the white envelope was typewritten, and read:

> Detective Tuck,
> Homicide Squad,
> City Hall,
> Los Angeles.

The *n* in "Angeles" had been struck heavily to cover an accidental *m* which had been first struck instead of the proper letter.

Tuck slit the envelope. The brief message inside was also typewritten, and its unevenness of touch again indicated a far from expert typist. The letter read:

> On the evening of November thirtieth last, a man entered Garnet Dillon's apartment at nine o'clock.
> The lights went out at nine-fifteen.
> The lights came on at one thirty-five.
> The man left at a quarter to two.
> The man was Kurt Schwann.

The message was unsigned.

The implication of a cold-eyed, watchful vigil in those carefully noted hours did something to the hairs on the back of Tuck's neck. He felt them rise, in aversion.

But the fact remained that at last he had something specific about which to question Kurt Schwann.

After noting that the paper was a low-grade typing paper, impossible to trace, and that the envelope was one of those long penny envelopes that can be bought at any drugstore, Tuck returned the message to its envelope which he stowed away in his inner breast pocket. He went to the ancient hatrack, settled his hat squarely on his long head, and stooped his way through the door leading to the outer office.

"Oh. Off again," commented Gufferty.

"That's right."

"Be back tonight," ordered Gufferty shortly.

Tuck opened the door leading to the marble hall outside, and bumped into Froody, coming in.

"Ugh!" groaned Froody, bouncing backward from the force of the collision.

Tuck felt in his inner breast pocket and drew out the letter he had just received. "I'm in a hurry, Froody. Will you please take this to Beavis? Tell him I want to know all he can find out about the machine this was typed on. And fast."

"Sure," mourned Froody. "Any odd job."

Kurt Schwann was bent over his microscope as he had been the first time Tuck saw him. He looked up, plainly annoyed at the interruption, and when he saw who it was the annoyance doubled. But he was polite, almost suave, as he said, "Please sit down. I shall have to ask you to wait one moment." With a pointed, glittering instrument he did something of a delicate nature to whatever was on the microscope slide. After a long look down the double tube, he jotted a brief note in the loose-leaf book open on the table. Then, carefully, he removed the slide, set it in one compartment of a wooden tray, and turned to Tuck. "Now. What can I do for you?"

Tuck's hands were clasped around his knees. He said, "This morning I received an anonymous note in the mail. I can't show it to you, because it's in the hands of a typewriting expert. But I can quote what it said. 'On the evening of November thirtieth last, a man entered Garnet Dillon's apartment at nine o'clock. The lights went out at nine-fifteen. The lights came on at one thirty-five.

The man left at a quarter to two. The man was Kurt Schwann.' "

As Tuck recited this, he watched Schwann's face closely. The expression altered as he spoke, but grew into something he did not expect. When he finished, Schwann was wearing a look of deep distaste, and nothing more.

"I shall have to ask you whether or not the statements made in this letter are true," said Tuck, quietly.

"Quite true," said Kurt, inclining his head.

Tuck's voice crisped. He leaned forward. "Then the implication of those statements—that you spent the night with Garnet Dillon—is also true."

"Quite true," said Kurt, nodding again, with the look of distaste more sharp on his sharp face than ever.

"You see," he added, with an extremely unkind smile, "we were married on November twenty-sixth. I have the license at home, if you should care to see it."

Tuck found himself sitting bolt upright in his hard chair. But his voice, long schooled not to show his feelings, was quite calm as he echoed, "Married."

"Yes," said Kurt. "Would you like to hear about it?"

"Yes."

Kurt leaned back in his chair, one thin arm dangling down over its back. "It was a runaway marriage. We chose Yuma, the local Gretna Green, and we borrowed John Greenwood's car. He did not know the purpose to which we intended putting it, however. He was spending the Thanksgiving holidays with his mother, who also has a car, and as he would not need his own he was glad to have me make use of it. On Wednesday, Thanksgiving Day, I drove him to his mother's— she lives in Hollywood—drove away with the car, and called for him late Sunday night to bring him back to campus. In the interim Garnet and I went to Yuma."

"And you didn't tell him of your marriage?" probed Tuck. "Your close friend?"

"No. I possess a rather large pride, Mr. Tuck. And I am very poor. Garnet's salary, although not particularly large, was four times what I earn. I did not wish anyone to know about the marriage until my professorship had been confirmed. You may not understand such an attitude. What I am telling you is nevertheless quite true."

"Go on," commanded Tuck.

"We drove all night, and were married in the early hours of the morning by a minister whose dwelling had a large neon sign announcing his availability at all times. It was the most incredible experience of my entire life."

"Why didn't you wait until you got your professorship?"

"Not for the reason you think," said Kurt Schwann, promptly. "We got married because we were infatuated with each other, and Garnet could see no reason for waiting. The subsequent silence was a compromise which Garnet made in return for my concession to her desire to be married during the Thanksgiving holidays. Don't ask me the why of that desire. Aside from the purely biological one, there were several very feminine reasons which I never fully understood. It was the only utterly foolish and *jejeune* action of my life. I am a rather grave person."

"You know of course that Miss Dillon—pardon me, Mrs. Schwann—was going to have a child when she died?"

For the first time, Kurt Schwann showed real surprise. He jerked straight involuntarily, and then, with an effort, relaxed again. "No. I did not."

"There is something else I must say. Why didn't

[183]

you tell me you and Garnet Dillon were married?"

"You didn't ask me."

"Still," said Tuck, allowing just a shade of sarcasm to creep into his voice, "I believe it must have occurred to you as being relevant information."

"I think," said Schwann, "that you're making the mistake of not looking at all this from my viewpoint. A young woman to whom I have been married approximately two months begins to behave very oddly toward me. She refuses to take me into her confidence in the slightest degree. She leaves me sitting at a table in a cafe and does not come back. The next day I find from her landlady that she moved the night before. Consider that, if you please, from my viewpoint."

"It was rather a shock," said Tuck.

Kurt Schwann gave a wintry smile. "I do not make a display of my feelings, Mr. Tuck, but we can agree that it was rather a shock. I was quite a burden to my friend Greenwood all day Saturday. I could do no work. I spent Sunday with some very bitter thoughts which we need not go into here. I spent Sunday trying to find some reason for what she had done, and failing utterly. My brother could not comfort me, because my brother does not yet know we were married. By Sunday night I realized that there were two roads open to me. I could abandon myself to grief and bitterness and fruitless hope, or I could go Monday morning to my laboratory and go on with the work that was waiting to be done. I chose that road."

"I can understand all that," said Tuck.

"Thank you. I must speak now about my wife. She was champagne, Mr. Tuck. Light. I did not marry to have an intellectual equal in my future home. I married to have a wife in my future home. I believe that a wise man looks for his intellectual

[184]

pleasures among men. That is not what women are for. Very well. On Monday a more or less intellectual woman made a suggestion which at the time I accepted as a solution of the puzzle of Garnet's behavior. Gladys Horstmann said that she believed that Garnet had found what I think she called 'a real, grown-up man,' had gone away to marry him, and would one day reappear wearing a very large diamond. That hit home. I remembered her frothiness, her fondness for the frilly things of life. I remembered her secrecy to me. I remembered how small a salary mine would be, even as a professor. Oh, I remembered a great deal. And I decided that for the sake of my own peace of mind I would accept that as the answer, in which case Garnet would either have to commit bigamy, which I did not believe she would do, or divorce me, probably in Reno, in which event I would soon learn of it. That was where I was when Sydney Vines came to me with the information that Garnet was dead and might have been murdered. When it sank in, it was superimposed on the other idea, and she was simply dead to me in a new way, scarcely more final than the old one."

"And you still told no one of your marriage?"

"What would have been the point? I had learned nothing to make me believe that the information would ease your labors. And I was frankly a trifle averse to being pointed at as the deserted husband. My pride again, you see."

Tuck thought for a minute. "Do you have any idea who could have written that note?"

"None." The look of distaste was on Kurt's face again, thin over a fiercer look. "I should like very much to know who it was. I should like to hit him in the face."

"The child," said Tuck, very quietly. "You are sure it was your child?"

[185]

Kurt stared straight into Tuck's eyes out of his green ones, and Tuck had the uncomfortable notion that Kurt Schwann's impulse to violence had transferred itself to a new object. His chin went out, just a trifle. He spoke very distinctly. "I said my wife was emotionally light. I did not say she was loose."

"I'd like to see your marriage license, as a matter of routine."

Kurt reached into his pocket, and drew out a flat leather key container from which he detached a key, handing it to Tuck. "My brother is not home. To the left of the front door are two other doors. One leads to a closet. The other leads to my bedroom. In the top left drawer of the highboy is a flat leather folder. That is the cover of my diploma. Under the diploma is the marriage license. You may bring the key back here if you wish. You must excuse my not accompanying you, but—" and here he made the only vague gesture Tuck had ever seen him use—"there is so little time, and so much to be done."

"Thank you," said Tuck, and turned to the door. Kurt stood tall and thin beside the microscope, in his white jacket, the sleeves of which had shrunk. "Please forgive the disorder. But as you know, when one is a bachelor . . ."

Tuck, standing with his hand on the knob of the door, saw the muscles of Kurt's throat suddenly tighten. He swallowed. He closed his eyes and at once opened them. Ignoring Tuck, he sat quickly before the microscope, and began looking down the barrel.

Tuck learned then that Kurt Schwann was not a convincing actor. There was no slide in the microscope.

Or was he a very good actor indeed?

Looking down at the marriage license of Kurt Schwann and Garnet Dillon, Tuck experienced an odd sensation. His stomach sank. Black ink on white paper brought home to him what spoken words had not, that it looked very much as though the bottom had dropped out of the case.

From Kurt's, he went to Dr. Uman's office. Gladys Horstmann told him that Uman was upstairs with his rats, and so Tuck plodded up to the little room through which he had passed five days before to look down at Garnet Dillon's body lying on a long table beyond one of the two long doors.

Dr. Uman was wearing his old white tennis sweater. His dusty hair was ruffled, and made Tuck think of cockatoos. He was squatting before one of the many tiers of cages, jotting a notation on the card attached to it, and when Tuck spoke his name, he looked up out of harassed eyes.

"Just a minute. GRIZZ!"

"Ya don't have to yell. I got ears. Good ears." And Grizz, like a soured troll, appeared around the end of the row of cages .

"You didn't increase the dose!" accused Uman.

"I did too!" stamped Grizz.

Uman made a thwarted gesture with his fountain pen at the frisky rat in the cage before which he had been stooping. "Then why is he still healthy?" he roared.

Grizz put his hands on his hips. "Could you be maybe wrong?" he asked, his wet blue eyes swimming with malice.

"Ach!" said Uman, and began screwing the top onto his fountain pen. He turned to Tuck, and Grizz, now a triumphant troll, vanished beyond the end of the row of cages.

"Yes?"asked Uman, unpleasantly, and with a vagueness already beginning to film his eyes.

Tuck abandoned all hope of subtlety. "How would marriage and children affect Kurt Schwann's career?"

The vagueness left Uman's eyes at once. He

[187]

cocked his head to one side and considered. Then he looked straight at Tuck. "That would depend on the wife, wouldn't it?"

Before Tuck could answer, he went on: "Now if you mean how would marriage with Garnet Dillon have affected his career, and I think you do, I will say that it would have been the best thing in the world for him. I told him so."

"Could we sit down?" asked Tuck, going to one of the two chairs at Griswold's table. "The chairs around here are all the hardest I've ever come across, but I think so badly on my feet."

Uman crouched uncomfortably on the chair opposite Tuck, and Tuck asked, "Might I have an elaboration?"

Uman nervously ran his thumbnail along a groove in the rough wooden top of the table. "Kurt is a German boy. He looks like a cross between Hamlet and the Lonely Scientist, and he enjoys looking that way. But I happen to know that he is one of a once typical German family, consisting of a momma and papa and four children. The tragic breaking up of that family because of the present regime in Germany is another story. Kurt is a German boy, then. And deep in him is an appreciation of good food, a good wife, good children, and good beer. He rather fought that, until he met Garnet Dillon. I don't know what you may have heard of her, and I don't give a hang, but I can tell you this: she would have made him a good wife, if only because she adored him."

Tuck began to feel sad. Uman stopped running his thumbnail along the groove, and nibbled at it. Then he abandoned that and sat still for a moment. It gave emphasis to what he next said, his hollow eyes full of a sort of cosmic amusement.

"Take animals. Take birds. The male is always more resplendent than the female. Why? To evoke admiration, to the end that propagation may follow. In the human sphere the women wear the fine feathers. But the men still need admiration. Some don't know it. Kurt does. Garnet Dillon admired him. She admired what he was doing, without understanding it. She thought he was wonderful, and showed it. She would have made him a perfect wife."

"Could Schwann afford a wife? And children?"

"With his professorship, yes."

"I'm rather interested in these fruit flies of his. Would a professorship allow him time to continue his work with them?"

"Yes."

"Hey, Uman," called Grizz, from somewhere beyond the cages. "Imogene is dead."

"Ah-ha!" said Uman, jumping up. His last look at Tuck said, quite plainly, "I remember your face, but the name escapes me."

As soon as he gave the key back to Kurt, Tuck pulled his notebook from his coat pocket, and began to thumb through its pages. "You know, I'm afraid I've forgotten the name of that chap in Pasadena—the one you spent the night of Friday the first with."

Kurt shook his head from side to side, an obscure amusement behind his green eyes. "No. You didn't forget. I didn't tell you. But I will, at once. His name is Charles Stuart, and the simplest way to reach him would be to phone Cal Tech and ask for the second floor of the Biology Department."

"Why, yes," said a voice not long from Dixie. "Ku't came ovah 'bout foah. We talked so doggoned long aftah dinnah that he missed the last train foah Los Angeles, so I asked him to spend the night with me. Then, in the mo'nin' he got so doggoned int'rested in some of the things we're doin' out heah that he stayed till 'most one. Is

[189]

theah anything moah ah could tell you?"

Tuck snatched at a straw. "Ah—I mean, *are* you sure this was on Friday the first of February, and Saturday, the second of February?"

"Oh, yes. You see, the fuhst is ma birthday."

Tuck hung up the receiver and stared at the round mouthpiece. "Happy birthday to you," he said, as an afterthought.

He wedged himself out of the phone booth and saw the turnstile leading to the Student Union Cafe just ahead of him. An urge for a great deal of strong black coffee gripped him.

The waitress said "Pardon?" when he asked for three cups of black coffee, so he looked up and explained, "I have some thinking to do."

"I see," she said, matter-of-factly. It was only when her starched pink skirt was bustling toward the long counter opposite the window where he was seated that he realized his explanation might not have exactly made sense.

He got out his notebook, opened it to a fresh page, and stared at it. He didn't see it. All he saw was the fact that the Coroner's inquest was tomorrow morning at nine o'clock and he was exactly where he had started.

When the waitress returned and with a nice precision lined up three thick cups of coffee in front of him, he took a long gulp that almost emptied the first cup. He set it into its saucer, and stared at it.

Moving all the cups one foot further back on the brown table, he spread out his notebook and took a pencil from his pocket. In square, firm handwriting, he began to set down the facts that still remained to him: the few survivors of the wreck.

1. Garnet Dillon died of digitalis poisoning. She became unconscious at a cafe near the station at eleven o'clock on the night of Friday, the eighth of February. She died at eleven-thirty, in the ambulance.

2. On the morning of Saturday, February the second, fifty-four grains of digitalis disappeared from Dean Calder's desk.

3. This digitalis was most probably taken by someone who had an exam that morning, or was in the building for some other ordinary reason. Kurt Schwann was not in the building that morning.

4. The digitalis which poisoned Garnet Dillon was administered before Monday, February fourth.

5. On the night of Friday, February first, Garnet Dillon came home at eight after a date with someone unknown. It was not Kurt Schwann, since he was in Pasadena at that time.

6. On the night of Saturday, February second, Garnet went out for dinner with a man. This, according to the testimony of Mrs. Nox, was not Kurt Schwann either, as his voice on the telephone had been instantly recognizable to her and she had not recognized this man's voice.

7. On Friday, the eighth, Garnet Dillon's driver's license, which she always carried, was found by Hitchlock on the table in the Hofbrau where she had earlier dined with Kurt Schwann.

8. Garnet Dillon had planned to leave town at least by three o'clock in the afternoon of Friday, February eighth, because at that time she drew all her funds from her bank.

9. She kept a date with Kurt Schwann on the night of Friday, February eighth, leaving abruptly and apparently without his knowledge. She hailed a taxi, drove home and got her packed bags, gave the key to Mrs. Nox, went to the station, bought a ticket to Grand Canyon, checked her bags, went to a cafe for coffee, became unconscious.

10. Her purse was then stolen, by a tall man in a black hat and a black overcoat who came in for coffee just after she did.

11. After diagnosing her death as a heart attack, the hospital held her unidentified body in its morgue until the morning of Monday, the eleventh of February, when it was sent out to the medical school where she had worked.

[191]

12. According to Dean Calder, who at her request examined her heart on Friday, February first, there was nothing wrong with her heart.
13. According to Dean Calder, she did not commit suicide.

Tuck drank his second cup of coffee, and thought. By the time he had finished thinking, the third cup was stone cold. He called the waitress and asked for another. When he had drunk it, he wrote a list of questions on a new page of his notebook.

1. Why did Garnet Dillon go away?
2. Why to Grand Canyon?
3. Why was she killed?
4. Who killed her?

Just four questions.

He began to laugh.

"Mr. Tuck," said a woman's voice. He looked up and saw Kathryn Farr standing beside the opposite chair. She looked very determined, and at the same time amazed, as though she were faced with something she had to believe but couldn't.

She drew out the chair and sat down. Leaning toward him, she said in a quiet, firm voice, "I think I know who killed Garnet Dillon. I am sure I know who sent that note to you."

TWENTY-TWO

OH?" SAID TUCK. "DO YOU want some coffee?"

"Thanks. I've had lunch."

Tuck looked at the clock over the counter and saw to his astonishment that it was almost one.

"It's the Horstmann thing all over again!" explained Kate Farr.

Tuck controlled his excitement. "What is the Horstmann thing all over again?"

"I had lunch with Kurt," said Kate Farr. "Johnny's out at the County Hospital today and Kurt needed someone to talk to. He told me everything. About the note you got this morning. About his marriage to Garnet. Everything. And, Mr. Tuck, you can't believe that he killed Garnet. He didn't."

"All right. He didn't. Go on."

She leaned still closer to him. She was speaking in a deliberately subdued voice, but there was excitement in it. "Why do people send the police anonymous accusing letters?"

"Because they're cranks, or because they want to point the finger of suspicion at someone else."

"That's what I thought. Do you know what kind of typewriter was used for the note you got this morning?"

"Not yet. I left it with our typewriting expert."

"Would he know by now?"

"Probably."

"Go phone him and find out."

Eyeing her speculatively, Tuck heaved himself up from his chair and walked past the cashier's desk toward the phone.

"Check, please, sir!" she called after him sharply.

He pointed to the phone booth. "I'll be right back."

"What did you find out about that letter Froody brought you this morning?" he asked when he had Beavis' ear.

"It was typed on a standard Royal machine, nineteen-forty model. The left serif on the h is missing. The p is partially clogged. The e is out of alignment. I've made enlargements, and if you'll bring me any samples I'll be glad to enlarge them and check them for you."

"Thanks."

He passed the watchful cashier again, and sat down opposite Kate Farr.

"Before you say anything, I want to talk," she said. "Last night I left the door of the Dean's office unlocked. When I came back to do some work after dinner, there was a light on. When I went up to the office, the light was out. Nothing had been disturbed except the typewriter on my desk. That was uncovered. I am sure that I covered it when I left. So I assume that someone, for some reason, used it. It is a nineteen-forty Royal. The *e* is out of line, and the *p* is clogged with goo. Does that check?"

"That checks. The note was typed on that machine." Tuck found that he was leaning toward her now. Their heads were nearly touching.

She looked elated. "I knew it! Here's where the Horstmann thing comes in. It *was* she who followed me in the park, wasn't it?"

"Yes."

"I was sure of that, too. She's been avoiding me like fury. All right. We lit on her as the masquerader because she was the only person who knew I would be there at a certain time, didn't we?"

The "we" made Tuck think of Brigit. He nodded.

Kate squirmed with eagerness. "Lookee. The Dean's office is never vacant during the day. One of us is always there. And it's never unlocked at night, because there are important papers on file. No one used that typewriter while I was in the office. After talking to Kurt, I asked the Dean, and no one used it while he was there. So the only time since the murder that anyone could have typed that anonymous letter was last night when I left the door unlocked. And there was only one person who knew I left the door unlocked; he was with me at the time. It was a fellow you've never laid eyes on. His name is Sydney Vines."

Tuck leaned slowly back in his chair.

"And if that's not enough, here's something more. When I was in the Science Building last night, someone played a joke on me. A nasty joke, with a lot of malice in it. Someone lured me into the anatomy lab by leaving the lights there burning. Then, while I was going down the room to the switch, he put a head on the table beside the door and went out and locked the door, leaving me with the head and not liking its company so much."

"A head?" echoed Tuck, feeling a little dazed.

"A dead head. From one of the pots of things like that under the windows."

"Why?" asked Tuck.

Kate opened her purse, and drew from it a very fat envelope. She opened the envelope and drew out a bulky letter, which she unfolded, turned to the last page, and laid before him. "There's the reason," she said. "And there's a pretty good description of the man who did it."

Below her pointing finger, he read, ". . . Sydney Vines, a fat white slug of a boy with glittering eyeglasses. And quite obviously, Garnet gave Sydney the brush-off, for which he hates her thoroughly. He's an elbow-massager, and it takes a considerable amount of dexterity to avoid his plump paw. I believe that he's a victim of an inferiority complex; he knows that women can't stand him, and covers it up with an assured manner and amusing babble. I dislike him thoroughly."

"I believe you do," said Tuck, as she refolded the letter and returned it to its envelope.

"This letter," she said, "was open to this page on the desk beside the typewriter. Do you see now the reason for the head?"

"It was certainly a childish revenge," Tuck mused.

"Is revenge childish?" asked Kate, wide-eyed. "Is malice confined to kindergarten?"

"I'm still a little vague about the mechanics of this—ah—prank."

"When I reached the head of the stairs, the light was out, the office door was closed and the office was empty. There is no way anyone inside the office could have heard me coming up the stairs. Therefore I'm starting by assuming that Vines had finished prying and using the typewriter and was outside the office while I was coming up the stairs. He heard me, and ducked into the Anatomy lab, to avoid being seen and to see who I was. He saw who I was when I went into the office. He had read the letter, and was furious at me because of what I had written about him. I believe he made up his joke as he went along. He lit the lights in the Anatomy lab, got the head from the pot, tucked it under his arm and lit the hall lights. The switch for those, I've since found, is right outside the door of the Anatomy lab. Then he ducked around the nearest corner and hid. I tumbled into his trap by going into the Anatomy lab to turn out the lights there, whereupon he sneaked in while my back was turned, deposited the head, clicked the switch on the door and shut it. And I imagine that he stood just the other side of that locked door, and heard me yell and liked it." She shivered a little.

"I think you've made that very clear, Miss Farr. And you've certainly convinced me that he used your typewriter. He undoubtedly knows that typing can be traced and picked a typewriter in a public place, only he didn't pick one quite public enough. But why do you think he might have killed Garnet Dillon?"

Kate frowned. "Perhaps I shouldn't have said that. I haven't a shred of proof to back it."

"I'm getting rather used to lack of proof," said Tuck, dryly. "Tell me what you think. Only not too much about his inferiority complex, please. I'm a little dubious about inferiority complexes as motives for murder."

Kate frowned again. "People . . ." She made a

[196]

jerky gesture. ". . . They're so funny. I mean, you see a person day after day, in certain circumstances. You work in the same office with him, or sit next to him in class. You get to think you know the person. 'Oh, yes,' you say. 'So-and-so is such and such.' But you don't know So-and-so at all. You don't know what they think or do when they're alone, or what they dream about. If you were to ask Hitchlock or Whittaker about Vines, they'd laugh and say, 'That crass son-of-a-gun. He thinks he's Lochinvar.' And they're right, maybe, but maybe wrong. They're judging him by what they see day after day, and that's only part of the pattern."

"What are you getting at?" asked Tuck, slowly.

As slowly, Kate Farr replied, "I was wondering if Vines is quite sane."

They looked at each other.

"I took some psychology courses, and I wasn't much impressed," Kate went on. "As a science, it's still in swaddling clothes. But you don't have to believe in all of psychology to know that there are varying degrees of sensitivity in people. What one man might laugh off, another might regard as a deadly insult."

Tuck found himself nodding. "Did Kurt Schwann give this Vines the black eye Dean Calder spoke of?"

"Oh, no! Hitchlock did." She giggled, and sobered at once. "That's not what I was thinking about. I was thinking of the morning I came here, and Sydney Vines' telling me about the departed Garnet. I keep remembering him saying, 'She played the field for a while, and spit in your eye when she felt like it, and then laughed as if it didn't matter at all.' He was trying to be light about it, trying to pretend it didn't matter, but the hatred he felt for her showed through like—like bones. And there's something else I keep remembering. Yesterday, just before dinner, he came to the office to ask me to eat with him. I refused. Then, when I was at the mirror putting on some lipstick, he said, very quietly in the dusky room, 'I used to watch Garnet do that.' " She gave a short laugh. "This is silly, but as I remember that now, it sounded like a threat."

Tuck stood up. "Where can I find Vines?"

Kate stood up too. "I've checked on that. He's out at the hospital today. I don't know where, but I'm sure you'll be able to find out."

Afternoon sunlight lay bright on the sprawling city across which Tuck's black sedan wove its way toward the multiple shallow steps and soaring verticals of the County Hospital.

A twisted mind behind the fat white face? Hatred gnawing its way inward, finding at last a way to vent itself?

Tuck shook his head. It was not a gesture of positive negation, he realized, but rather a gesture of doubt.

Of one thing he was certain. He would see Sydney Vines.

That involved time, and patience, and repeated displayings of his badge. At last a starched person at a large desk reluctantly told him that Sydney Vines was on duty in a tuberculosis ward on the third floor; that since visiting hours were now in effect, Tuck might see him; and that Tuck would do well to hold his handkerchief before his mouth and nose while in the ward.

Sydney Vines was sitting at a small table near the door. He was wearing a white jacket, and he was cleaning his fingernails.

The ward was a long narrow room, each wall flanked by white beds on which quiet bodies lay. Beside several beds dark figures sat. As Tuck entered someone coughed.

Vines turned a bland face up at Tuck, and

[198]

slipped the nail file into his coat pocket. "Yes?" he asked.

Tuck showed his badge. "I want to talk to you."

Vines' face remained bland. There was a calm insolence in the pale eyes behind the glasses. "Yes?"

"Yes." Somehow the shielding handkerchief made Tuck feel on the defensive, which annoyed him. "I suggest that you have someone replace you. We're going to have quite a long talk. All about the letter you sent me."

"What letter?" asked Sydney Vines, without the slightest change of expression.

"The letter you typed on Miss Farr's typewriter last night."

Sydney Vines' expression altered at that. But it altered to a look of commiseration. "Look here, old chap. I'm afraid you're barking up the wrong tree."

There were two expressions in the English language which rubbed Tuck the wrong way. One was "old chap." The other was "barking up the wrong tree."

Tuck ignored them. "The question is, do you talk here, or do I take you down to headquarters?"

"On what charge?" asked Vines, innocently.

"Suspicion of murder."

That did it. Cold alertness showed for a minute in Sydney Vines' gray eyes. "You have no proof."

"That's where the 'suspicion' comes in."

Vines clasped his white hands on the table and regarded them thoughtfully.

"Listen, boy," Tuck said, making his voice as insulting as he could. "I don't have time to waste. I know you typed that letter. There are several reasons why you did it. One of them may be that you killed Garnet Dillon. You're in a bad spot, and I advise you to talk, and talk fast, and start thinking about a good lawyer."

Tuck made no effort to talk confidentially. At the word "killed," several of the quiet heads turned toward them. A fine sweat broke out on Vines' pallid forehead.

His tone was conciliatory when he said, "Listen. I can explain everything."

"Where have I heard that before?" Tuck asked the ceiling.

Vines stood up. "We can't talk here. Just a minute."

"Oh, no. I'll come right along."

The starched person at the desk agreed to send another student to the ward.

"Come on," said Vines. "I need a weed."

Tuck followed him to a small cement balcony, offering a fine view of the city and displaying two buckets and a mop in a sheltered corner.

Vines offered Tuck a cigarette, which Tuck refused, and lighted one for himself. When he had it going, he took an inhalation which must have filtered through the uttermost lobes of his lungs. "I'm not saying I wrote that letter, understand. I'm . . ."

"You don't have to. I know you did. You're telling me why you wrote it. Name? I have it. Address?"

Vines looked suspiciously at Tuck's notebook. "410 Fargo Lane."

"Beverly Hills, huh?" Tuck snapped, trying to make it sound as discrediting as possible. Evidently he did, for Vines' reply was far from bland, and the fine dew on his forehead was more pronounced. "Look. So I wrote the letter. I did you a favor. I knew you were having one hell of a time . . ."

"How did you know that?"

"You started in on Monday, and by Thursday nothing had happened. No story in the papers, no arrest—nothing. I was in a bad spot. I knew some-

[200]

thing which would help you, but naturally I couldn't give you that information in person, so . . ."

"Why not?"

Vines looked unhappy. "Well, it would have looked kind of ratty to . . ."

Tuck smiled unkindly. "So you wrote an anonymous letter. I see. Go on."

"I suppose you're wondering how I happened to have the information I gave you."

"That had occurred to me."

"It was this way. And I leave you to judge if I did anything you wouldn't have done yourself. I dropped by to see Garnet on the night of November thirtieth. As I went into the lower hall of the apartment house I saw the elevator door just closing after Kurt Schwann. I called to him but the door had shut. I waited for him to get out on the third floor—I knew of course that he had come to see Garnet—and then I punched the button and waited for it to come down. Then I rode up to Garnet's floor, got out, and knocked at her door. She opened it after a long wait. She was wearing a negligee—peach satin crawling with lace. That floored me. Before I could say anything she said in the quick voice she used to slap people down with, 'Sorry, Sydney. I'm just going to bed.' Well! I mumbled something, and went away. I realized that she didn't know I'd seen Kurt going into the elevator, and didn't realize she was giving anything away. Then I thought maybe I was doing her an injustice, maybe Kurt hadn't been going to see her after all. So I waited. There weren't any lights on in the private house next door, so I just went and sat on the front steps and waited."

"And looked at your watch," supplemented Tuck.

"And looked at my watch. I figured out which windows were Garnet's. The lights were on. In a few minutes someone pulled down the shades. It wasn't Garnet, and I'm not saying it was Kurt; I couldn't see that well. But it was definitely and positively a man. I waited some more. In a little while, the lights went out."

"That was at nine-fifteen."

Vines looked a little uncomfortable. "Yes. So I waited some more."

"Four hours and twenty minutes."

"No. I waited for a few minutes, and then I thought, 'Nuts to this. It's her business.' So I went to the library and did some collateral reading for a course I'm taking. The library closes at ten, and I went over to a cafe near campus for some beer. I met some of the boys, and had a few, and pretty soon it was one o'clock. I was a little lit, and the whole thing seemed like a joke to me. I thought, 'I wonder if that guy is still there.' So I went back to Garnet's place and sat on the steps some more. The lights were still out, so either he'd gone home, or . . . I was just deciding to serenade them—I said I was tight, didn't I?—when the lights went on again. I looked at my watch, and it was one thirty-five. By then I was plenty sure, but I stuck around some more, and after a while, sure enough, Schwann came out."

"At a quarter to two," finished Tuck.

"Yeah. He walked right past me, whistling."

"Why did you note the time so carefully?"

"I'm a methodical guy."

"You had no idea of using this information against them?"

"Hell, no! What kind of person do you think I am?"

Tuck smiled. Very placidly, he asked, "And why did you think this information would be of any interest to me?"

"I'll tell you why! Garnet Dillon was pregnant when she died!"

[202]

"And how do you know that?"

"For chrissake stop trying to trip me up! Sorry . . ." Vines took out a crumpled handkerchief and mopped his forehead, managing at the same time a flabby smile. "Where were we? Oh, yes. This is how I know the way Garnet was. Time lapse of two months, more or less. On Friday, February first . . ."

Something in Tuck pricked up its ears.

". . . I went into the Dean's office for an exam schedule. I'd lost mine. It was noontime, and the Dean was gone. Garnet was sitting at her desk, and she looked like hell. I asked her if anything was wrong, and she said nothing was. But she said it as if she didn't mean it much, and she looked scared to death. I said nobody felt good and looked like she did, but she put me off again. I thought 'What the hell, I'll be a Good Samaritan anyway.' So I said, 'Don't try to kid an old pal, honey. And don't fool around with something serious. Go to a reputable doctor, and see what he has to say.' She said she'd been thinking of doing that, but she didn't know any doctor to go to. I gave her the name and address and phone number of mine. He's been the family M.D. for years, and he's a pretty good guy. She thanked me, and I told her to skip it. As I left the office, I heard her dialing a number on the phone, very brisk and definite, if ' you get me.

"The next afternoon I went over to Gordon's office to have him take a look at my sinus; I've got sinus trouble to beat hell!

"After Gordon had sprayed my nose, I said, 'I told a friend of mine to have you take a look at her. Garnet Dillon. Has she been in?' He said she had, Friday afternoon at four-thirty. I said, 'What's wrong there, Doc? Man to man.' And do you know what he said? He said, 'None of your damned business!' "

Vines was perspiring again. Very earnestly, he said, "Now I ask you! What would you have thought? I mean, if she'd had a sore throat, or something like that, he'd have told me, wouldn't he?" Vines used the crumpled handkerchief briefly, and put it away. "So I said, 'O.K., doc. I can guess.' And he said, 'You can guess until you're blue. That girl's trouble is that girl's business.'" Vines shrugged. "If he wanted to lay the professional ethics on thick, O.K. But I knew, all right. I knew."

"And so when you listened outside the Dean's door on Monday, February eleventh, and learned that she was dead and might have been murdered, you decided that Kurt Schwann had done it."

Vines raised a protesting palm. "Not at first! That's not one of those things you jump at. First I thought she'd killed herself."

"Then why did you go to Schwann with your information?"

"If she did kill herself, he was still responsible, wasn't he? I wanted to see how he'd take it. He never batted an eye. That's when I started to add things up."

"And what made you decide to inform me of all this?"

Vines said eagerly, "It was something I saw in Farr's letter to her mother . . ." He checked himself, looking rather shocked, and then obviously realizing that what was said, was said: "Something about Kurt not being the sort of person you could browbeat into telling the truth, without proof. I decided to give you the proof."

"Give me the address and phone number of this Dr. Gordon."

"2020 Wilshire Boulevard. Crescent 4109."

Tuck wrote, and closed his notebook. "Vines, your anonymous effort in my behalf was very much in vain."

Vines' brow clouded.

"Since last Thanksgiving Garnet Dillon's legal name has been Mrs. Kurt Schwann."

Vines' eyes opened very wide behind his thick glasses. "No foolin'!" He sounded, Tuck noticed, almost disappointed.

"No fooling. And Vines. You had a final exam on the morning of Saturday, February second, didn't you?"

"Yes. I did. But what . . . ?"

"And Vines."

"Yes?"

"That little joke with the head wasn't a good idea. It made me wonder about you. I'm still wondering."

Tuck turned, and went away from there, carrying with him the last glimpse he had had of Vines' face. A fat face screwed up against strong sunlight, and in the small eyes a reflection of the confusion that comes to minds which habitually think evil and find evil replaced with decency.

TWENTY-THREE

It was four o'clock when he entered Dr. Gordon's office. A starched voice spoke from a desk beside the door, and he turned to face a nurse who obviously placed time at a high value. "Did you wish to see Dr. Gordon?"

"Yes." He thought, I'm getting tired of white.

"Dr. Gordon is seeing a patient this afternoon." She looked up at him sharply. "You don't have an appointment?"

"No. Do you expect him back?"

"No. He will go directly to the Lutheran Hospital, where he is performing an operation this evening. Do you wish to make an appointment for tomorrow?"

"Thanks, no. I didn't want to see him professionally. I want to ask him some questions about a patient of his."

The nurse looked so outraged that Tuck hastily fished his badge up from the side pocket of his coat. On seeing it she looked slightly mollified, and more than slightly interested. "What is the patient's name? Perhaps I can help you."

"Garnet Dillon. Or maybe Garnet Schwann. She came in on the afternoon of Friday, the first of February."

The nurse opened a large book on her desk, and went back a number of pages. Then she read something, and nodded. "Yes. It's Garnet Dillon, here. Friday the first, at four-thirty. I'm sorry, but I don't know another thing to tell you. She was not one of the doctor's regular patients."

"Do you suppose I could see the doctor before he performs this operation?"

"No, that would be impossible."

"After?"

She looked doubtful. "I don't know . . . perhaps if you could tell me what this is all about . . ."

Tuck leaned down with quiet drama. "Do you remember this Dillon girl at all?"

"Wasn't she an extremely pretty blonde?"

"She was. She's been murdered."

The nurse's mouth was a perfect O.

"My name's Richard Tuck, and I'm investigating her death. I have just learned that she came to Dr. Gordon, and I'm hoping that he may be able to tell me something which will help me."

"Isn't that *terrible!*" marveled the nurse. "She was so pretty, too. Well. This *is* important. I'll tell you what I'll do, Mr. Tuck. Dr. Gordon will telephone me before he goes to the hospital. I'll tell him that you will be waiting in the sunroom, east wing, third floor, and for him to meet you there as soon as the operation is over."

[206]

"Fine! What time would that be?"

The nurse smiled an inscrutable, professional smile. "I suggest that you arrive at ten, and be prepared to wait some time." She leaned forward. "Gall stones," she confided.

Tuck telephoned to Brigit and told her that because of an unexpected development he would be unable to help her lay a trap for Black Overcoat at eleven that evening. He recommended Froody, who was a far better shot than he was. He also suggested that the evening of the following day would find him completely at her service.

"You're a crumb-bun!" declared Brigit.

"A what?"

"Froody!" complained Brigit, bitterly. "And this guy I'm after is about six feet four!"

"What you need is a good shot, who can wing him from the rear window of the car at the first crack, and height has nothing to do with that."

"Gufferty!" yelled Brigit. "Tuck thinks he's Sherlock Holmes again. He says he won't . . ."

Tuck heard Gufferty's faint roar distinctly. "Oh, *won't* he . . ."

Tuck pressed the receiver hook down quietly, just as Gufferty's voice smote his eardrum with: "Listen, Tuck! You're going to . . ."

Tuck then went to a large, homely cafeteria, where he methodically ate his way through a large, homely dinner. This was in accordance with a favorite theory of his, to the effect that the brain is an organ of the body and must be nourished in order to function properly. Another theory of his was that thinking and eating belong in separate categories of action; you can't do both at once and do justice to either. But tonight he forgot that theory entirely.

"The pattern of Dillon's actions prior to her death is now enlarged," he said to himself. "And

[207]

some minor mysteries are explained. The appointment that made her leave work at four on Friday the first—I should have paid more attention to that appointment—was with this Dr. Gordon, who undoubtedly told her that she was going to have a baby. Yes. But why the bottle of whisky that so outraged Mrs. Nox? Whisky is a primitive means of escape from unpleasant reality. Why would the discovery that she, a married woman, was going to have a perfectly legitimate child, cause her to want to ease her mind with drink? Maybe she didn't want the child. Maybe Kurt didn't want the child. Uman says that a normal, pleasant childhood in the bosom of a large German family made Kurt into a family man, but Uman may be wrong. Still, that's no good. Schwann was in Pasadena that night. He could not yet have known he was a prospective father. Unless . . . could Garnet have phoned him after leaving the doctor's?"

Tuck did an unusual thing. He left his dessert half eaten, with a firm command to the bus boy to leave it on the table, and went to the phone booth by the cashier's desk. Charles Stuart had left his laboratory for the day, but some patient persuasion procured his home phone number.

"No," said Charles Stuart. "No one phoned Ku't while he was heah. Ah can say that definitely, because he was with me the whole time."

Tuck was happy to find his pie where he had left it. "That's out, then," he told himself. "Kurt didn't know about the child. And I don't know why she bought a bottle of whisky. Wait! Celebration of a happy event? Hardly."

Tuck took out his notebook. "I won't theorize. I'll list all the questions that occur to me." He began to write.

Why did she ask Dean Calder to examine her heart?
Why did she buy that whisky?
Was she really dead drunk when Kurt telephoned
    from Pasadena? Or had she gone out, Mrs. Nox's
    second and more charitable suggestion? If so,
    where? Why?
Who took the digitalis from Dean Calder's desk on
    Saturday morning?
Why did this person want to kill Garnet Dillon
    Schwann?
How was the poison administered?
Who was the man with whom Garnet went out to
    dinner on the night of Saturday, February second?
Why did not Garnet tell him they were going to have
    a baby, if Kurt Schwann was telling the truth?
Why was the last dose of the poison, found in the in-
    testine by the medical examiner, given to Garnet?
Why did she keep the date with Kurt Schwann?
Why did she plan to go away, and of all places, to
    Grand Canyon?

Tuck closed his notebook. There was an answer
which covered the majority of the questions. It
was not a pretty answer. It concerned a young
wife, betraying a young husband.

He thought, Vines is only a little worse than the
rest of us. We're all too quick to believe evil about
another human being. That's why I'm no nearer a
solution than I was on Monday. I accepted the idea
that Garnet was bad, without proof. No more of
that.

At half past eleven, Tuck was sitting on a wicker
rocker in the sunroom on the third floor of the
east wing of the Lutheran Hospital. He was reading a pamphlet called "Advice To Young
Mothers."

The other occupant of the room, seated on another wicker rocker, was a pale young man, who
had been smoking cigarettes chain fashion for an
hour, and who gave every indication of being an
expectant father. At twenty-five minutes to mid-

night, Tuck's guess was confirmed when a smiling young nurse appeared in the doorway, causing the young man to leap from his chair as though it had suddenly pinched him. She said, "It's a lovely little girl."

The young man, wearing a confused smile, went away.

So it goes, thought Tuck.

A moment after the young father's exit, a small, spare man of about forty-five, looking weary, came in. He had on a dark business suit, and his tie had been tied in a hurry. On seeing Tuck he went straight to him, and held out his hand. "Mr. Tuck? I'm Dr. Gordon. My nurse tells me you wish to ask me some questions about Garnet Dillon Schwann."

"I do, Dr. Gordon. It's kind of you to help me."

Dr. Gordon made a movement of negation with one hand. "We might as well sit down. It's a short story." He looked at Tuck out of dark-brown eyes which were at once alert and kindly. "Do you know anything about leukemia?"

A gong rang in Tuck's head. What had the medical examiner said? "She had anemia, maybe leukemia, but she didn't die of that . . ."

"No, I don't, Dr. Gordon."

"The briefest way I can describe it to you is to say that it is sometimes called cancer of the blood. The normal white blood count is around 8,000 per cubic millimeter. Leukemia ups it to as much as five hundred thousand. These white blood cells invade the spleen, and it swells enormously, sometimes until it fills over half of the abdominal cavity. This is often painful. Death comes by an uncontrollable hemorrhage into a vital organ, such as the brain. Acute leukemia kills in a few hours. Chronic leukemia takes longer, say six months to a'year, or thereabouts. It is one hundred per cent fatal, Mr. Tuck. I had the unpleasant task of telling Mrs. Schwann what I am telling you. **She** had chronic leukemia.

"I furthermore had to tell her that there is no known cure for this terrible disease. X-ray and radium prolong life by a few months, but sooner or later the patient becomes inured to radiation and the blood count does not drop. From then on, his days are numbered.

"You may wonder that I told her all this. There is a school of thought, I know, which believes that in such cases a doctor should tell a white lie. Hold out false hope. I do not believe in that. It is in the long run far more unkind. Mrs. Schwann was an adult. She had not only herself to consider, but her husband as well. I felt it best to let her know exactly where she stood. I did."

For the first time, Tuck was able to frame words. "How did she take it?"

"How would you expect a pretty young woman to take such news? After the first shock wore off she began to ask questions that were really pleadings that I tell her a lie that would make it easier to bear. This I did not do. I told her that many other human beings had faced her problem, and faced it bravely. I pointed out that we all know that death will come for us one day, and that her case was dreadful only in that she knew her death would be soon."

"You found that she was pregnant?"

"Yes. I told her that, too. I gave her a sedative, and said that I would be glad to arrange for X-ray treatments if she should so decide."

Tuck spoke slowly. "I know that it must have taken courage to do what you did. But surely you could see that she was very young. Weren't you asking her to grow up all at once?"

"She had to, Mr. Tuck. She had to."

"Yes," said Tuck.

There was a silence.

[211]

"My nurse told me that you believe she has been murdered. You can see now, I think, what more probably happened. She couldn't face her problem. She didn't grow up. She killed herself."

The small and dingy cafe down the street from the Lutheran Hospital was reminiscent of another small, dingy cafe—the one where Death had laid his hand on Garnet Dillon's shoulder. There was the long tan counter, the counterman with his circling damp cloth, the chrome of the huge coffeemaker. This counterman was not redhaired, and his name was not Joe; this was the last act of the tragedy, instead of the first.

"Coffee," Tuck ordered, and drew his black notebook from his pocket. With the first gulp from the steaming cup came the thought that here was the setting for tragedy in modern dress; not the halls of a castle—Elsinore, Rimini; not the tapestried opulence of a drawing room; but a cheap place, a glaring place, a place where low comedy lurked behind the counter—that was where Garnet Dillon Schwann had felt Death approach, and with her last conscious breath must have wondered whether she would awake in heaven or in hell for having given herself to death a little sooner than life was ready to relinquish her.

If she had killed herself.

He opened his notebook to the list of questions he had jotted down at dinner time, before he had talked to Dr. Gordon, before he had learned that Garnet Dillon had not died because of life growing within her body but because of death growing there, in the wildly proliferating white blood cells.

"Why did she ask Dean Calder to examine her heart?"

The enlarged spleen, of course. Its pressure had been mistaken by her, in view of her father's death, for a heart ailment.

"Why did she buy the whisky?"

How plain the answer was, now. The knowledge of imminent death, too terrible to be borne without the oldest solace for immature minds face to face with some tragic immensity.

"Was she really dead drunk when Kurt Schwann telephoned from Pasadena? Or had she gone out, Mrs. Nox's second and more charitable suggestion? If so, where? Why?"

One fact was very plain now. Drunk or sober, she certainly would not have answered that summons to the telephone.

"Who took the digitalis from Dean Calder's desk on Saturday morning?"

Garnet took it. After a night of agony, the solution to her problem, in three little glass vials, plain on a desk not five feet from her own.

"Why did this person want to kill Garnet Dillon Schwann?"

Enough said.

"How was the poison administered?"

Rather haphazardly, certainly, since, according to Dean Calder, Garnet knew nothing of poison and its ways. Probably, the first dose producing no effect, she had taken repeated doses, arriving finally by accident at the dose fatal to her.

"Who was the man with whom Garnet went out to dinner on the night of Saturday, February second?"

That, it would seem, no longer mattered.

"Why did not Garnet tell Kurt Schwann they were going to have a baby, if he was telling the truth?"

Again, the answer was plain. She had kept both the secret of the leukemia and the secret of the child from her husband, having already formulated the plan of killing herself, or going away, or both. Why had she not confided in her husband?

Two fragments of testimony gave the answer to that. Tuck remembered Whittaker saying of Theodor, Kurt's brother, "He's a sad son-of-a-gun who lost his wife and never got over it." Dr. Uman had said, "She admired what he was doing, without understanding it. . . . She adored him." It certainly looked, then, as though her decision to take her own life had been motivated not only by inability to face the death within her, but by a thoroughly noble desire to spare her husband for his work rather than have him go the way Theodor had gone.

"Why was the last dose of poison, found in the intestine by the medical examiner, given her?"

Answer: It was not given her. She took it herself. She took two or three little green pills in a glass of water when she was alone. And the problem of skulduggery over her glass of beer vanished like mist before the dawn.

"Why did she keep the date with Kurt Schwann?"

Tuck was not a sentimental man, but something gentle in him was stirred at the reason for that last rendezvous. Good-by, forever. Her forced gaiety at the Hofbrau on her last night on earth, the tears Whittaker had seen in her eyes while she and Kurt were dancing—these were explained now.

"Why did she plan to go away, and of all places, to Grand Canyon?"

She went away either because she had become convinced that for some reason the poison was not going to kill her, and wanted to leave before her will power could break, before she found herself weeping out the truth on her husband's shoulder; or because she wanted to die far away from him, so that even the shock of a sudden death might be spared him. Or perhaps a combination of the two. Certainly there were enough reasons to convince a Coroner's jury. And Grand Canyon? Again pity

[214]

stirred within Tuck's case-hardened heart. **Why** not? There was no place better or worse for dying.

Tuck slowly closed his notebook. All questions answered. All except two, not included on that list.

Dean Calder had said that she didn't know arsenic from aspirin. Were those vials of digitalis labeled with a red skull and cross-bones, with the red letters: POISON?

Dean Calder has said that she was incapable of taking her own life. What would he say to that now?

Tuck wedged himself into a drugstore phone booth and made two calls. The first was to Dean Calder's home. The Dean himself answered the phone, after prolonged ringing.

"I want to see you at once, Dean Calder. I can be at your house in twenty minutes. Will that be satisfactory?"

"Why . . . yes, certainly. Have you found out something new?"

"I've found out everything," Tuck said.

The second phone call was to the Homicide Bureau. He asked for Brigit Estees.

Her voice was shrill with excitement. "We've got him!"

"Black Overcoat?"

"Yep."

"You're kidding me!"

"Nope. You were right about Froody. What an eye! It worked like a charm."

"Are you all right, Brigit?"

"Oh, sure. I felt him coming at me out of the alley. I ducked in time, and then Froody's revolver went off." A shiver came in Brigit's voice. "He's crazy, of course. He's sitting in front of Gufferty's desk right now. His name's Roger Hink, and he's not sure whether his 'trouble'—that's what he calls it, so help me—is due to environment or heredity. Says his childhood was very unhappy.

smiles a lot, and his smile is pretty bad, too. Oh,
Rotten home life, he says. And little girls used to
call him 'Skinny.' You can't believe it without
seeing it." The shiver in her voice accentuated.
"He's as tall as you are, with a white face and a
long neck. His eyes are horrible. Don't laugh.
They are. They make me think of snakes' eyes—
flat yellow-green, with no expression to them. He
yes. Something else . . ."

The shiver left her voice, and mockery took its
place. "He was the man who sat next to Garnet
Dillon, all right. And he took her purse. I have it
on my desk now. Black suede with a gold 'G.D.' "

"You have it on your desk now!"

"Yep. He didn't throw any of the purses away,
you see. 'That would have been too dangerous,' he
said. I suppose he meant that his landlady might
begin to wonder things. Or maybe they were
fetishes. And oh, Tucker old man, wouldn't you
like to know what's in Garnet's purse! *Wouldn't*
you, though!"

"Brigit! This is no time for jokes!"

"You crumb-bun," said Brigit.

"I was right about Froody, wasn't I? Didn't I
say he was a good shot? Didn't I?"

"Ha, ha," said Brigit.

"Oh all right," said Tuck nonchalantly. "In
twenty minutes I'll know who killed Garnet Dillon. And that isn't her name, by the way, and . . ."

"What!"

"Yep," said Tuck.

"If I tell you what I found in Garnet's purse, do
you swear that as soon as you know who killed
her, you'll tell me?"

"I will."

"All right. In her purse is a perfectly ordinary
pill box. And in the pill box . . ."

Tuck experienced an odd feeling. It was akin to
being pushed along by a force too powerful to

resist. "Digitalis."

". . . Two tablets."

"Thanks, Brigit." He hung up.

Dean Calder opened the door for Tuck. Over striped pajamas, he was wearing a maroon bathrobe. "Come in! Excuse my robe—I was in bed when you called!" He led Tuck through an archway into a high-ceilinged, pleasant living room, with a fire burning in the grate, and a silver tray on a low table before it bearing a decanter, siphon, ice and two glasses. "Thought you might like a drink." He busied himself filling the glasses "Well now. What's all this? I'm very interested, naturally."

. When his palm was cold around a tall glass, Tuck seated himself in one of the two chairs at at each side of the fireplace, and Calder took the other. The writhing flames warmed the side of his face nearest the fire; the other was by contrast almost in shadow. His eyes watched Tuck with calm interest.

"I'll be brief," Tuck said. "Garnet Dillon had leukemia."

Calder simply stared at Tuck.

"The appointment she left at four to keep was with a Dr. Gordon. I have just talked with him. He told Garnet exactly what was wrong with her, and that her days were numbered. He believes that she was not murdered, but killed herself. Her purse has been found—I'll not go into details—and in it is a pill box containing two digitalis tablets. I've come to ask you two questions. The first is this: Was there a poison label on the digitalis vials which were on your desk Friday afternoon and Saturday morning?"

Calder rubbed his brow with a hand that was not quite steady. Then he looked squarely at Tuck. "I'm sorry, but I can't remember. The pharmacist at the Campus Drugstore has known me for a number of years; sometimes there was a poison sticker on the digitalis I bought from him, and sometimes there wasn't I really can't remember which was the case this time."

"Thank you. This is the other question: Knowing that Garnet Dillon was the victim of an incurable and fatal disease, do you believe she would have committed suicide? Or do you stick to your original statement that suicide was impossible?"

"I don't know," said Calder, in a dull voice. "I don't know."

There was silence, and Tuck took a drink. The ice clanked loudly against the side of his glass.

He said, "She was married to Kurt Schwann, by the way."

Calder's brows rose. "Schwann? Kurt Schwann?" Then he nodded. "He used to stop in to see her, occasionally. Well."

Tuck finished his drink and set the glass down on the silver tray. "I'll tell you just where things stand, Calder. I'll ask you to put yourself in the place of a Coroner's juryman, although none of them will have a tenth of your intelligence. Let that pass. This is what the Coroner's jury will hear. On Friday, the first of February, late in the afternoon, a pretty young girl learns that she is in the grip of a disease as remorseless as the guillotine. She is faced with growing physical pain, coupled with the mental anguish of knowing that each breath she draws brings her closer to early death. She has a young husband who is a scientist with a future, whom she loves deeply, and whose talent she admires. Her husband has a brother, who was once a promising young scientist, too, but who suffered the anguish of watching his wife die of cancer, and who never recovered from that ordeal. Her husband is out of town on the night she learns that she is doomed, which gives her time to control her first impulse to tell him everything. The next

[218]

morning she manages to go to work, as usual. On your desk are three vials of poison. You later find that someone took that poison, and on that very morning. She behaves strangely; she will not tell her husband what is wrong. On Friday, February eighth, one week after her visit to the doctor, she leaves her husband, goes to the station, buys a ticket. Where? What does that matter? Grand Canyon. Waiting for her train, she goes to a cafe for coffee. The poison strikes at last. She dies in the ambulance. Her purse, which was stolen from the counter as she was dying, is found by the police. It contains a pill box in which are two digitalis tablets. There were thirty-six tablets in those vials which disappeared from your desk. It is quite plain what the Coroner's jury will think. Now, you take the stand. 'Do you adhere to your original statement that this young woman was incapable of suicide, Dean Calder?' "

Firmly, Dean Calder said, "I cannot, in honesty, do so, Tuck. I cannot presume to say what effect such terrible knowledge would have on another human being. I cannot even say what I myself might do."

Tuck stood up. Looking straight into Calder's bright blue eyes, he said, "I can tell you, then, what the Coroner's verdict will be. I did this once before, you remember. But this time I'm right. The Coroner's verdict will be suicide."

It was.

TWENTY-FOUR

KATE NEVER FORGOT GARNET's funeral. It was held on the gray Sunday following Saturday's inquest, in a cold chapel in a big green cemetery. Most of the mourners were young.

The minister, who undoubtedly read the papers, showed in his voice that he was conscious of added tragedy in this death. He may also have been conscious of two reporters sitting in the last row. Hidden birds twittered unceasingly throughout the service; their plaintive, uncertain cries bothered Kate. If they were there to remind those left behind of the life everlasting they failed miserably to do so. They sounded like caged birds and that was all.

Kate cringed as they filed past the coffin. In a brief glimpse she saw Garnet Dillon for the second time; a small white face, quiet and beautiful, framed by carefully arranged golden hair.

Then they all found their cars and drove in slow procession to a hillside.

On the slow way to the grave Kate sat silent between Kurt and Johnny. Johnny had his driving to busy himself with, but Kate clasped her idle hands in her lap and wished that there was something kind she could say to Kurt. Once she looked up at his face and saw that as soon as he was alone he would cry.

Standing beside the grave, beside the mass of flowers that covered the lowered coffin, listening to the minister's voice, Kate found herself looking around the circle of faces. Dean Calder, in a dark overcoat, pale and calm, and beside him a frail lady in black. Whittaker, his face composed as ever, but one hand clenched at his side. Hitchlock, with grief plain and young and unashamed in his eyes. Horstmann, beside him, looking stoically at the flowers. Grizz, his blue eyes more moist than ever, looking very uncomfortable in a tight little navy-blue suit. Dr. Uman, his dusty hair combed neatly. Vines, in a dark suit, staring at the coffin through his thick glasses. Kurt, immobile, head stiffly bowed. And Johnny, his lips tight, his eyes full of shadows. These faces stood out from the faces that were strange to her.

"And after this life, comes the life everlasting."

As they turned away from the grave, Kate heard Horstmann say to Hitchlock, "I think funerals are among our most horrible survivals." She saw the look Hitchlock gave Gladys. She thought, "Horstmann just lost Hitch, and she'll never know why."

Driving back to campus, Kurt watched the road ahead. Suddenly, he said, "You have no notion how odd it feels to know that someone died in order to save you for science. I'm wondering what it's going to be like—the nine days' wonder of being pointed at and whispered about. They didn't do it at the funeral, of course; they were busy trying to wear the expression proper to funerals. But after today . . ."

Kate couldn't help it. She said. "I'm wondering whether what you just said is really uppermost in your mind, or whether you're pretending. I hope you're pretending, Kurt."

He turned his eyes from the road to hers. He smiled his thin, not pleasant smile. "I'm pretending," he said. There was something in his voice— not exactly a quaver, but something almost humble and unsure of itself—that made her know he was telling the truth.

Johnny turned a corner, easily and competently, and said, "I think that she killed herself partly out of funk. I'm not minimizing the heroic side of it; there's no doubt in my mind that she also wanted to keep you from cracking up as Theodor did; the fact that she left you in the dark and went away proves that absolutely. But she was afraid, too. Afraid of the coming days and nights. Remember that, Kurt."

Kate couldn't help it again. "I think Garnet Dillon was the bravest person I've ever known about. I doubt whether any of us sitting here would have thought of someone else if we were to find ourselves in her particular hell."

To her surprise, Johnny cursed softly. Then he

[221]

looked down at her, and over at Kurt. She looked too. Kurt was still staring at the road ahead, but tears were beginning to wet his thin cheeks.

"Get me home fast," he commanded in a smothered voice.

TWENTY-FIVE

JOHNNY," ASKED KATE, "will you marry me? Not in three years. Now."

Johnny looked up from the medical book he was reading. Lamplight was bright on his hair, his forehead; his eyes were in shadow. Kate looked steadily at him across the room, the book she had been pretending to read neglected ·in her lap. She ·was conscious of the curtains blowing into the room, dim except for his lamp and hers. There was a peculiar desolation to those blowing curtains, making her know that, remembering this place, she would remember them. But she had wanted the windows open so that she could hear the fraternity men singing from the steps of the Library across the street. She had always liked the "Spring Sing."

Johnny looked at her for a long time before he spoke. "I was afraid that you might say that. I think that from the minute I looked down and saw you walking beside me again I was afraid of this."

"There's nothing to be afraid of," said Kate. "I've thought it all out. I could keep my job, and there'd be only one rent to pay instead of two. It's probably one of the few known cases where two can live as cheaply as one."

"It probably is," agreed Johnny mildly. He marked his place, and set his book down beside the radio. "How would you like some Beethoven, Kate?"

An uneasy feeling stired in Kate. But she managed to smile as she said, "Are you trying to avoid my question?"

[222]

"Yes," said Johnny. "I am."

Something of the sudden hurt that surged strongly through her must have shown on Kate's face because he said with a forced smile, "But I see that I can't."

She could hear her own voice tremble. "I thought I had known you long enough to be perfectly honest. I was wrong. I'm sorry." she closed her book, laid it beside her on the couch and stood up.

"Don't go," said Johnny. She hesitated, and he said, "Sit down, Kate."

Faintly came the sound of young men's voices singing.

"The girl of my dreams is the sweetest girl,
Of all the girls I know . . ."

"Kate," said Johnny. "I killed Garnet."

They looked at each other steadily. There was dust on the gleaming brown of the radio on the table beside Johnny's chair. The colored backs of the books in the tall case behind him glared in the lamplight. Kate was conscious of these, and of the fact that all her bodily functions seemed to have ceased. She had stopped breathing. Her blood was standing still in her veins.

"May I tell you about it?" he asked.

She couldn't nod. He looked at her for a moment, and then went on: "Garnet came here at nine-thirty on the night of Friday, February first. She was a little drunk. Her face is something I'll never forget. It made me think of only one thing— the face of a person who is dying. I thought, 'Something's happened to Kurt.' I tried not to show my fear, because I knew that if that was true she would need someone to lean on for a while.

"So I said, 'You'll have to excuse the mess. I

have an exam tomorrow. Sit down.'

"She sat down where you are, and I asked her what was wrong.

" 'I'm dying,' she said. Her voice was so shrill it hurt my ears. 'I'm dying. Day by day, hour by hour, and there's nothing anyone can do.' She began to cry. I've heard women cry before, but I never heard crying like that. I got her a glass of water, and gave it to her as soon as her sobs died down a little. I had no idea what she meant. She drank the water, looking up at me over the rim of the glass the way a child looks up at you. Then she handed it back to me and said, 'It's something called leukemia. Your blood goes wacky. It kills you in something like a year. I'm going to have a baby.' "

He paused. His face was strange while he remembered.

"I won't bother to tell you how shocked I was. I asked her how she had learned this, and she told me about going to Dr. Gordon for an examination, because of the pain in her side. I know of Gordon. He's a good doctor. It was true, all right. I remember I thought, 'What a hell of a mess!' over and over again.

" 'Does Kurt know?' I asked her.

" 'No. I went to him before I came here. His brother told me he's in Pasadena. He said he didn't know where. I couldn't be alone any longer, so I came to you.'

" 'What are you going to do?' I asked her.

"She just shook her head from side to side, and then she said in a still little voice, 'I'd like to kill myself.'

"I said nothing.

" 'Johnny,' she asked, still in that tiny voice, 'do you believe in God?'

"I said, 'Not in a stern father who puts down black marks against us in his big book.'

[224]

"'I do,' she said. She waited a minute, and then added, 'I wish I didn't. But I do. That's why I won't kill myself. That's why I'll wait to die. Oh, Johnny, if only it would happen tonight!'

"That got me. I thought of the days and nights ahead of her, and I felt something I haven't felt since I watched my father fuming against the tuberculosis that finally killed him. It was pity. It was painful."

He was still looking at her out of those shadowed, somber eyes. She still felt as though she had been chiseled from stone. Only the curtains moved.

"I had some benzidrine sulfate in my pocket. You've heard of it. They call it 'anti-suicide pills.' I use it when I'm studying; you can work much longer that way. I gave her one in a glass of water, and took her home. It was then that she told me she and Kurt had been married since Thanksgiving. I told her I'd guessed that when I saw the mileage on my car.

"I went back to my books. I couldn't study. I couldn't sleep. I spent most of the night thinking. About Garnet. And about Kurt. I remember that when I finally fell asleep just before dawn I was thinking how strange it was that the same situation that finished Theodor should catch up with Kurt. I tried to tell myself that he would pull through. I knew he wouldn't.

"I got through the exam somehow; I still don't remember what I put down. I was the last one to leave the class. I went to the Dean's office. She was still there, alone, writing something on that blue stationery of hers. She looked up and gave me a funny smile.

"'Kurt spent the night in Pasadena, Theodor tells me, I'm writing a note to the Dean. I'm going away.'

"She showed me the note she had been writing.

[225]

It was extremely incoherent, but it explained about the leukemia. 'I tried to write it last night, at home, but I was too shaky. I kept making blots.'

"I read the note and handed it back to her. 'Why are you going away?' I asked.

" 'I've been thinking,' she said. 'About what happened to Theodor. I don't want that to happen to Kurt, too. But if I stay here, I'll tell him.'

" 'I think you're right,' I said. 'But in that case do you think you'd better tell the Dean? It seems to me that the fewer people who know about it, the less chance there'll be of Kurt ever learning.'

"She saw that. 'You're a great help to me, Johnny,' she said. 'I'll only tell Dean Calder that I have to leave town. But what shall I say to Kurt?'

"I knew the answer to that. 'Nothing.'

"She looked at me, as though she didn't understand. 'But what will he think?'

"I said, 'That's not what matters. So long as he doesn't think the truth, anything will do.'

" 'He'll hate me,' she said, with tears beginning to fill her voice.

"I said, 'I think you love him enough even for that.'

"She'd been sitting sort of slumped over. She straightened. 'I do.'

"Then she dropped her head into her hands. Her voice was so choked it was hard to hear her, but that didn't matter, because somehow I knew what she was going to say. She said, 'Oh, God, God, I'm not big enough! Why didn't you let me die last night?'

"Along with the pity I was feeling for her, I was embarrassed; the kind of embarrassment you feel when you're intruding on someone's private grief. And then I thought, But it's not her private grief any more. I'm part of it. It's mine, too.

"I said, 'Since Kurt's in Pasadena, let me take you to lunch. Some food will do you good.'

[226]

" 'I can't eat,' she said.

" 'You'll have to do a lot of things you can't do before this is over,' I told her. 'Put on some lipstick. I'm going to take you to some place very nice.'

"She stood up. While she was standing at her mirror, I moved around the office. It was then that I saw the digitalis on the Dean's desk. It was like a reflex action. My hand went out and took it, and I put it into my pocket. It was just then that she said, 'You may not believe in God, Johnny, but you're a good person, just the same.'

"I'm not particularly poetic, but I shall always think that it was odd that she said that just then.

"At lunch I asked her where she planned to go.

"She tilted her head to one side in the funny way she had. 'I think I'll go to Grand Canyon,' she said. 'I've always wanted to see the Grand Canyon.' Then she smiled, and the tears began to stream down her cheeks. 'Oh,' she whispered, 'isn't this terrible!'

"I put my hand into my pocket to get a handkerchief for her. I felt those three vials of digitalis.

"While I was driving her home, I said, 'Are you going out with Kurt tonight?'

" 'I don't know,' she said. 'He'll probably work tonight.'

" 'I'll come over at six,' I told her. 'If you haven't heard from him by then I'll take you to dinner.'

"That's the way it worked out. I learned later that Kurt worked in the lab that night, to make up for his excursion the day before.

"I thought all afternoon. I thought of all the aspects of her problem. I decided that her wish to die soon ought to come true. I knew that the disease might kill her at any moment. It also might let her live for a year—maybe a little longer, but not much. A year, Kate! I switched the digitalis to a

[227]

big pill box that I had in the medicine chest.

"At dinner, she said, 'Johnny. Would you kill a person who was . . . would you kill me? It would be so kind. And you don't believe in heaven anyway.'

"I managed to keep my surprise under cover. I said, "Why, Garnet! Don't you care whether I go to hell or not?'

" 'Don't joke,' she said, very earnestly. And then, 'Perhaps it was selfish of me. And it was too much to ask of anyone, wasn't it?' Her voice was piteous, and she was searching my face as though to see whether I might do it, after all.

" 'Much too much,' I told her. 'But here's something I can do for you.' I took the pill box with the digitalis tablets in it and shoved it across the tablecloth. 'It's something to make you feel better. I use it at finals time; that's how I happen to have it. Take a couple of pills every two hours.'

"She put the box in her purse. 'Thank you, Johnny,' she said."

Kate spoke for the first time. She found that her lips moved stiffly. "Do you think that she guessed it was poison?"'

After a pause, Johnny said, "No."

"Oh," said Kate.

"The next thing she said rather floored me. I had thought, you see, that she was leaving that week end. But she said, 'I've decided to wait until the end of this coming week. It's partly on account of Dean Calder; I hate to leave him helpless in the middle of exams. He's been good to me. And then, there's that date you and Kurt and I have next Friday. I want to dance with him again.'

" 'Aren't you afraid you'll——?' I began.

"She straightened. 'No. I won't tell him. I want to dance with him again. He dances so well.'

"I saw that she was going to cry. I got her out to the car just in time.

"I kept thinking that I ought to ask her to give back the digitalis. But I couldn't do it. I was so sure it was the right thing to do. I haven't been sure since.

"I won't bother you with details of that next week. I had an exam every day, and every night I lay down with the fear that she would die before she went away. I had begun to think of other facets of the situation, you see. I had begun to realize that in the eyes of the law I was a murderer.

"On the Friday she died, I went to her apartment at five-thirty. I went to say good-by, because I had decided that she should have Kurt alone. She told me that she had just taken two more of the pills I'd given her. She told me that she'd taken all but four by Monday night, and that then she'd stopped. 'They didn't seem to do me any good,' she said.

"Oh, I thought, but they did.

"Kurt came then, and I said good-by and went away.

"Then, on Monday, I saw her body in the embalming room. I knew what I had been afraid of had happened. I knew that from then on I would have to be careful. I was. That's all, Kate."

Kate looked at him for a long time.

Then she stood up.

"So you're going," he said.

"Yes."

He stood up too. "And you're not coming back." His voice was empty.

"No."

"You think I was wrong."

She moved toward the door. "Yes."

"Why?"

"No one has the right to take life. You can't give it back again."

"She didn't want it, Kate!"

She stopped with her hand on the knob of the door, memorizing his face. Thinking it out as she spoke, she said, "It's so easy to forgive the people you love, and so unfair."

"Where are you going?" Johnny asked.

She shrugged, and then smiled. The smile felt strange and bitter. "You know, of course, that I won't tell anyone what you've told me. You know that."

"Yes."

She opened the door.

His voice was almost a whisper. "Good-by, Kate."

"Good-by."

As she closed the door, she looked back. He was standing in the center of the room, watching her go. The curtains blew into the room, and then dropped back to stillness.

He'll be alone for the rest of his life, she thought, as she went down the stairs.

"Euthanasia?"

Tuck looked down at his hands, busy removing the closely written pages of his little black notebook. His hands were suddenly still.

He leaned back in his chair, and frowned at the hat-rack. What he knew of mercy-killing began to spill over some dam in his mind.

To begin with, it's logically indefensible. Make mercy-killing valid in the case of a person suffering unbearable agony from an incurable disease. As soon as you've created a starting point, the range of euthanasiac activity opens out like a fan. Look at Germany. Next come incurable mental diseases. And what we don't know about mental diseases is really something. Schizophrenia was completely incurable ten years ago. Now, insulin shock is effective in, say, one case out of five. And new cures are being found for physical ailments.

A disease listed as incurable this year may have its cure next year. A doctor who might feel justified in the use of mercy killing this year might next year find that he could cure the man he had killed. Replace the solution "Cure!" with the solution "Kill!" and what happens to medical research?

Maybe that's what Hippocrates had in mind. How does the doctor's oath start? "I swear by Apollo . . ." and somewhere it says, "Neither will I administer a poison to anybody when asked to do so, nor will I suggest such a course."

But juries have been consistently lenient in the rare cases of proved mercy-killing. Emotional, of course. But maybe that's fair. Because a person who kills mercifully certainly surrenders to his emotions. Pity, usually. Maybe it's more fair to judge him on an emotional basis. I don't know.

"I'll pretend, for the moment, that Garnet Dillon was killed out of pity, by someone she had told of the leukemia. Someone who liked her, and liked Kurt Schwann, and saw only one way out for both of them.

Who would that person have been?

Dr. Calder?

No. Granted that he is capable of such an emotional gesture, granted that he called me in on the case in order to deliberately mislead me, he is certainly not a fool. If he killed Garnet Dillon out of pity with the digitalis he bought for his wife, he would surely have said she *would* have killed herself on learning she had leukemia. And top that by saying there *was* a poison label on those vials on his desk. He would have known that the pharmacist would not deny it. But instead he was very dubious on both those points. And furthermore, he had no interest whatever in Kurt. And the saving of Kurt Schwann was certainly part of the pattern.

Theodor Schwann? Kurt's brother. What had he said about Garnet? "She makes me think of a statue of the Lorelei made in Hoboken." He had never spoken ten words to her. And one thing was sure. If someone killed her out of pity, that some-one liked her. Theodor did not. And the only way the mercy killer could have learned about the leu-kemia was from Garnet's own lips. Would she have gone to Theodor? No. Nor to Horstmann. Nor to Vines.

Hitchlock? Gentle, kind, emotional. But very young. And if Hitchlock killed her, then he did not come by the driver's license accidentally. And would he have carried such incriminating evi-dence around in his wallet, when he could have so easily burned it? No.

Someone who knew Garnet, and liked her. Someone who knew Kurt and liked him. Someone to whom Garnet could have gone for solace. Some-one who had access to the poison. Kurt didn't have access to the poison. Whittaker was a small quiet man of thirty. He was fond of Garnet. He admired Kurt. Maybe . . .

Whom did that leave?

John Greenwood.

John Greenwood had access to the digitalis. He was Kurt's best friend. He liked Garnet. He lived down the street from her. *He lived two blocks away.*

What had Mrs. Nox said? "There was a phone call for her, from Pasadena, at nine-thirty. I buzzed her three times but she didn't answer. She may have gone out."

John Greenwood lived two blocks away.

She would have gone first to Kurt. He was in Pasadena. On the way back she would have passed Johnny's apartment house; she would have seen his light burning. Kurt's best friend. And there-fore her friend.

[232]

Tuck became conscious of the hatrack. He looked down at his hands still resting against the black notebook.

"Hey," said Gufferty's voice.

He looked up and saw him standing in the doorway.

Gufferty came quickly toward him.

"Listen," he said. "I think the wife did it. She was in love with the other guy. That's as plain as a pipe-stem. Now, the way I see it, the fact that the poison was sent to the husband through the mail actually points to her. I mean, it looks to me like she was trying too hard to make it look like murder from an outside source. Do you think—— Hey! Are you listening?"

Tuck's hands became busy. He lifted the notebook's pages out of their three metal rings. He dropped them into the wastebasket.

No proof. No way of getting any. Circumstantial evidence. You can't deduce the facts from theory. You must induce the theory from the facts. No facts here. Guesses.

"I'm listening," he said.

Kate found that she had walked the length of campus, and into the park. The bright plume of the fountain was ahead of her, and the odor of roses filled the night. A breeze was blowing from the west. She turned to go home.

She thought, How quiet it is. It's late.

As she passed the Science Building she looked up and saw one lighted window. The last window on the third floor. Kurt's laboratory.

That window has such a lonely look, she thought.

Three fraternity men were coming toward her. Their arms were locked, and they were singing. She was glad it was dark. She knew that the storm of thoughts that had come and gone within her

[233]

mind must have left traces on her face.

When they reached her, they stepped off the sidewalk to let her pass. Their voices faded.

Then she saw the building where Johnny lived, straight ahead of her. One window was a yellow square in the darkness. A second-floor window. Johnny's window.

She stood for a long time, looking up at it. She thought of Kurt, alone in his laboratory. She thought of Johnny, as she had last seen him.

Then she walked quickly toward his room.

THE END